A Lady of Quality

Published by Hesperus Press Limited
28 Mortimer Street, London W1W 7RD
www.hesperuspress.com

A Lady of Quality first published, 1896
First published by Hesperus Press, 2014

Typeset by Sarah Newitt
Printed and bound in Italy by 🦁 Grafica Veneta

ISBN: 978-1-84391-529-4

A Lady of Quality

Frances Hodgson Burnett

Being a most curious, hitherto unknown history,
as related by Mr Isaac Bickerstaff but not presented
to the World of Fashion through the pages
of *The Tatler*, and now for the first time written
down by Francis Hodgson Burnett

Were Nature just to Man from his first hour,
he need not ask for Mercy; then 'tis for us –
the toys of Nature – to be both just and merciful,
for so only can the wrongs she does be undone.

The Twenty-Fourth Day
of November 1690

On a wintry morning at the close of 1690, the sun shining faint
and red through a light fog, there was a great noise of baying
dogs, loud voices, and trampling of horses in the courtyard at
Wildairs Hall; Sir Jeoffry being about to go forth a-hunting, and
being a man with a choleric temper and big, loud voice, and
given to oaths and noise even when in good humour, his riding
forth with his friends at any time was attended with boisterous
commotion. This morning it was more so than usual, for he had
guests with him who had come to his house the day before, and
had supped late and drunk deeply, whereby the day found them,
some with headaches, some with a nausea at their stomachs,
and some only in an evil humour which made them curse at
their horses when they were restless, and break into loud surly
laughs when a coarse joke was made. There were many such
jokes, Sir Jeoffry and his boon companions being renowned
throughout the county for the freedom of their conversation as
for the scandal of their pastimes, and this day 'twas well indeed,
as their loud-voiced, oath-besprinkled jests rang out on the cold
air, that there were no ladies about to ride forth with them.

'Twas Sir Jeoffry who was louder than any other, he having
drunk even deeper than the rest, and though 'twas his boast that
he could carry a bottle more than any man, and see all his guests
under the table, his last night's bout had left him in ill humour
and boisterous. He strode about, casting oaths at the dogs and
rating the servants, and when he mounted his big black horse
'twas amid such a clamour of voices and baying hounds that the
place was like Pandemonium.

He was a large man of florid good looks, black eyes, and full
habit of body, and had been much renowned in his youth for
his great strength, which was indeed almost that of a giant, and

for his deeds of prowess in the saddle and at the table when the bottle went round. There were many evil stories of his roisterings, but it was not his way to think of them as evil, but rather to his credit as a man of the world, for, when he heard that they were gossiped about, he greeted the information with a loud triumphant laugh. He had married, when she was fifteen, the blooming toast of the county, for whom his passion had long died out, having indeed departed with the honeymoon, which had been of the briefest, and afterwards he having borne her a grudge for what he chose to consider her undutiful conduct. This grudge was founded on the fact that, though she had presented him each year since their marriage with a child, after nine years had passed none had yet been sons, and, as he was bitterly at odds with his next of kin, he considered each of his offspring an ill turn done him.

He spent but little time in her society, for she was a poor, gentle creature of no spirit, who found little happiness in her lot, since her lord treated her with scant civility, and her children one after another sickened and died in their infancy until but two were left. He scarce remembered her existence when he did not see her face, and he was certainly not thinking of her this morning, having other things in view, and yet it so fell out that, while a groom was shortening a stirrup and being sworn at for his awkwardness, he by accident cast his eye upward to a chamber window peering out of the thick ivy on the stone. Doing so he saw an old woman draw back the curtain and look down upon him as if searching for him with a purpose.

He uttered an exclamation of anger.

'Damnation! Mother Posset again,' he said. 'What does she there, old frump?'

The curtain fell and the woman disappeared, but in a few minutes more an unheard-of thing happened – among the servants in the hall, the same old woman appeared making her way with a hurried fretfulness, and she descended haltingly the stone steps and came to his side where he sat on his black horse.

'The Devil!' he exclaimed – 'what are you here for? 'Tis not time for another wench upstairs, surely?'

''Tis not time,' answered the old nurse acidly, taking her tone from his own. 'But there is one, but an hour old, and my lady –'

'Be damned to her!' quoth Sir Jeoffry savagely. 'A ninth one – and 'tis nine too many. 'Tis more than man can bear. She does it but to spite me.'

''Tis ill treatment for a gentleman who wants an heir,' the old woman answered, as disrespectful of his spouse as he was, being a time-serving crone, and knowing that it paid but poorly to coddle women who did not as their husbands would have them in the way of offspring. 'It should have been a fine boy, but it is not, and my lady –'

'Damn her puling tricks!' said Sir Jeoffry again, pulling at his horse's bit until the beast reared.

'She would not let me rest until I came to you,' said the nurse resentfully. 'She would have you told that she felt strangely, and before you went forth would have a word with you.'

'I cannot come, and am not in the mood for it if I could,' was his answer. 'What folly does she give way to? This is the ninth time she hath felt strangely, and I have felt as squeamish as she – but nine is more than I have patience for.'

'She is light-headed, mayhap,' said the nurse. 'She lieth huddled in a heap, staring and muttering, and she would leave me no peace till I promised to say to you, "For the sake of poor little Daphne, whom you will sure remember." She pinched my hand and said it again and again.'

Sir Jeoffry dragged at his horse's mouth and swore again.

'She was fifteen then, and had not given me nine yellow-faced wenches,' he said. 'Tell her I had gone a-hunting and you were too late,' and he struck his big black beast with the whip, and it bounded away with him, hounds and huntsmen and fellow-roisterers galloping after, his guests, who had caught at the reason of his wrath, grinning as they rode.

In a huge chamber hung with tattered tapestries and barely set forth with cumbersome pieces of furnishing, my lady lay in a gloomy, canopied bed, with her newborn child at her side, but not looking at or touching it, seeming rather to have withdrawn herself from the pillow on which it lay in its swaddling-clothes.

She was but a little lady, and now, as she lay in the large bed, her face and form shrunken and drawn with suffering, she looked scarce bigger than a child. In the brief days of her happiness those who toasted her had called her Titania for her fairy slightness and delicate beauty, but then her fair wavy locks had been of a length that touched the ground when her woman unbound them, and she had had the colour of a wild rose and the eyes of a tender little fawn. Sir Jeoffry for a month or so had paid tempestuous court to her, and had so won her heart with his dashing way of lovemaking and the daringness of his reputation, that she had thought herself – being child enough to think so – the luckiest young lady in the world that his black eye should have fallen upon her with favour. Each year since, with the bearing of each child, she had lost some of her beauty. With each one her lovely hair fell out still more, her wild-rose colour faded, and her shape was spoiled. She grew thin and yellow, only a scant covering of the fair hair was left her, and her eyes were big and sunken. Her marriage having displeased her family, and Sir Jeoffry having a distaste for the ceremonies of visiting and entertainment, save where his own cronies were concerned, she had no friends, and grew lonelier and lonelier as the sad years went by. She being so without hope and her life so dreary, her children were neither strong nor beautiful, and died quickly, each one bringing her only the anguish of birth and death. This wintry morning her ninth lay slumbering by her side; the noise of baying dogs and boisterous men had died away with the last sound of the horses' hoofs; the little light which came into the room through the ivied window was a faint yellowish red; she was cold, because the fire in the chimney was but a scant, failing one; she was alone – and she knew that the time had come for her death. This she knew full well.

She was alone, because, being so disrespected and deserted by her lord, and being of a timid and gentle nature, she could not command her insufficient retinue of servants, and none served her as was their duty. The old woman Sir Jeoffry had dubbed Mother Posset had been her sole attendant at such times as these for the past five years, because she would come to her for a less fee than a better woman, and Sir Jeoffry had sworn he would not pay for wenches being brought into the world. She was a slovenly, guzzling old crone, who drank caudle from morning till night, and demanded good living as a support during the performance of her trying duties; but these last she contrived to make wondrous light, knowing that there was none to reprove her.

'A fine night I have had,' she had grumbled when she brought back Sir Jeoffry's answer to her lady's message. 'My old bones are like to break, and my back will not straighten itself. I will go to the kitchen to get victuals and somewhat to warm me; your ladyship's own woman shall sit with you.'

Her ladyship's 'own woman' was also the sole attendant of the two little girls, Barbara and Anne, whose nursery was in another wing of the house, and my lady knew full well she would not come if she were told, and that there would be no message sent to her.

She knew, too, that the fire was going out, but, though she shivered under the bedclothes, she was too weak to call the woman back when she saw her depart without putting fresh fuel upon it.

So she lay alone, poor lady, and there was no sound about her, and her thin little mouth began to feebly quiver, and her great eyes, which stared at the hangings, to fill with slow cold tears, for in sooth they were not warm, but seemed to chill her poor cheeks as they rolled slowly down them, leaving a wet streak behind them which she was too far gone in weakness to attempt to lift her hand to wipe away.

'Nine times like this,' she panted faintly, 'and 'tis for naught but oaths and hard words that blame me. I was but a child myself and he loved me. When 'twas "My Daphne," and "My beauteous little Daphne," he loved me in his own man's way. But now –' she faintly rolled her head from side to side. 'Women are poor things' – a chill salt tear sliding past her lips so that she tasted its bitterness – 'only to be kissed for an hour, and then like this – only for this and nothing else. I would that this one had been dead.'

Her breath came slower and more pantingly, and her eyes stared more widely.

'I was but a child,' she whispered – 'a child – as – as this will be – if she lives fifteen years.'

Despite her weakness, and it was great and woefully increasing with each panting breath, she slowly laboured to turn herself towards the pillow on which her offspring lay, and, this done, she lay staring at the child and gasping, her thin chest rising and falling convulsively. Ah, how she panted, and how she stared, the glaze of death stealing slowly over her wide-opened eyes; and yet, dimming as they were, they saw in the sleeping infant a strange and troublous thing – though it was but a few hours old 'twas not as red and crumple visaged as newborn infants usually are, its little head was covered with thick black silk, and its small features were of singular definiteness. She dragged herself nearer to gaze.

'She looks not like the others,' she said. 'They had no beauty – and are safe. She – she will be like – Jeoffry – and like *me*.'

The dying fire fell lower with a shuddering sound.

'If she is – beautiful, and has but her father, and no mother!' she whispered, the words dragged forth slowly, 'only evil can come to her. From her first hour – she will know naught else, poor heart, poor heart!'

There was a rattling in her throat as she breathed, but in her glazing eyes a gleam like passion leaped, and gasping, she dragged nearer.

''Tis not fair,' she cried. 'If I – if I could lay my hand upon thy mouth – and stop thy breathing – thou poor thing, 'twould be fairer – but – I have no strength.'

She gathered all her dying will and brought her hand up to the infant's mouth. A wild look was on her poor, small face, she panted and fell forward on its breast, the rattle in her throat growing louder. The child awakened, opening great black eyes, and with her dying weakness its newborn life struggled. Her cold hand lay upon its mouth, and her head upon its body, for she was too far gone to move if she had willed to do so. But the tiny creature's strength was marvellous. It gasped, it fought, its little limbs struggled beneath her, it writhed until the cold hand fell away, and then, its baby mouth set free, it fell a-shrieking. Its cries were not like those of a newborn thing, but fierce and shrill, and even held the sound of infant passion. 'Twas not a thing to let its life go easily, 'twas of those born to do battle.

Its lusty screaming pierced her ear perhaps – she drew a long, slow breath, and then another, and another still – the last one trembled and stopped short, and the last cinder fell dead from the fire.

When the nurse came bustling and fretting back, the chamber was cold as the grave's self – there were only dead embers on the hearth, the newborn child's cries filled all the desolate air, and my lady was lying stone dead, her poor head resting on her offspring's feet, the while her open glazed eyes seemed to stare at it as if in asking Fate some awful question.

In Which Sir Jeoffry
Encounters His Offspring

In a remote wing of the house, in barren, ill-kept rooms, the poor
infants of the dead lady had struggled through their brief lives,
and given them up, one after the other. Sir Jeoffry had not wished
to see them, nor had he done so, but upon the rarest occasions,
and then nearly always by some untoward accident. The six who
had died, even their mother had scarcely wept for; her weeping
had been that they should have been fated to come into the world,
and when they went out of it she knew she need not mourn
their going as untimely. The two who had not perished, she had
regarded sadly day by day, seeing they had no beauty and that
their faces promised none. Naught but great beauty would have
excused their existence in their father's eyes, as beauty might have
helped them to good matches which would have rid him of them.
But 'twas the sad ill fortune of the children Anne and Barbara to
have been treated by Nature in a way but niggardly. They were
pale young misses, with insignificant faces and snub noses, resem-
bling an aunt who died a spinster, as they themselves seemed most
likely to. Sir Jeoffry could not bear the sight of them, and they fled
at the sound of his footsteps, if it so happened that by chance they
heard it, huddling together in corners, and slinking behind doors
or anything big enough to hide them. They had no playthings and
no companions and no pleasures but such as the innocent inven-
tion of childhood contrives for itself.

After their mother's death a youth desolate and strange indeed
lay before them. A spinster who was a poor relation was the
only person of respectable breeding who ever came near them.
To save herself from genteel starvation, she had offered herself
for the place of governess to them, though she was fitted for the
position neither by education nor character. Mistress Margery
Wimpole was a poor, dull creature, having no wilful harm in her,

but endowed with neither dignity nor wit. She lived in fear of Sir Jeoffry, and in fear of the servants, who knew full well that she was an humble dependant, and treated her as one. She hid away with her pupils in the bare schoolroom in the west wing, and taught them to spell and write and work samplers. She herself knew no more.

The child who had cost her mother her life had no happier prospect than her sisters. Her father felt her more an intruder than they had been, he being of the mind that to house and feed and clothe, howsoever poorly, these three burdens on him was a drain scarcely to be borne. His wife had been a toast and not a fortune, and his estate not being great, he possessed no more than his drinking, roistering, and gambling made full demands upon.

The child was baptised Clorinda, and bred, so to speak, from her first hour, in the garret and the servants' hall. Once only did her father behold her during her infancy, which event was a mere accident, as he had expressed no wish to see her, and only came upon her in the nurse's arms some weeks after her mother's death. 'Twas quite by chance. The woman, who was young and buxom, had begun an intrigue with a groom, and having a mind to see him, was crossing the stable-yard, carrying her charge with her, when Sir Jeoffry came by to visit a horse.

The woman came plump upon him, entering a stable as he came out of it; she gave a frightened start, and almost let the child drop, at which it set up a strong, shrill cry, and thus Sir Jeoffry saw it, and seeing it, was thrown at once into a passion which expressed itself after the manner of all his emotion, and left the nurse quaking with fear.

'Thunder and damnation!' he exclaimed, as he strode away after the encounter; ''tis the ugliest yet. A yellow-faced girl brat, with eyes like an owl's in an ivy-bush, and with a voice like a very peacock's. Another mawking, plain slut that no man will take off my hands.'

He did not see her again for six years. But little wit was needed to learn that 'twas best to keep her out of his sight, as her sisters were kept, and this was done without difficulty, as he avoided the wing of the house where the children lived, as if it were stricken with the plague.

But the child Clorinda, it seemed, was of lustier stock than her older sisters, and this those about her soon found out to their grievous disturbance. When Mother Posset had drawn her from under her dead mother's body she had not left shrieking for an hour, but had kept up her fierce cries until the roof rang with them, and the old woman had jogged her about and beat her back in the hopes of stifling her, until she was exhausted and dismayed. For the child would not be stilled, and seemed to have such strength and persistence in her as surely infant never showed before.

'Never saw I such a brat among all I have brought into the world,' old Posset quavered. 'She hath the voice of a six-months boy. It cracks my very ears. Hush thee, then, thou little wild cat.'

This was but the beginning. From the first she grew apace, and in a few months was a bouncing infant, with a strong back, and a power to make herself heard such as had not before appeared in the family. When she desired a thing, she yelled and roared with such a vigour as left no peace for any creature about her until she was humoured, and this being the case, rather than have their conversation and lovemaking put a stop to, the servants gave her her way. In this they but followed the example of their betters, of whom we know that it is not to the most virtuous they submit or to the most learned, but to those who, being crossed, can conduct themselves in a manner so disagreeable, shrewish or violent, that life is a burden until they have their will. This the child Clorinda had the infant wit to discover early, and having once discovered it, she never ceased to take advantage of her knowledge. Having found in the days when her one desire was pap, that she had but to roar lustily enough to find it beside her in her porringer, she tried the game upon all other occasions. When she had reached but a twelve-month, she stood stoutly upon her little feet, and beat her sisters to gain their playthings, and her nurse for wanting to change her smock. She was so easily thrown into furies, and so raged and stamped in her baby way that she was a sight to behold, and the men-servants found amusement in badgering her. To set Mistress Clorinda in their midst on a winter's night when they were dull, and to torment her until her little face grew scarlet with the blood which flew up into it, and she ran from one to the other beating them and screaming like a young spitfire, was among them a favourite entertainment.

'Ifackens!' said the butler one night, 'but she is as like Sir Jeoffry in her temper as one pea is like another. Ay, but she grows blood red just as he does, and curses in her little way as he does in man's words among his hounds in their kennel.'

'And she will be of his build, too,' said the housekeeper. 'What mishap changed her to a maid instead of a boy, I know not. She would have made a strapping heir. She has the thigh and shoulders of a handsome man-child at this hour, and she is not three years old.'

'Sir Jeoffry missed his mark when he called her an ugly brat,' said the woman who had nursed her. 'She will be a handsome woman – though large in build, it may be. She will be a brown beauty, but she will have a colour in her cheeks and lips like the red of Christmas holly, and her owl's eyes are as black as sloes, and have fringes on them like the curtains of a window. See how her hair grows thick on her little head, and how it curls in great rings. My lady, her poor mother, was once a beauty, but she was no such beauty as this one will be, for she has her father's long limbs and fine shoulders, and the will to make every man look her way.'

'Yes,' said the housekeeper, who was an elderly woman, 'there will be doings – there will be doings when she is a ripe young maid. She will take her way, and God grant she mayn't be *too* like her father and follow his.'

It was true that she had no resemblance to her plain sisters, and bore no likeness to them in character. The two elder children, Anne and Barbara, were too meek-spirited to be troublesome; but during Clorinda's infancy Mistress Margery Wimpole watched her rapid growth with fear and qualms. She dare not reprove the servants who were ruining her by their treatment, and whose manners were forming her own. Sir Jeoffry's servants were no more moral than their master, and being brought up as she was among them, their young mistress became strangely familiar with many sights and sounds it is not the fortune of most young misses of breeding to see and hear. The cooks and kitchen-wenches were flighty with the grooms and men-servants, and little Mistress Clorinda, having a passion for horses and dogs, spent many an hour in the stables with the women who, for reasons of their own, were pleased enough to take her there as an excuse for seeking amusement for themselves. She played in the kennels and among the horses' heels, and learned to use oaths as roundly as any Giles or Tom whose work was to wield the curry comb. It was indeed a curious thing to hear her red baby mouth pour forth curses and unseemly words as she would at anyone who crossed her. Her temper and hot-headedness carried all before them, and the grooms and stable boys found great sport in the language my young lady used in her innocent furies. But balk her in a whim, and she would pour forth the eloquence of a fish-wife or a lady of easy virtue in a pot-house quarrel. There was no human creature near her who had mind or heart enough to see the awfulness of her condition, or to strive to teach her to check her passions; and in the midst of these perilous surroundings the little virago grew handsomer and of finer carriage every hour, as if on the rank diet that fed her she throve and flourished.

There came a day at last when she had reached six years old, when by a trick of chance a turn was given to the wheel of her fate.

She had not reached three when a groom first set her on a horse's back and led her about the stable-yard, and she had so delighted in her exalted position, and had so shouted for pleasure and clutched her steed's rein and clucked at him, that her audience had looked on with roars of laughter. From that time she would be put up every day, and as time went on showed such unchildish courage and spirit that she furnished to her servant companions a new pastime. Soon she would not be held on, but riding astride like a boy, would sit up as straight as a man and swear at her horse, beating him with her heels and little fists if his pace did not suit her. She knew no fear, and would have used a whip so readily that the men did not dare to trust her with one, and knew they must not mount her on a steed too mettlesome. By the time she passed her sixth birthday she could ride as well as a grown man, and was as familiar with her father's horses as he himself, though he knew nothing of the matter, it being always contrived that she should be out of sight when he visited his hunters.

It so chanced that the horse he rode the oftenest was her favourite, and many were the tempests of rage she fell into when she went to the stable to play with the animal and did not find him in his stall, because his master had ordered him out. At such times she would storm at the men in the stable-yard and call them ill names for their impudence in letting the beast go, which would cause them great merriment, as she knew nothing of who the man was who had balked her, since she was, in truth, not so much as conscious of her father's existence, never having seen or even heard more of him than his name, which she in no manner connected with herself.

'Could Sir Jeoffry himself but once see and hear her when she storms at us and him, because he dares to ride his own beast,' one of the older men said once, in the midst of their laughter, 'I swear he would burst forth laughing and be taken with her impudent spirit, her temper is so like his own. She is his own flesh and blood, and as full of hellfire as he.'

Upon this morning which proved eventful to her, she had gone to the stables, as was her daily custom, and going into the stall where the big black horse was wont to stand, she found it empty. Her spirit rose hot within her in the moment. She clenched her fists, and began to stamp and swear in such a manner as it would be scarce fitting to record.

'Where is he now?' she cried. 'He is my own horse, and shall not be ridden. Who is the man who takes him? Who? Who?'

''Tis a fellow who hath no manners,' said the man she stormed at, grinning and thrusting his tongue in his cheek. 'He says 'tis his beast, and not yours, and he will have him when he chooses.'

''Tis not his – 'tis mine!' shrieked Miss, her little face inflamed with passion. 'I will kill him! 'Tis my horse. He *shall* be mine!'

For a while the men tormented her, to hear her rave and see her passion, for, in truth, the greater tempest she was in, the better she was worth beholding, having a colour so rich, and eyes so great and black and flaming. At such times there was naught of the feminine in her, and indeed always she looked more like a handsome boy than a girl, her growth being for her age extraordinary. At length a lad who was a helper said to mock her –

'The man hath him at the door before the great steps now. I saw him stand there waiting but a moment ago. The man hath gone in the house.'

She turned and ran to find him. The front part of the house she barely knew the outside of, as she was kept safely in the west wing and below stairs, and when taken out for the air was always led privately by a side way – never passing through the great hall, where her father might chance to encounter her.

She knew best this side-entrance, and made her way to it, meaning to search until she found the front. She got into the house, and her spirit being roused, marched boldly through corridors and into rooms she had never seen before, and being so mere a child, notwithstanding her strange wilfulness and daring, the novelty of the things she saw so far distracted her mind from the cause of her anger that she stopped more than once to stare up at a portrait on a wall, or to take in her hand something she was curious concerning.

When she at last reached the entrance-hall, coming into it through a door she pushed open, using all her childish strength, she stood in the midst of it and gazed about her with a new curiosity and pleasure. It was a fine place, with antlers, and arms, and foxes' brushes hung upon the walls, and with carved panels of black oak, and oaken floor and furnishings. All in it was disorderly and showed rough usage; but once it had been a notable feature of the house, and well worth better care than had been bestowed upon it. She discovered on the walls many trophies that attracted her, but these she could not reach, and could only gaze and wonder at; but on an old oaken settle she found some things she could lay hands on, and forthwith seized and sat down upon the floor to play with them. One of them was a hunting-crop, which she brandished grandly, until she was more taken with a powder-flask which it so happened her father, Sir Jeoffry, had lain down but a few minutes before, in passing through. He was going forth coursing, and had stepped into the dining hall to toss off a bumper of brandy.

When he had helped himself from the buffet, and came back in haste, the first thing he clapped eyes on was his offspring pouring forth the powder from his flask upon the oaken floor. He had never seen her since that first occasion after the unfortunate incident of her birth, and beholding a child wasting his good powder at the moment he most wanted it and had no time to spare, and also not having had it recalled to his mind for years that he was a parent, except when he found himself forced reluctantly to pay for some small need, he beheld in the young offender only some impudent servant's brat, who had strayed into his domain and applied itself at once to mischief.

He sprang upon her, and seizing her by the arm, whirled her to her feet with no little violence, snatching the powder-flask from her, and dealing her a sound box on the ear.

'Blood and damnation on thee, thou impudent little baggage!' he shouted. 'I'll break thy neck for thee, little scurvy beast,' and pulled the bell as he were like to break the wire.

But he had reckoned falsely on what he dealt with. Miss uttered a shriek of rage which rang through the roof like a clarion. She snatched the crop from the floor, rushed at him, and fell upon him like a thousand little devils, beating his big legs with all the strength of her passion, and pouring forth oaths such as would have done credit to Doll Lightfoot herself.

'Damn *thee*! – damn *thee*!' – she roared and screamed, flogging him. 'I'll tear thy eyes out! I'll cut thy liver from thee! Damn thy soul to hell!'

And this choice volley was with such spirit and fury poured forth, that Sir Jeoffry let his hand drop from the bell, fell into a great burst of laughter, and stood thus roaring while she beat him and shrieked and stormed.

The servants, hearing the jangled bell, attracted by the tumult, and of a sudden missing Mistress Clorinda, ran in consternation to the hall, and there beheld this truly pretty sight – Miss beating her father's legs, and tearing at him tooth and nail, while he stood shouting with laughter as if he would split his sides.

'Who is the little cockatrice?' he cried, the tears streaming down his florid cheeks. 'Who is the young she-devil? Ods bodikins, who is she?'

For a second or so the servants stared at each other aghast, not knowing what to say, or venturing to utter a word; and then the nurse, who had come up panting, dared to gasp forth the truth.

''Tis Mistress Clorinda, Sir Jeoffry,' she stammered – 'my lady's last infant – the one of whom she died in childbed.'

His big laugh broke in two, as one might say. He looked down at the young fury and stared. She was out of breath with beating him, and had ceased and fallen back apace, and was staring up at him also, breathing defiance and hatred. Her big black eyes were flames, her head was thrown up and back, her cheeks were blood scarlet, and her great crop of crow-black hair stood out about her beauteous, wicked little virago face, as if it might change into Medusa's snakes.

'Damn thee!' she shrieked at him again. 'I'll kill thee, devil!'

Sir Jeoffry broke into his big laugh afresh.

'Clorinda do they call thee, wench?' he said. 'Jeoffry thou shouldst have been but for thy mother's folly. A fiercer little devil for thy size I never saw – nor a handsomer one.'

And he seized her from where she stood, and held her at his big arms' length, gazing at her uncanny beauty with looks that took her in from head to foot.

Wherein Sir Jeoffry's
Boon Companions Drink a Toast

Her beauty of face, her fine body, her strength of limb, and
great growth for her age, would have pleased him if she had
possessed no other attraction, but the daring of her fury
and her stable boy breeding so amused him and suited his
roistering tastes that he took to her as the finest plaything
in the world.

He set her on the floor, forgetting his coursing, and would
have made friends with her, but at first she would have none of
him, and scowled at him in spite of all he did. The brandy by
this time had mounted to his head and put him in the mood for
frolic, liquor oftenest making him gamesome. He felt as if he
were playing with a young dog or marking the spirit of a little
fighting cock. He ordered the servants back to their kitchen,
who stole away, the women amazed, and the men concealing
grins which burst forth into guffaws of laughter when they
came into their hall below.

''Tis as we said,' they chuckled. 'He had but to see her beauty
and find her a bigger devil than he, and 'twas done. The mettle
of her – damning and flogging him! Never was there a finer
sight! She feared him no more than if he had been a spaniel –
and he roaring and laughing till he was like to burst.'

'Dost know who I am?' Sir Jeoffry was asking the child, grinning himself as he stood before her where she sat on the oaken
settle on which he had lifted her.

'No,' quoth little Mistress, her black brows drawn down, her
handsome owl's eyes verily seeming to look him through and
through in search of somewhat; for, in sooth, her rage abating
before his jovial humour, the big burly laugher attracted her
attention, though she was not disposed to show him that she
leaned towards any favour or yielding.

'I am thy Dad,' he said. ''Twas thy Dad thou gavest such a trouncing. And thou hast an arm, too. Let's cast an eye on it.'

He took her wrist and pushed up her sleeve, but she dragged back.

'Will not be mauled,' she cried. 'Get away from me!'

He shouted with laughter again. He had seen that the little arm was as white and hard as marble, and had such muscles as a great boy might have been a braggart about.

'By Gad!' he said, elated. 'What a wench of six years old. Wilt have my crop and trounce thy Dad again!'

He picked up the crop from the place where she had thrown it, and forthwith gave it in her hand. She took it, but was no more in the humour to beat him, and as she looked still frowning from him to the whip, the latter brought back to her mind the horse she had set out in search of.

'Where is my horse?' she said, and 'twas in the tone of an imperial demand. 'Where is he?'

'Thy horse!' he echoed. 'Which is thy horse then?'

'Rake is my horse,' she answered – 'the big black one. The man took him again,' and she ripped out a few more oaths and unchaste expressions, threatening what she would do for the man in question; the which delighted him more than ever. 'Rake is my horse,' she ended. 'None else shall ride him.'

'None else?' cried he. 'Thou canst not ride him, baggage!'

She looked at him with scornful majesty.

'Where is he?' she demanded. And the next instant hearing the beast's restless feet grinding into the gravel outside as he fretted at having been kept waiting so long, she remembered what the stable boy had said of having seen her favourite standing before the door, and struggling and dropping from the settle, she ran to look out; whereupon having done so, she shouted in triumph.

'He is here!' she said. 'I see him,' and went pell-mell down the stone steps to his side.

Sir Jeoffry followed her in haste. 'Twould not have been to his humour now to have her brains kicked out.

'Hey!' he called, as he hurried. 'Keep away from his heels, thou little devil.'

But she had run to the big beast's head with another shout, and caught him round his foreleg, laughing, and Rake bent his head down and nosed her in a fumbling caress, on which, the bridle coming within her reach, she seized it and held his head that she might pat him, to which familiarity the beast was plainly well accustomed.

'He is my horse,' quoth she grandly when her father reached her. 'He will not let Giles play so.'

Sir Jeoffry gazed and swelled with pleasure in her.

'Would have said 'twas a lie if I had not seen it,' he said to himself. ''Tis no girl this, I swear. I thought 'twas my horse,' he said to her, 'but 'tis plain enough he is thine.'

'Put me up!' said his newfound offspring.

'Hast rid him before?' Sir Jeoffry asked, with some lingering misgiving. 'Tell thy Dad if thou hast rid him.'

She gave him a look askance under her long fringed lids – a surly yet half-slyly relenting look, because she wanted to get her way of him, and had the cunning wit and shrewdness of a child witch.

'Ay!' quoth she. 'Put me up – Dad!'

He was not a man of quick mind, his brain having been too many years bemuddled with drink, but he had a rough instinct which showed him all the wondrous shrewdness of her casting that last word at him to wheedle him, even though she looked sullen in the saying it. It made him roar again for very exultation.

'Put me up, Dad!' he cried. 'That will I – and see what thou wilt do.'

He lifted her, she springing as he set his hands beneath her arms, and flinging her legs over astride across the saddle when she reached it. She was all fire and excitement, and caught the reins like an old huntsman, and with such a grasp as was amazing. She sat up with a straight, strong back, her whole face glowing and sparkling with exultant joy. Rake seemed to answer to her excited little laugh almost as much as to her hand. It seemed to wake his spirit and put him in good humour. He started off with her down the avenue at a light, spirited trot, while she, clinging with her little legs and sitting firm and fearless, made him change into canter and gallop, having actually learned all his paces like a lesson, and knowing his mouth as did his groom, who was her familiar and slave. Had she been of the build ordinary with children of her age, she could not have stayed upon his back; but she sat him like a child jockey, and Sir Jeoffry, watching and following her, clapped his hands boisterously and hallooed for joy.

'Lord, Lord!' he said. 'There's not a man in the shire has such another little devil – and Rake, "her horse",' grinning – 'and she to ride him so. I love thee, wench – hang me if I do not!'

She made him play with her and with Rake for a good hour, and then took him back to the stables, and there ordered him about finely among the dogs and horses, perceiving that somehow this great man she had got hold of was a creature who was in power and could be made use of.

When they returned to the house, he had her to eat her midday meal with him, when she called for ale, and drank it, and did good trencher duty, making him the while roar with laughter at her impudent child-talk.

'Never have I so split my sides since I was twenty,' he said. 'It makes me young again to roar so. She shall not leave my sight, since by chance I have found her. 'Tis too good a joke to lose, when times are dull, as they get to be as a man's years go on.'

He sent for her woman and laid strange new commands on her.

'Where hath she hitherto been kept?' he asked.

'In the west wing, where are the nurseries, and where Mistress Wimpole abides with Mistress Barbara and Mistress Anne,' the woman answered, with a frightened curtsey.

'Henceforth she shall live in this part of the house where I do,' he said. 'Make ready the chambers that were my lady's, and prepare to stay there with her.'

From that hour the child's fate was sealed. He made himself her playfellow, and romped with and indulged her until she became fonder of him than of any groom or stable boy she had been companions with before. But, indeed, she had never been given to bestowing much affection on those around her, seeming to feel herself too high a personage to show softness. The ones she showed most favour to were those who served her best; and even to them it was always *favour* she showed, not tenderness. Certain dogs and horses she was fond of, Rake coming nearest to her heart, and the place her father won in her affections was somewhat like to Rake's. She made him her servant and tyrannised over him, but at the same time followed and imitated him as if she had been a young spaniel he was training. The life the child led, it would have broken a motherly woman's heart to hear about; but there was no good woman near her, her mother's relatives, and even Sir Jeoffry's own, having cut themselves off early from them – Wildairs Hall and its master being no great credit to those having the misfortune to be connected with them. The neighbouring gentry had gradually ceased to visit the family some time before her ladyship's death, and since then the only guests who frequented the place were a circle of hunting, drinking, and guzzling boon companions of Sir Jeoffry's own, who joined him in all his carousals and debaucheries.

To these he announced his discovery of his daughter with tumultuous delight. He told them, amid storms of laughter, of his first encounter with her; of her flogging him with his own crop, and cursing him like a trooper; of her claiming Rake as her own horse, and swearing at the man who had dared to take him from the stable to ride; and of her sitting him like an infant jockey, and seeming, by some strange power, to have mastered him as no other had been able heretofore to do. Then he had her brought into the dining room, where they sat over their bottles drinking deep, and setting her on the table, he exhibited her to them, boasting of her beauty, showing them her splendid arm and leg and thigh, measuring her height, and exciting her to test the strength of the grip of her hand and the power of her little fist.

'Saw you ever a wench like her?' he cried, as they all shouted with laughter and made jokes not too polite, but such as were of the sole kind they were given to. 'Has any man among you begot a boy as big and handsome? Hang me! if she would not knock down any lad of ten if she were in a fury.'

'We wild dogs are out of favour with the women,' cried one of the best pleased among them, a certain Lord Eldershawe, whose seat was a few miles from Wildairs Hall – 'women like nincompoops and chaplains. Let us take this one for our toast, and bring her up as girls should be brought up to be companions for men. I give you, Mistress Clorinda Wildairs – Mistress Clorinda, the enslaver of six years old – bumpers, lads! – bumpers!'

And they set her in the very midst of the big table and drank her health, standing, bursting into a jovial, ribald song; and the child, excited by the noise and laughter, actually broke forth and joined them in a high, strong treble, the song being one she was quite familiar with, having heard it often enough in the stable to have learned the words pat.

Two weeks after his meeting with her, Sir Jeoffry was seized with the whim to go up to London and set her forth with finery. 'Twas but rarely he went up to town, having neither money to waste, nor finding great attraction in the more civilised quarters of the world. He brought her back such clothes as for richness and odd, unsuitable fashion child never wore before. There were brocades that stood alone with splendour of fabric, there was rich lace, fine linen, ribands, farthingales, swansdown tippets, and little slippers with high red heels. He had a wardrobe made for her such as the finest lady of fashion could scarcely boast, and the tiny creature was decked out in it, and on great occasions even strung with her dead mother's jewels.

Among these strange things, he had the fantastical notion to have made for her several suits of boy's clothes: pink and blue satin coats, little white, or amber, or blue satin breeches, ruffles of lace, and waistcoats embroidered with colours and silver or gold. There was also a small scarlet-coated hunting costume and all the paraphernalia of the chase. It was Sir Jeoffry's finest joke to bid her woman dress her as a boy, and then he would have her brought to the table where he and his fellows were dining together, and she would toss off her little bumper with the best of them, and rip out childish oaths, and sing them, to their delight, songs she had learned from the stable boys. She cared more for dogs and horses than for finery, and when she was not in the humour to be made a puppet of, neither tire-woman nor devil could put her into her brocades; but she liked the excitement of the dining room, and, as time went on, would be dressed in her flowered petticoats in a passion of eagerness to go and show herself, and coquet in her lace and gewgaws with men old enough to be her father, and loose enough to find her premature airs and graces a fine joke indeed. She ruled them all with her temper and her shrewish will. She would have her way in all things, or there should be no sport with her, and she would sing no songs for them, but would flout them bitterly, and sit in a great chair with her black brows drawn down, and her whole small person breathing rancour and disdain.

Sir Jeoffry, who had bullied his wife, had now the pleasurable experience of being henpecked by his daughter; for so, indeed, he was. Miss ruled him with a rod of iron, and wielded her weapon with such skill that before a year had elapsed he obeyed her as the servants below stairs had done in her infancy. She had no fear of his great oaths, for she possessed a strangely varied stock of her own upon which she could always draw, and her voice being more shrill than his, if not of such bigness, her ear-piercing shrieks and indomitable perseverance always proved too much for him in the end. It must be admitted likewise that her violence of temper and power of will were somewhat beyond his own, notwithstanding her tender years and his reputation. In fact, he found himself obliged to observe this, and finally made something of a merit and joke of it.

'There is no managing of the little shrew,' he would say. 'Neither man nor devil can bend or break her. If I smashed every bone in her carcass, she would die shrieking hell at me and defiance.'

If one admits the truth, it must be owned that if she had not had bestowed upon her by nature gifts of beauty and vivacity so extraordinary, and had been cursed with a thousandth part of the vixenishness she displayed every day of her life, he would have broken every bone in her carcass without a scruple or a qualm. But her beauty seemed but to grow with every hour that passed, and it was by exceeding good fortune exactly the fashion of beauty which he admired the most. When she attained her tenth year she was as tall as a fine boy of twelve, and of such a shape and carriage as young Diana herself might have envied. Her limbs were long, and most divinely moulded, and of a strength that caused admiration and amazement in all beholders. Her father taught her to follow him in the hunting-field, and when she appeared upon her horse, clad in her little breeches and top-boots and scarlet coat, child though she was, she set the field on fire. She learned full early how to coquet and roll her fine eyes; but it is also true that she was not much of a languisher, as all her ogling was of a destructive or proudly attacking kind. It was her habit to leave others to languish, and herself to lead them with disdainful vivacity to doing so. She was the talk, and, it must be admitted, the scandal, of the county by the day she was fifteen. The part wherein she lived was a boisterous hunting shire where there were wide ditches and high hedges to leap, and rough hills and moors to gallop over, and within the region neither polite life nor polite education were much thought of; but even in the worst portions of it there were occasional virtuous matrons who shook their heads with much gravity and wonder over the beautiful Mistress Clorinda.

Lord Twemlow's Chaplain Visits
His Patron's Kinsman, and Mistress Clorinda
Shines on Her Birthday Night

Uncivilised and almost savage as her girlish life was, and unregulated by any outward training as was her mind, there were none who came in contact with her who could be blind to a certain strong, clear wit, and unconquerableness of purpose, for which she was remarkable. She ever knew full well what she desired to gain or to avoid, and once having fixed her mind upon any object, she showed an adroitness and brilliancy of resource, a control of herself and others, the which there was no circumventing. She never made a blunder because she could not control the expression of her emotions; and when she gave way to a passion, 'twas because she chose to do so, having naught to lose, and in the midst of all their riotous jesting with her the boon companions of Sir Jeoffry knew this.

'Had she a secret to keep, child though she is,' said Eldershawe, 'there is none – man or woman – who could scare or surprise it from her; and 'tis a strange quality to note so early in a female creature.'

She spent her days with her father and his dissolute friends, treated half like a boy, half a fantastical queen, until she was fourteen. She hunted and coursed, shot birds, leaped hedges and ditches, reigned at the riotous feastings, and coquetted with these mature, and in some cases elderly, men, as if she looked forward to doing naught else all her life.

But one day, after she had gone out hunting with her father, riding Rake, who had been given to her, and wearing her scarlet coat, breeches, and top-boots, one of the few remaining members of her mother's family sent his chaplain to remonstrate and advise her father to command her to forbear from appearing in such impudent attire.

There was, indeed, a stirring scene when this message was delivered by its bearer. The chaplain was an awkward, timid creature, who had heard stories enough of Wildairs Hall and its master to undertake his mission with a quaking soul. To have refused to obey any behest of his patron would have cost him his living, and knowing this beyond a doubt, he was forced to gird up his loins and gather together all the little courage he could muster to beard the lion in his den.

The first thing he beheld on entering the big hall was a beautiful tall youth wearing his own rich black hair, and dressed in scarlet coat for hunting. He was playing with a dog, making it leap over his crop, and both laughing and swearing at its clumsiness. He glanced at the chaplain with a laughing, brilliant eye, returning the poor man's humble bow with a slight nod as he plainly hearkened to what he said as he explained his errand.

'I come from my Lord Twemlow, who is your master's kinsman,' the chaplain faltered; 'I am bidden to see and speak to him if it be possible, and his lordship much desires that Sir Jeoffry will allow it to be so. My Lord Twemlow –'

The beautiful youth left his playing with the dog and came forward with all the air of the young master of the house.

'My Lord Twemlow sends you?' he said. ''Tis long since his lordship favoured us with messages. Where is Sir Jeoffry, Lovatt?'

'In the dining hall,' answered the servant. 'He went there but a moment past, Mistress.'

The chaplain gave such a start as made him drop his shovel hat. 'Mistress!' And this was she – this fine young creature who was tall and grandly enough built and knit to seem a radiant being even when clad in masculine attire. He picked up his hat and bowed so low that it almost swept the floor in his obeisance. He was not used to female beauty which deigned to cast great smiling eyes upon him, for at my Lord Twemlow's table he sat so far below the salt that women looked not his way.

This beauty looked at him as if she was amused at the thought of something in her own mind. He wondered tremblingly if she guessed what he came for and knew how her father would receive it.

'Come with me,' she said; 'I will take you to him. He would not see you if I did not. He does not love his lordship tenderly enough.'

She led the way, holding her head jauntily and high, while he cast down his eyes lest his gaze should be led to wander in a way unseemly in one of his cloth. Such a foot and such – ! He felt it more becoming and safer to lift his eyes to the ceiling and keep them there, which gave him somewhat the aspect of one praying.

Sir Jeoffry stood at the buffet with a flagon of ale in his hand, taking his stirrup cup. At the sight of a stranger and one attired in the garb of a chaplain, he scowled surprisedly.

'What's this?' quoth he. 'What dost want, Clo? I have no leisure for a sermon.'

Mistress Clorinda went to the buffet and filled a tankard for herself and carried it back to the table, on the edge of which she half sat, with one leg bent, one foot resting on the floor.

'Time thou wilt have to take, Dad,' she said, with an arch grin, showing two rows of gleaming pearls. 'This gentleman is my Lord Twemlow's chaplain, whom he sends to exhort you, requesting you to have the civility to hear him.'

'Exhort be damned, and Twemlow be damned too!' cried Sir Jeoffry, who had a great quarrel with his lordship and hated him bitterly. 'What does the canting fool mean?'

'Sir,' faltered the poor message-bearer, 'his lordship hath – hath been concerned – having heard –'

The handsome creature balanced against the table took the tankard from her lips and laughed.

'Having heard thy daughter rides to field in breeches, and is an unseemly-behaving wench,' she cried, 'his lordship sends his chaplain to deliver a discourse thereon – not choosing to come himself. Is not that thy errand, reverend sir?'

The chaplain, poor man, turned pale, having caught, as she spoke, a glimpse of Sir Jeoffry's reddening visage.

'Madam,' he faltered, bowing – 'Madam, I ask pardon of you most humbly! If it were your pleasure to deign to – to – allow me –'

She set the tankard on the table with a rollicking smack, and thrust her hands in her breeches-pockets, swaying with laughter; and, indeed, 'twas ringing music, her rich great laugh, which, when she grew of riper years, was much lauded and written verses on by her numerous swains.

'If 'twere my pleasure to go away and allow you to speak, free from the awkwardness of a young lady's presence,' she said. 'But 'tis not, as it happens, and if I stay here, I shall be a protection.'

In truth, he required one. Sir Jeoffry broke into a torrent of blasphemy. He damned both kinsman and chaplain, and raged at the impudence of both in daring to approach him, swearing to horsewhip my lord if they ever met, and to have the chaplain kicked out of the house, and beyond the park gates themselves. But Mistress Clorinda chose to make it her whim to take it in better humour, and as a joke with a fine point to it. She laughed at her father's storming, and while the chaplain quailed before it with pallid countenance and fairly hangdog look, she seemed to find it but a cause for outbursts of merriment.

'Hold thy tongue a bit, Dad,' she cried, when he had reached his loudest, 'and let his reverence tell us what his message is. We have not even heard it.'

'Want not to hear it!' shouted Sir Jeoffry. 'Dost think I'll stand his impudence? Not I!'

'What was your message?' demanded the young lady of the chaplain. 'You cannot return without delivering it. Tell it to me. I choose it shall be told.'

The chaplain clutched and fumbled with his hat, pale, and dropping his eyes upon the floor, for very fear.

'Pluck up thy courage, man,' said Clorinda. 'I will uphold thee. The message?'

'Your pardon, madam – 'twas this,' the chaplain faltered. 'My lord commanded me to warn your honoured father – that if he did not beg you to leave off wearing – wearing –'

'Breeches,' said Mistress Clorinda, slapping her knee.

The chaplain blushed with modesty, though he was a man of sallow countenance.

'No gentleman,' he went on, going more lamely at each word – 'notwithstanding your great beauty – no gentleman –'

'Would marry me?' the young lady ended for him, with merciful good humour.

'For if you – if a young lady be permitted to bear herself in such a manner as will cause her to be held lightly, she can make no match that will not be a dishonour to her family – and – and –'

'And may do worse!' quoth Mistress Clo, and laughed until the room rang.

Sir Jeoffry's rage was such as made him like to burst; but she restrained him when he would have flung his tankard at the chaplain's head, and amid his storm of curses bundled the poor man out of the room, picking up his hat which in his hurry and fright he let fall, and thrusting it into his hand.

'Tell his lordship,' she said, laughing still as she spoke the final words, 'that I say he is right – and I will see to it that no disgrace befalls him.'

'Forsooth, Dad,' she said, returning, 'perhaps the old son of a –' – something unmannerly – 'is not so great a fool. As for me, I mean to make a fine marriage and be a great lady, and I know of none hereabouts to suit me but the old Earl of Dunstanwolde, and 'tis said he rates at all but modest women, and, in faith, he might not find breeches mannerly. I will not hunt in them again.'

She did not, though once or twice when she was in a wild mood, and her father entertained at dinner those of his companions whom she was the most inclined to, she swaggered in among them in her daintiest suits of male attire, and caused their wine-shot eyes to gloat over her boyish-maiden charms and jaunty airs and graces.

On the night of her fifteenth birthday Sir Jeoffry gave a great dinner to his boon companions and hers. She had herself commanded that there should be no ladies at the feast; for she chose to announce that she should appear at no more such, having the wit to see that she was too tall a young lady for childish follies, and that she had now arrived at an age when her market must be made.

'I shall have women enough henceforth to be dull with,' she said. 'Thou art but a poor matchmaker, Dad, or wouldst have thought of it for me. But not once has it come into thy pate that I have no mother to angle in my cause and teach me how to cast sheep's eyes at bachelors. Long-tailed petticoats from this time for me, and hoops and patches, and ogling over fans – until at last, if I play my cards well, some great lord will look my way and be taken by my shape and my manners.'

'With thy shape, Clo, God knows every man will,' laughed Sir Jeoffry, 'but I fear me not with thy manners. Thou hast the manners of a baggage, and they are second nature to thee.'

'They are what I was born with,' answered Mistress Clorinda. 'They came from him that begot me, and he has not since improved them. But now' – making a great sweeping curtsey, her impudent bright beauty almost dazzling his eyes – 'now, after my birth-night, they will be bettered; but this one night I will have my last fling.'

When the men trooped into the black oak wainscotted dining hall on the eventful night, they found their audacious young hostess awaiting them in greater and more daring beauty than they had ever before beheld. She wore knee-breeches of white satin, a pink satin coat embroidered with silver roses, white silk stockings, and shoes with great buckles of brilliants, revealing a leg so round and strong and delicately moulded, and a foot so arched and slender, as surely never before, they swore one and all, woman had had to display. She met them standing jauntily astride upon the hearth, her back to the fire, and she greeted each one as he came with some pretty impudence. Her hair was tied back and powdered, her black eyes were like lodestars, drawing all men, and her colour was that of a ripe pomegranate. She had a fine, haughty little Roman nose, a mouth like a scarlet bow, a wonderful long throat, and round cleft chin. A dazzling mien indeed she possessed, and ready enough she was to shine before them. Sir Jeoffry was now elderly, having been a man of forty when united to his conjugal companion. Most of his friends were of his own age, so that it had not been with unripe youth Mistress Clorinda had been in the habit of consorting. But upon this night a newcomer was among the guests. He was a young relation of one of the older men, and having come to his kinsman's house upon a visit, and having proved himself, in spite of his youth, to be a young fellow of humour, high courage in the hunting-field, and by no means averse either to entering upon or discussing intrigue and gallant adventure, had made himself something of a favourite. His youthful beauty for a man almost equalled that of Mistress Clorinda herself. He had an elegant, fine shape, of great strength and vigour, his countenance was delicately ruddy and handsomely featured, his curling fair hair flowed loose upon his shoulders, and, though masculine in mould, his ankle was as slender and his buckled shoe as arched as her own.

He was, it is true, twenty-four years of age and a man, while she was but fifteen and a woman, but being so tall and built with such unusual vigour of symmetry, she was a beauteous match for him, and both being attired in fashionable masculine habit, these two pretty young fellows standing smiling saucily at each other were a charming, though singular, spectacle.

This young man was already well known in the modish world of town for his beauty and adventurous spirit. He was indeed already a beau and conqueror of female hearts. It was suspected that he cherished a private ambition to set the modes in beauties and embroidered waistcoats himself in time, and be as renowned abroad and as much the town talk as certain other celebrated beaux had been before him. The art of ogling tenderly and of uttering soft nothings he had learned during his first season in town, and as he had a great melting blue eye, the figure of an Adonis, and a white and shapely hand for a ring, he was well equipped for conquest. He had darted many an inflaming glance at Mistress Clorinda before the first meats were removed. Even in London he had heard a vague rumour of this hand-some young woman, bred among her father's dogs, horses, and boon companions, and ripening into a beauty likely to make town faces pale. He had almost fallen into the spleen on hearing that she had left her boy's clothes and vowed she would wear them no more, as above all things he had desired to see how she carried them and what charms they revealed. On hearing from his host and kinsman that she had said that on her birth-night she would bid them farewell for ever by donning them for the last time, he was consumed with eagerness to obtain an invitation. This his kinsman besought for him, and, behold! the first glance the beauty shot at him pierced his inflammable bosom like a dart. Never before had it been his fortune to behold female charms so dazzling and eyes of such lustre and young majesty. The lovely baggage had a saucy way of standing with her white jewelled hands in her pockets like a pretty fop, and throwing up her little head like a modish beauty who was of royal blood; and these two tricks alone, he felt, might have set on fire the heart of a man years older and colder than himself.

If she had been of the order of soft-natured charmers, they would have fallen into each other's eyes before the wine was changed; but this Mistress Clorinda was not. She did not fear to meet the full battery of his enamoured glances, but she did not choose to return them. She played her part of the pretty young fellow who was a high-spirited beauty, with more of wit and fire than she had ever played it before. The rollicking hunting-squires, who had been her playfellows so long, devoured her with their delighted glances and roared with laughter at her sallies. Their jokes and flatteries were not of the most seemly, but she had not been bred to seemliness and modesty, and was no more ignorant than if she had been, in sooth, some gay young springald of a lad. To her it was part of the entertainment that upon this last night they conducted themselves as beseemed her boyish masquerading. Though country-bred, she had lived among companions who were men of the world and lived without restraints, and she had so far learned from them that at fifteen years old she was as worldly and as familiar with the devices of intrigue as she would be at forty. So far she had not been pushed to practising them, her singular life having thrown her among few of her own age, and those had chanced to be of a sort she disdainfully counted as country bumpkins.

But the young gallant introduced tonight into the world she lived in was no bumpkin, and was a dandy of the town. His name was Sir John Oxon, and he had just come into his title and a pretty property. His hands were as white and bejewelled as her own, his habit was of the latest fashionable cut, and his fair flowing locks scattered a delicate French perfume she did not even know the name of.

But though she observed all these attractions and found them powerful, young Sir John remarked, with a slight sinking qualm, that her great eye did not fall before his amorous glances, but met them with high smiling readiness, and her colour never blanched or heightened a whit for all their masterly skilfulness. But he had sworn to himself that he would approach close enough to her to fire off some fine speech before the night was ended, and he endeavoured to bear himself with at least an outward air of patience until he beheld his opportunity.

When the last dish was removed and bottles and bumpers stood upon the board, she sprang up on her chair and stood before them all, smiling down the long table with eyes like flashing jewels. Her hands were thrust in her pockets with her pretty young fop's air, and she drew herself to her full comely height, her beauteous lithe limbs and slender feet set smartly together. Twenty pairs of masculine eyes were turned upon her beauty, but none so ardently as the young one's across the table.

'Look your last on my fine shape,' she proclaimed in her high, rich voice. 'You will see but little of the lower part of it when it is hid in farthingales and petticoats. Look your last before I go to don my fine lady's furbelows.'

And when they filled their glasses and lifted them and shouted admiring jests to her, she broke into one of her stable boy songs, and sang it in the voice of a skylark.

No man among them was used to showing her the courtesies of polite breeding. She had been too long a boy to them for that to have entered any mind, and when she finished her song, sprang down, and made for the door, Sir John beheld his long-looked-for chance, and was there before her to open it with a great bow, made with his hand upon his heart and his fair locks falling.

'You rob us of the rapture of beholding great beauties, madam,' he said in a low, impassioned voice. 'But there should be indeed but one happy man whose bliss it is to gaze upon such perfections.'

'I am fifteen years old tonight,' she answered; 'and as yet I have not set eyes upon him.'

'How do you know that, madam?' he said, bowing lower still.

She laughed her great rich laugh.

'Forsooth, I do not know,' she retorted. 'He may be here this very night among this company; and as it might be so, I go to don my modesty.'

And she bestowed on him a parting shot in the shape of one of her prettiest young fop waves of the hand, and was gone from him.

When the door closed behind her and Sir John Oxon returned to the table, for a while a sort of dullness fell upon the party. Not being of quick minds or sentiments, these country roisterers failed to understand the heavy cloud of spleen and lack of spirit they experienced, and as they filled their glasses and tossed off one bumper after another to cure it, they soon began again to laugh and fell into boisterous joking.

They talked mostly, indeed, of their young playfellow, of whom they felt, in some indistinct manner, they were to be bereft; they rallied Sir Jeoffry, told stories of her childhood and made pictures of her budding beauties, comparing them with those of young ladies who were celebrated toasts.

'She will sail among them like a royal frigate,' said one; 'and they will pale before her lustre as a tallow dip does before an illumination.'

The clock struck twelve before she returned to them. Just as the last stroke sounded the door was thrown open, and there she stood, a woman on each side of her, holding a large silver candelabra bright with wax tapers high above her, so that she was in a flood of light.

She was attired in rich brocade of crimson and silver, and wore a great hooped petticoat, which showed off her grandeur, her waist of no more bigness than a man's hands could clasp, set in its midst like the stem of a flower; her black hair was rolled high and circled with jewels, her fair long throat blazed with a collar of diamonds, and the majesty of her eye and lip and brow made up a mien so dazzling that every man sprang to his feet beholding her.

She made a sweeping obeisance and then stood up before them, her head thrown back and her lips curving in the triumphant mocking smile of a great beauty looking upon them all as vassals.

'Down upon your knees,' she cried, 'and drink to me kneeling. From this night all men must bend so – all men on whom I deign to cast my eyes.'

'Not I,' said she.
'There thou mayst trust me.
I would not be found out.'

She went no more a-hunting in boy's clothes, but from this time forward wore brocades and paduasoys, fine lawn and lace. Her tirewoman was kept so busily engaged upon making rich habits, fragrant waters and essences, and so running at her bidding to change her gown or dress her head in some new fashion, that her life was made to her a weighty burden to bear, and also a painful one. Her place had before been an easy one but for her mistress' choleric temper, but it was so no more. Never had young lady been so exacting and so tempestuous when not pleased with the adorning of her face and shape. In the presence of polite strangers, whether ladies or gentlemen, Mistress Clorinda in these days chose to chasten her language and give less rein to her fantastical passions, but alone in her closet with her woman, if a riband did but not suit her fancy, or a hoop not please, she did not fear to be as scurrilous as she chose. In this discreet retirement she rapped out oaths and boxed her woman's ears with a vigorous hand, tore off her gowns and stamped them beneath her feet, or flung pots of pomade at the poor woman's head. She took these freedoms with such a readiness and spirit that she was served with a despatch and humbleness scarcely to be equalled, and, it is certain, never excelled.

The high courage and undaunted will which had been the engines she had used to gain her will from her infant years aided her in these days to carry out what her keen mind and woman's wit had designed, which was to take the county by storm with her beauty, and reign toast and enslaver until such time as she won the prize of a husband of rich estates and notable rank.

It was soon bruited abroad, to the amazement of the county, that Mistress Clorinda Wildairs had changed her strange and unseemly habits of life, and had become as much a young lady of fashion and breeding as her birth and charm demanded. This was first made known by her appearing one Sunday morning at church, accompanied – as though attended with a retinue of servitors – by Mistress Wimpole and her two sisters, whose plain faces, awkward shape, and still more awkward attire were such a foil to her glowing loveliness as set it in high relief. It was seldom that the coach from Wildairs Hall drew up before the lychgate, but upon rare Sunday mornings Mistress Wimpole and her two charges contrived, if Sir Jeoffry was not in an ill humour and the coachman was complaisant, to be driven to service. Usually, however, they trudged afoot, and, if the day chanced to be sultry, arrived with their snub-nosed faces of a high and shiny colour, or if the country roads were wet, with their petticoats bemired.

This morning, when the coach drew up, the horses were well groomed, the coachman smartly dressed, and a footman was in attendance, who sprang to earth and opened the door with a flourish.

The loiterers in the churchyard, and those who were approaching the gate or passing towards the church porch, stared with eyes wide stretched in wonder and incredulity. Never had such a thing before been beheld or heard of as what they now saw in broad daylight.

Mistress Clorinda, clad in highest town fashion, in brocades and silver lace and splendid furbelows, stepped forth from the chariot with the air of a queen. She had the majestic composure of a young lady who had worn nothing less modish than such raiment all her life, and who had prayed decorously beneath her neighbours' eyes since she had left her nurse's care.

Her sisters and their governess looked timorous, and as if they knew not where to cast their eyes for shamefacedness; but not so Mistress Clorinda, who moved forward with a stately, swimming gait, her fine head in the air. As she stepped into the porch a young gentleman drew back and made a profound obeisance to her. She cast her eyes upon him and returned it with a grace and condescension which struck the beholders dumb with admiring awe. To some of the people of a commoner sort he was a stranger, but all connected with the gentry knew he was Sir John Oxon, who was staying at Eldershawe Park with his relative, whose estate it was.

How Mistress Clorinda contrived to manage it no one was aware but herself, but after a few appearances at church she appeared at other places. She was seen at dinners at fine houses, and began to be seen at routs and balls. Where she was seen she shone, and with such radiance as caused matchmaking matrons great dismay, and their daughters woeful qualms. Once having shone, she could not be extinguished or hidden under a bushel; for, being of rank and highly connected through mother as well as father, and playing her cards with great wit and skill, she could not be thrust aside.

At her first hunt ball she set aflame every male breast in the shire, unmasking such a battery of charms as no man could withstand the fire of. Her dazzling eye, her wondrous shape, the rich music of her laugh, and the mocking wit of her sharp saucy tongue were weapons to have armed a dozen women, and she was but one, and in the first rich tempting glow of blooming youth.

She turned more heads and caused more quarrels than she could have counted had she sat up half the night. She went to her coach with her father followed by a dozen gallants, each ready to spit the other for a smile. Her smiles were wondrous, but there seemed always a touch of mockery or disdain in them which made them more remembered than if they had been softer.

One man there was, who perchance found something in her high glance not wholly scornful, but he was used to soft treatment from women, and had, in sooth, expected milder glances than were bestowed upon him. This was young Sir John Oxon, who had found himself among the fair sex that night as great a beau as she had been a belle; but two dances he had won from her, and this was more than any other man could boast, and what other gallants envied him with darkest hatred.

Sir Jeoffry, who had watched her as she queened it amongst rakes and fops and honest country squires and knights, had marked the vigour with which they plied her with an emotion which was a new sensation to his drink-bemuddled brain. So far as it was in his nature to love another than himself, he had learned to love this young lovely virago of his own flesh and blood, perchance because she was the only creature who had never quailed before him, and had always known how to bend him to her will.

When the chariot rode away, he looked at her as she sat erect in the early morning light, as unblenching, bright, and untouched in bloom as if she had that moment risen from her pillow and washed her face in dew. He was not so drunk as he had been at midnight, but he was a little maudlin.

'By God, thou art handsome, Clo!' he said. 'By God, I never saw a finer woman!'

'Nor I,' she answered back, 'which I thank Heaven for.'

'Thou pretty, brazen baggage,' her father laughed. 'Old Dunstanwolde looked thee well over tonight. He never looked away from the moment he clapped eyes on thee.'

'That I knew better than thee, Dad,' said the beauty; 'and I saw that he could not have done it if he had tried. If there comes no richer, younger great gentleman, he shall marry me.'

'Thou hast a sharp eye and a keen wit,' said Sir Jeoffry, looking askance at her with a new maggot in his brain. 'Wouldst never play the fool, I warrant. They will press thee hard and 'twill be hard to withstand their lovemaking, but I shall never have to mount and ride off with pistols in my holsters to bring back a man and make him marry thee, as Chris Crowell had to do for his youngest wench. Thou wouldst never play the fool, I warrant – wouldst thou, Clo?'

She tossed her head and laughed like a young scornful devil, showing her white pearl teeth between her lips' scarlet.

'Not I,' she said. 'There thou mayst trust me. I would not be found out.'

She played her part as triumphant beauty so successfully that the cleverest managing mother in the universe could not have bettered her position. Gallants brawled for her; honest men fell at her feet; romantic swains wrote verses to her, praising her eyes, her delicate bosom, the carnation of her cheek, and the awful majesty of her mien. In every revel she was queen, in every contest of beauties Venus, in every spectacle of triumph empress of them all.

The Earl of Dunstanwolde, who had the oldest name and the richest estates in his own county and the six adjoining ones, who, having made a love-match in his prime, and lost wife and heir but a year after his nuptials, had been the despair of every maid and mother who knew him, because he would not be melted to a marriageable mood. After the hunt ball this mourning nobleman, who was by this time of ripe years, had appeared in the world again as he had not done for many years. Before many months had elapsed, it was known that his admiration of the new beauty was confessed, and it was believed that he but waited further knowledge of her to advance to the point of laying his title and estates at her feet.

But though, two years before, the entire county would have rated low indeed the wit and foresight of the man who had even hinted the possibility of such honour and good fortune being in prospect for the young lady, so great was Mistress Clorinda's brilliant and noble beauty, and with such majesty she bore herself in these times, that there were even those who doubted whether she would think my lord a rich enough prize for her, and if, when he fell upon his knees, she would deign to become his countess, feeling that she had such splendid wares to dispose of as might be bartered for a duke, when she went to town and to court.

During the length of more than one man's lifetime after, the reign of Mistress Clorinda Wildairs was a memory recalled over the bottle at the dining-table among men, some of whom had but heard their fathers vaunt her beauties. It seemed as if in her person there was not a single flaw, or indeed a charm, which had not reached the highest point of beauty. For shape she might have vied with young Diana, mounted side by side with her upon a pedestal; her raven locks were of a length and luxuriance to clothe her as a garment, her great eye commanded and flashed as Juno's might have done in the goddess' divinest moments of lovely pride, and though it was said none ever saw it languish, each man who adored her was maddened by the secret belief that Venus' self could not so melt in love as she if she would stoop to loving – as each one prayed she might – himself. Her hands and feet, her neck, the slimness of her waist, her mantling crimson and ivory white, her little ear, her scarlet lip, the pearls between them and her long white throat, were perfection each and all, and catalogued with oaths of rapture.

'She hath such beauties,' one admirer said, 'that a man must toast them all and cannot drink to her as to a single woman. And she hath so many that to slight none her servant must go from the table reeling.'

There was but one thing connected with her which was not a weapon to her hand, and this was, that she was not a fortune. Sir Jeoffry had drunk and rioted until he had but little left. He had cut his timber and let his estate go to rack, having, indeed, no money to keep it up. The great Hall, which had once been a fine old place, was almost a ruin. Its carved oak and noble rooms and galleries were all of its past splendours that remained. All had been sold that could be sold, and all the outcome had been spent. The county, indeed, wondered where Mistress Clorinda's fine clothes came from, and knew full well why she was not taken to court to kneel to the Queen. That she was waiting for this to make her match, the envious were quite sure, and did not hesitate to whisper pretty loudly.

The name of one man of rank and fortune after another was spoken of as that of a suitor to her hand, but in some way it was discovered that she refused them all. It was also known that they continued to worship her, and that at any moment she could call even the best among them back. It seemed that, while all the men were enamoured of her, there was not one who could cure himself of his passion, however hopeless it might be.

Her wit was as great as her beauty, and she had a spirit before which no man could stand if she chose to be disdainful. To some she was so, and had the whim to flout them with great brilliancy. Encounters with her were always remembered, and if heard by those not concerned, were considered worthy both of recollection and of being repeated to the world; she had a tongue so nimble and a wit so full of fire.

Young Sir John Oxon's visit to his relative at Eldershawe being at an end, he returned to town, and remaining there through a few weeks of fashionable gaiety, won new reputations as a triumpher over the female heart. He made some renowned conquests and set the mode in some new essences and sword knots. But even these triumphs appeared to pall upon him shortly, since he deserted the town and returned again to the country, where, on this occasion, he did not stay with his relative, but with Sir Jeoffry himself, who had taken a boisterous fancy to him.

It had been much marked since the altered life of Mistress Clorinda that she, who had previously defied all rules laid down on behaviour for young ladies, and had been thought to do so because she knew none of them, now proved that her wild fashion had been but wilfulness, since it was seen that she must have observed and marked manners with the best. There seemed no decorum she did not know how to observe with the most natural grace. It was, indeed, all grace and majesty, there being no suggestion of the prude about her, but rather the manner of a young lady having been born with pride and stateliness, and most carefully bred. This was the result of her wondrous wit, the highness of her talents, and the strength of her will, which was of such power that she could carry out without fail anything she chose to undertake. There are some women who have beauty, and some who have wit or vigour of understanding, but she possessed all three, and with them such courage and strength of nerve as would have well equipped a man.

Quick as her wit was and ready as were her brilliant quips and sallies, there was no levity in her demeanour, and she kept Mistress Margery Wimpole in discreet attendance upon her, as if she had been the daughter of a Spanish Hidalgo, never to be approached except in the presence of her duenna. Poor Mistress Margery, finding her old fears removed, was overpowered with new ones. She had no lawlessness or hoyden manners to contend with, but instead a haughtiness so high and demands so great that her powers could scarcely satisfy the one or her spirit stand up before the other.

'It is as if one were lady-in-waiting to Her Majesty's self,' she used to whimper when she was alone and dare do so. 'Surely the Queen has not such a will and such a temper. She will have me toil to look worthy of her in my habit, and bear myself like a duchess in dignity. Alack! I have practised my obeisance by the hour to perfect it, so that I may escape her wrath. And I must know how to look, and when and where to sit, and with what air of being near at hand, while I must see nothing! And I must drag my failing limbs hither and thither with genteel ease while I ache from head to foot, being neither young nor strong.'

The poor lady was so overawed by, and yet so admired, her charge, that it was piteous to behold.

'She is an arrant fool,' quoth Mistress Clorinda to her father. 'A nice duenna she would be, forsooth, if she were with a woman who needed watching. She could be hoodwinked as it pleased me a dozen times a day. It is I who am her guard, not she mine! But a beauty must drag some spy about with her, it seems, and she I can make to obey me like a spaniel. We can afford no better, and she is well born, and since I bought her the purple paduasoy and the new lappets she has looked well enough to serve.'

'Dunstanwolde need not fear for thee now,' said Sir Jeoffry. 'Thou art a clever and foreseeing wench, Clo.'

'Dunstanwolde nor any man!' she answered. 'There will be no gossip of me. It is Anne and Barbara thou must look to, Dad, lest their plain faces lead them to show soft hearts. My face is my fortune!'

When Sir John Oxon paid his visit to Sir Jeoffry the days of Mistress Margery were filled with carking care. The night before he arrived, Mistress Clorinda called her to her closet and laid upon her her commands in her own high way. She was under her woman's hands, and while her great mantle of black hair fell over the back of her chair and lay on the floor, her tirewoman passing the brush over it, lock by lock, she was at her greatest beauty. Either she had been angered or pleased, for her cheek wore a bloom even deeper and richer than usual, and there was a spark like a diamond under the fringe of her lashes.

At her first timorous glance at her, Mistress Margery thought she must have been angered, the spark so burned in her eyes, and so evident was the light but quick heave of her bosom; but the next moment it seemed as if she must be in a pleasant humour, for a little smile deepened the dimples in the corner of her bowed, full lips. But quickly she looked up and resumed her stately air.

'This gentleman who comes to visit tomorrow,' she said, 'Sir John Oxon – do you know aught of him?'

'But little, Madame,' Mistress Margery answered with fear and humility.

'Then it will be well that you should, since I have commands to lay upon you concerning him,' said the beauty.

'You do me honour,' said the poor gentlewoman.

Mistress Clorinda looked her straight in the face.

'He is a gentleman from town, the kinsman of Lord Elder-shawe,' she said. 'He is a handsome man, concerning whom many women have been fools. He chooses to allow it to be said that he is a conqueror of female hearts and virtue, even among women of fashion and rank. If this be said in the town, what may not be said in the country? He shall wear no such graces here. He chooses to pay his court to me. He is my father's guest and a man of fashion. Let him make as many fine speeches as he has the will to. I will listen or not as I choose. I am used to words. But see that we are not left alone.'

The tirewoman pricked up her ears. Clorinda saw her in the glass.

'Attend to thy business if thou dost not want a box o' the ear,' she said in a tone which made the woman start.

'You would not be left alone with the gentleman, madam?' faltered Mistress Margery.

'If he comes to boast of conquests,' said Mistress Clorinda, looking at her straight again and drawing down her black brows, 'I will play as cleverly as he. He cannot boast greatly of one whom he never makes his court to but in the presence of a kinswoman of ripe years. Understand that this is to be your task.'

'I will remember, madam,' answered Mistress Margery. 'I will bear myself as you command.'

'That is well,' said Mistress Clorinda. 'I will keep you no more. You may go.'

Relating How Mistress Anne
Discovered a Miniature

The good gentlewoman took her leave gladly. She had spent a life in timid fears of such things and persons as were not formed by Nature to excite them, but never had she experienced such humble terrors as those with which Mistress Clorinda inspired her. Never did she approach her without inward tremor, and never did she receive permission to depart from her presence without relief. And yet her beauty and wit and spirit had no admirer regarding them with more of wondering awe.

In the bare west wing of the house, comfortless though the neglect of its master had made it, there was one corner where she was unafraid. Her first charges, Mistress Barbara and Mistress Anne, were young ladies of gentle spirit. Their sister had said of them that their spirit was as poor as their looks. It could not be said of them by anyone that they had any pretension to beauty, but that which Mistress Clorinda rated at as poor spirit was the one element of comfort in their poor dependent kinswoman's life. They gave her no ill words, they indulged in no fantastical whims and vapours, and they did not even seem to expect other entertainment than to walk the country roads, to play with their little lapdog Cupid, wind silks for their needlework, and please themselves with their embroidery-frames.

To them their sister appeared a goddess whom it would be presumptuous to approach in any frame of mind quite ordinary. Her beauty must be heightened by rich adornments, while their plain looks were left without the poorest aid. It seemed but fitting that what there was to spend must be spent on her. They showed no signs of resentment, and took with gratitude such cast-off finery as she deigned at times to bestow upon them, when it was no longer useful to herself. She was too full of the occupations of pleasure to have had time to notice them, even if her nature had inclined her to the observance of family affections. It was their habit, when they knew of her going out in state, to watch her incoming and outgoing through a peephole in a chamber window. Mistress Margery told them stories of her admirers and of her triumphs, of the county gentlemen of fortune who had offered themselves to her, and of the modes of life in town of the handsome Sir John Oxon, who, without doubt, was of the circle of her admiring attendants, if he had not fallen totally her victim, as others had.

Of the two young women, it was Mistress Anne who had the more parts, and the attraction of the mind the least dull. In sooth, Nature had dealt with both in a niggardly fashion, but Mistress Barbara was the plainer and the more foolish. Mistress Anne had, perchance, the tenderer feelings, and was in secret given to a certain sentimentality. She was thin and stooping, and had but a muddy complexion; her hair was heavy, it is true, but its thickness and weight seemed naught but an ungrateful burden; and she had a dull, soft eye. In private she was fond of reading such romances as she could procure by stealth from the library of books gathered together in past times by some ancestor Sir Jeoffry regarded as an idiot. Doubtless she met with strange reading in the volumes she took to her closet, and her simple virgin mind found cause for the solving of many problems; but from the pages she contrived to cull stories of lordly lovers and cruel or kind beauties, whose romances created for her a strange world of pleasure in the midst of her loneliness. Poor, neglected young female, with every guileless maiden instinct withered at birth, she had need of some tender dreams to dwell upon, though Fate herself seemed to have decreed that they must be no more than visions.

It was, in sooth, always the beauteous Clorinda about whose charms she builded her romances. In her great power she saw that for which knights fought in tourney and great kings committed royal sins, and to her splendid beauty she had in secrecy felt that all might be forgiven. She cherished such fancies of her, that one morning, when she believed her absent from the house, she stole into the corridor upon which Clorinda's apartment opened. Her first timid thought had been, that if a chamber door were opened she might catch a glimpse of some of the splendours her sister's woman was surely laying out for her wearing at a birth-night ball, at the house of one of the gentry of the neighbourhood. But it so happened that she really found the door of entrance open, which, indeed, she had not more than dared to hope, and finding it so, she stayed her foot steps to gaze with beating heart within. On the great bed, which was of carved oak and canopied with tattered tapestry, there lay spread such splendours as she had never beheld near to before. 'Twas blue and silver brocade Mistress Clorinda was to shine in tonight; it lay spread forth in all its dimensions. The beautiful bosom and shoulders were to be bared to the eyes of scores of adorers, but rich lace was to set their beauties forth, and strings of pearls. Why Sir Jeoffry had not sold his lady's jewels before he became enamoured of her six-year-old child it would be hard to explain. There was a great painted fan with jewels in the sticks, and on the floor – as if peeping forth from beneath the bravery of the expanded petticoats – was a pair of blue and silver shoes, high-heeled and arched and slender. In gazing at them Mistress Anne lost her breath, thinking that in some fashion they had a regal air of being made to trample hearts beneath them.

To the gentle, hapless virgin, to whom such possessions were as the wardrobe of a queen, the temptation to behold them near was too great. She could not forbear from passing the threshold, and she did with heaving breast. She approached the bed and gazed; she dared to touch the scented gloves that lay by the outspread petticoat of blue and silver; she even laid a trembling finger upon the pointed bodice, which was so slender that it seemed small enough for even a child.

'Ah me,' she sighed gently, 'how beautiful she will be! How beautiful! And all of them will fall at her feet, as is not to be wondered at. And it was always so all her life, even when she was an infant, and all gave her her will because of her beauty and her power. She hath a great power. Barbara and I are not so. We are dull and weak, and dare not speak our minds. It is as if we were creatures of another world; but He who rules all things has so willed it for us. He has given it to us for our portion – our portion.'

Her dull, poor face dropped a little as she spoke the words, and her eyes fell upon the beauteous tiny shoes, which seemed to trample even when no foot was within them. She stooped to take one in her hand, but as she was about to lift it something which seemed to have been dropped upon the floor, and to have rolled beneath the valance of the bed, touched her hand. It was a thing to which a riband was attached – an ivory miniature – and she picked it up wondering. She stood up gazing at it, in such bewilderment to find her eyes upon it that she scarce knew what she did. She did not mean to pry; she would not have had the daring so to do if she had possessed the inclination. But the instant her eyes told her what they saw, she started and blushed as she had never blushed before in her tame life. The warm rose mantled her cheeks, and even suffused the neck her chaste kerchief hid. Her eye kindled with admiration and an emotion new to her indeed.

'How beautiful!' she said. 'He is like a young Adonis, and has the bearing of a royal prince! How can it – by what strange chance hath it come here?'

She had not regarded it more than long enough to have uttered these words, when a fear came upon her, and she felt that she had fallen into misfortune.

'What must I do with it?' she trembled. 'What will she say, whether she knows of its being within the chamber or not? She will be angry with me that I have dared to touch it. What shall I do?'

She regarded it again with eyes almost suffused. Her blush and the sensibility of her emotion gave to her plain countenance a new liveliness of tint and expression.

'I will put it back where I found it,' she said, 'and the one who knows it will find it later. It cannot be she – it cannot be she! If I laid it on her table she would rate me bitterly – and she can be bitter when she will.'

She bent and placed it within the shadow of the valance again, and as she felt it touch the hard oak of the polished floor her bosom rose with a soft sigh.

'It is an unseemly thing to do,' she said; ''tis as though one were uncivil; but I dare not – I dare not do otherwise.'

She would have turned to leave the apartment, being much overcome by the incident, but just as she would have done so she heard the sound of horses' feet through the window by which she must pass, and looked out to see if it was Clorinda who was returning from her ride. Mistress Clorinda was a matchless horsewoman, and a marvel of loveliness and spirit she looked when she rode, sitting upon a horse such as no other woman dared to mount – always an animal of the greatest beauty, but of so dangerous a spirit that her riding whip was loaded like a man's.

This time it was not she; and when Mistress Anne beheld the young gentleman who had drawn rein in the court she started backward and put her hand to her heart, the blood mantling her pale cheek again in a flood. But having started back, the next instant she started forward to gaze again, all her timid soul in her eyes.

''Tis he!' she panted; ''tis he himself! He hath come in hope to speak with my sister, and she is abroad. Poor gentleman, he hath come in such high spirit, and must ride back heavy of heart. How comely, and how finely clad he is!'

He was, in sooth, with his rich riding habit, his handsome face, his plumed hat, and the sun shining on the fair luxuriant locks which fell beneath it. It was Sir John Oxon, and he was habited as when he rode in the park in town and the court was there. Not so were attired the country gentry whom Anne had been wont to see, though many of them were well mounted, knowing horseflesh and naught else, as they did.

She pressed her cheek against the side of the oriel window, over which the ivy grew thickly. She was so intent that she could not withdraw her gaze. She watched him as he turned away, having received his dismissal, and she pressed her face closer that she might follow him as he rode down the long avenue of oak trees, his servant riding behind.

Thus she bent forward gazing, until he turned and the oaks hid him from her sight; and even then the spell was not dissolved, and she still regarded the place where he had passed, until a sound behind her made her start violently. It was a peal of laughter, high and rich, and when she so started and turned to see whom it might be, she beheld her sister Clorinda, who was standing just within the threshold, as if movement had been arrested by what had met her eye as she came in. Poor Anne put her hand to her side again.

'Oh sister!' she gasped; 'oh sister!' but could say no more.

She saw that she had thought falsely, and that Clorinda had not been out at all, for she was in home attire; and even in the midst of her trepidation there sprang into Anne's mind the awful thought that through some servant's blunder the comely young visitor had been sent away. For herself, she expected but to be driven forth with wrathful, disdainful words for her presumption. For what else could she hope from this splendid creature, who, while of her own flesh and blood, had never seemed to regard her as being more than a poor superfluous underling? But strangely enough, there was no anger in Clorinda's eyes; she but laughed, as though what she had seen had made her merry.

'You here, Anne,' she said, 'and looking with light-mindedness after gallant gentlemen! Mistress Margery should see to this and watch more closely, or we shall have unseemly stories told. You, sister, with your modest face and bashfulness! I had not thought it of you.'

Suddenly she crossed the room to where her sister stood drooping, and seized her by the shoulder, so that she could look her well in the face.

'What,' she said, with a mocking not quite harsh – 'What is this? Does a glance at a fine gallant, even taken from behind an oriel window, make such change indeed? I never before saw this look, nor this colour, forsooth; it hath improved thee wondrously, Anne – wondrously.'

'Sister,' faltered Anne, 'I so desired to see your birth-night ballgown, of which Mistress Margery hath much spoken – I so desired – I thought it would not matter if, the door being open and it spread forth upon the bed – I – I stole a look at it. And then I was tempted – and came in.'

'And then was tempted more,' Clorinda laughed, still regarding her downcast countenance shrewdly, 'by a thing far less to be resisted – a fine gentleman from town, with lovelocks falling on his shoulders and ladies' hearts strung at his saddle-bow by scores. Which found you the most beautiful?'

'Your gown is splendid, sister,' said Anne, with modest shyness. 'There will be no beauty who will wear another like it, or should there be one, she will not carry it as you will.'

'But the man – the man, Anne,' Clorinda laughed again. 'What of the man?'

Anne plucked up just enough of her poor spirit to raise her eyes to the brilliant ones that mocked at her.

'With such gentlemen, sister,' she said, 'is it like that I have aught to do?'

Mistress Clorinda dropped her hand and left laughing.

''Tis true,' she said, 'it is not; but for this one time, Anne, thou lookest almost a woman.'

''Tis not beauty alone that makes womanhood,' said Anne, her head on her breast again. 'In some book I have read that – that it is mostly pain. I am woman enough for that.'

'You have read – you have read,' quoted Clorinda. 'You are the bookworm, I remember, and filch romances and poems from the shelves. And you have read that it is mostly pain that makes a woman? 'Tis not true. 'Tis a poor lie. I am a woman and I do not suffer – for I will not, that I swear! And when I take an oath I keep it, mark you! It is men women suffer for; that was what your scholar meant – for such fine gentlemen as the one you have just watched while he rode away. More fools they! No man shall make me womanly in such a fashion, I promise you! Let them wince and kneel; I will not.'

'Sister,' Anne faltered, 'I thought you were not within. The gentleman who rode away – did the servants know?'

'That did they,' quoth Clorinda, mocking again. 'They knew that I would not receive him today, and so sent him away. He might have known as much himself, but he is an arrant popinjay, and thinks all women wish to look at his fine shape, and hear him flatter them when he is in the mood.'

'You would not – let him enter?'

Clorinda threw her graceful body into a chair with more light laughter.

'I would not,' she answered. 'You cannot understand such ingratitude, poor Anne; you would have treated him more softly. Sit down and talk to me, and I will show thee my furbelows myself. All women like to chatter of their laced bodices and petticoats. That is what makes a woman.'

Anne was tremulous with relief and pleasure. It was as if a queen had bid her to be seated. She sat almost with the humble lack of ease a servingwoman might have shown. She had never seen Clorinda wear such an air before, and never had she dreamed that she would so open herself to any fellow creature. She knew but little of what her sister was capable – of the brilliancy of her charm when she chose to condescend, of the deigning softness of her manner when she chose to please, of her arch-pleasantries and cutting wit, and of the strange power she could wield over any human being, gentle or simple, with whom she came in contact. But if she had not known of these things before, she learned to know them this morning. For some reason best known to herself, Mistress Clorinda was in a high good humour. She kept Anne with her for more than an hour, and was dazzling through every moment of its passing. She showed her the splendours she was to shine in at the birth-night ball, even bringing forth her jewels and displaying them. She told her stories of the house of which the young heir today attained his majority, and mocked at the poor youth because he was ungainly, and at a distance had been her slave since his nineteenth year.

'I have scarce looked at him,' she said. 'He is a lout, with great eyes staring, and a red nose. It does not need that one should look at men to win them. They look at us, and that is enough.'

To poor Mistress Anne, who had seen no company and listened to no wits, the entertainment bestowed upon her was as wonderful as a night at the playhouse would have been. To watch the vivid changing face; to hearken to jesting stories of men and women who seemed like the heroes and heroines of her romances; to hear love itself – the love she trembled and palpitated at the mere thought of – spoken of openly as an experience which fell to all; to hear it mocked at with dainty or biting quips; to learn that women of all ages played with, enjoyed, or lost themselves for it – it was with her as if a nun had been withdrawn from her cloister and plunged into the vortex of the world.

'Sister,' she said, looking at the beauty with humble, adoring eyes, 'you make me feel that my romances are true. You tell such things. It is like seeing pictures of things to hear you talk. No wonder that all listen to you, for indeed 'tis wonderful the way you have with words. You use them so that 'tis as though they had shapes of their own and colours, and you builded with them. I thank you for being so gracious to me, who have seen so little, and cannot tell the poor, quiet things I have seen.'

And being led into the loving boldness by her gratitude, she bent forward and touched with her lips the fair hand resting on the chair's arm.

Mistress Clorinda fixed her fine eyes upon her in a new way.

'I' faith, it doth not seem fair, Anne,' she said. 'I should not like to change lives with thee. Thou hast eyes like a shot pheasant – soft, and with the bright hid beneath the dull. Some man might love them, even if thou art no beauty. Stay,' suddenly; 'methinks –'

She uprose from her chair and went to the oaken wardrobe, and threw the door of it open wide while she looked within.

'There is a gown and tippet or so here, and a hood and some ribands I might do without,' she said. 'My woman shall bear them to your chamber, and show you how to set them to rights. She is a nimble-fingered creature, and a gown of mine would give almost stuff enough to make you two. Then some days, when I am not going abroad and Mistress Margery frets me too much, I will send for you to sit with me, and you shall listen to the gossip when a visitor drops in to have a dish of tea.'

Anne would have kissed her feet then, if she had dared to do so. She blushed red all over, and adored her with a more worshipping gaze than before.

'I should not have dared to hope so much,' she stammered. 'I could not – perhaps it is not fitting – perhaps I could not bear myself as I should. I would try to show myself a gentlewoman and seemly. I – I am a gentlewoman, though I have learned so little. I could not be aught but a gentlewoman, could I, sister, being of your own blood and my parents' child?' half afraid to presume even this much.

'No,' said Clorinda. 'Do not be a fool, Anne, and carry yourself too humbly before the world. You can be as humble as you like to me.'

'I shall – I shall be your servant and worship you, sister,' cried the poor soul, and she drew near and kissed again the white hand which had bestowed with such royal bounty all this joy. It would not have occurred to her that a cast-off robe and riband were but small largesse.

It was not a minute after this grateful caress that Clorinda made a sharp movement – a movement which was so sharp that it seemed to be one of dismay. At first, as if involuntarily, she had raised her hand to her tucker, and after doing so she started – though 'twas but for a second's space, after which her face was as it had been before.

'What is it?' exclaimed Anne. 'Have you lost anything?'

'No,' quoth Mistress Clorinda quite carelessly, as she once more turned to the contents of the oaken wardrobe; 'but I thought I missed a trinket I was wearing for a wager, and I would not lose it before the bet is won.'

'Sister,' ventured Anne before she left her and went away to her own dull world in the west wing, 'there is a thing I can do if you will allow me. I can mend your tapestry hangings which have holes in them. I am quick at my needle, and should love to serve you in such poor ways as I can; and it is not seemly that they should be so worn. All things about you should be beautiful and well kept.'

'Can you make these broken things beautiful?' said Clorinda. 'Then indeed you shall. You may come here to mend them when you will.'

'They are very fine hangings, though so old and ill cared for,' said Anne, looking up at them; 'and I shall be only too happy sitting here thinking of all you are doing while I am at my work.'

'Thinking of all I am doing?' laughed Mistress Clorinda. 'That would give you such wondrous things to dream of, Anne, that you would have no time for your needle, and my hangings would stay as they are.'

'I can think and darn also,' said Mistress Anne, 'so I will come.'

'Twas the Face of Sir John Oxon
the Moon Shone Upon

From that time henceforward into the young woman's dull life there came a little change. It did not seem a little change to her, but a great one, though to others it would have seemed slight indeed. She was an affectionate, housewifely creature, who would have made the best of wives and mothers if it had been so ordained by Fortune, and something of her natural instincts found outlet in the furtive service she paid her sister, who became the empress of her soul. She darned and patched the tattered hangings with a wonderful neatness, and the hours she spent at work in the chamber were to her almost as sacred as hours spent at religious duty, or as those nuns and novices give to embroidering altar-cloths. There was a brightness in the room that seemed in no other in the house, and the lingering essences in the air of it were as incense to her. In secrecy she even busied herself with keeping things in better order than Rebecca, Mistress Clorinda's woman, had ever had time to do before. She also contrived to get into her own hands some duties that were Rebecca's own. She could mend lace cleverly and arrange riband knots with taste, and even change the fashion of a gown. The hard-worked tirewoman was but too glad to be relieved, and kept her secret well, being praised many times for the set or fashion of a thing into which she had not so much as set a needle. Being a shrewd baggage, she was wise enough always to relate to Anne the story of her mistress' pleasure, having the wit to read in her delight that she would be encouraged to fresh effort.

At times it so befell that, when Anne went into the bed-chamber, she found the beauty there, who, if she chanced to be in the humour, would detain her in her presence for a space and bewitch her over again. In sooth, it seemed that she took a pleasure in showing her female adorer how wondrously full of all fascinations she could be. At such times Anne's plain face would almost bloom with excitement, and her shot pheasant's eyes would glow as if beholding a goddess.

She neither saw nor heard more of the miniature on the riband. It used to make her tremble at times to fancy that by some strange chance it might still be under the bed, and that the handsome face smiled and the blue eyes gazed in the very apartment where she herself sat and her sister was robed and disrobed in all her beauty.

She used all her modest skill in fitting to her own shape and refurnishing the cast-off bits of finery bestowed upon her. It was all set to rights long before Clorinda recalled to mind that she had promised that Anne should sometime see her chance visitors take their dish of tea with her.

But one day, for some cause, she did remember, and sent for her.

Anne ran to her bedchamber and donned her remodelled gown with shaking hands. She laughed a little hysterically as she did it, seeing her plain snub-nosed face in the glass. She tried to dress her head in a fashion new to her, and knew she did it ill and untidily, but had no time to change it. If she had had some red she would have put it on, but such vanities were not in her chamber or Barbara's. So she rubbed her cheeks hard, and even pinched them, so that in the end they looked as if they were badly rouged. It seemed to her that her nose grew red too, and indeed 'twas no wonder, for her hands and feet were like ice.

'She must be ashamed of me,' the humble creature said to herself. 'And if she is ashamed she will be angered and send me away and be friends no more.'

She did not deceive herself, poor thing, and imagine she had the chance of being regarded with any great lenience if she appeared ill.

'Mistress Clorinda begged that you would come quickly,' said Rebecca, knocking at the door.

So she caught her handkerchief, which was scented, as all her garments were, with dried rose leaves from the garden, which she had conserved herself, and went down to the chintz parlour trembling.

It was a great room with white panels, and flowered coverings to the furniture. There were a number of ladies and gentlemen standing talking and laughing loudly together. The men outnumbered the women, and most of them stood in a circle about Mistress Clorinda, who sat upright in a great flowered chair, smiling with her mocking, stately air, as if she defied them to dare to speak what they felt.

Anne came in like a mouse. Nobody saw her. She did not, indeed, know what to do. She dared not remain standing all alone, so she crept to the place where her sister's chair was, and stood a little behind its high back. Her heart beat within her breast till it was like to choke her.

They were only country gentlemen who made the circle, but to her they seemed dashing gallants. That some of them had red noses as well as cheeks, and that their voices were big and their gallantries boisterous, was no drawback to their manly charms, she having seen no other finer gentlemen. They were specimens of the great conquering creature Man, whom all women must aspire to please if they have the fortunate power; and each and all of them were plainly trying to please Clorinda, and not she them.

And so Anne gazed at them with admiring awe, waiting until there should come a pause in which she might presume to call her sister's attention to her presence; but suddenly, before she had indeed made up her mind how she might best announce herself, there spoke behind her a voice of silver.

'It is only goddesses,' said the voice, 'who waft about them as they move the musk of the rose-gardens of Araby. When you come to reign over us in town, madam, there will be no perfume in the mode but that of rose leaves, and in all drawing rooms we shall breathe but their perfume.'

And there, at her side, was bowing, in cinnamon and crimson, with jewelled buttons on his velvet coat, the beautiful being whose fair locks the sun had shone on the morning she had watched him ride away – the man whom the imperial beauty had dismissed and called a popinjay.

Clorinda looked under her lashes towards him without turning, but in so doing beheld Anne standing in waiting.

'A fine speech lost,' she said, 'though 'twas well enough for the country, Sir John. 'Tis thrown away, because 'tis not I who am scented with rose leaves, but Anne there, whom you must not ogle. Come hither, sister, and do not hide as if you were ashamed to be looked at.'

And she drew her forward, and there Anne stood, and all of them stared at her poor, plain, blushing face, and the Adonis in cinnamon and crimson bowed low, as if she had been a duchess, that being his conqueror's way with gentle or simple, maid, wife, or widow, beauty or homespun uncomeliness.

It was so with him always; he could never resist the chance of luring to himself a woman's heart, whether he wanted it or not, and he had a charm, a strange and wonderful one, it could not be denied. Anne palpitated indeed as she made her curtsey to him, and wondered if Heaven had ever before made so fine a gentleman and so beautiful a being.

She went but seldom to this room again, and when she went she stood always in the background, far more in fear that someone would address her than that she should meet with neglect. She was used to neglect, and to being regarded as a nonentity, and aught else discomfited her. All her pleasure was to hear what was said, though 'twas not always of the finest wit – and to watch Clorinda play the queen among her admirers and her slaves. She would not have dared to speak of Sir John Oxon frequently – indeed, she let fall his name but rarely; but she learned a curious wit in contriving to hear all things concerning him. It was her habit cunningly to lead Mistress Margery to talking about him and relating long histories of his conquests and his grace. Mistress Wimpole knew many of them, having, for a staid and prudent matron, a lively interest in his ways. It seemed, truly – if one must believe her long-winded stories – that no duchess under seventy had escaped weeping for him and losing rest, and that ladies of all ranks had committed follies for his sake.

Mistress Anne, having led her to this fruitful subject, would sit and listen, bending over her embroidery frame with strange emotions, causing her virgin breast to ache with their swelling. She would lie awake at night thinking in the dark, with her heart beating. Surely, surely there was no other man on earth who was so fitted to Clorinda, and to whom it was so suited that this empress should give her charms. Surely no woman, however beautiful or proud, could dismiss his suit when he pressed it. And then, poor woman, her imagination strove to paint the splendour of their mutual love, though of such love she knew so little. But it must, in sooth, be bliss and rapture; and perchance, was her humble thought, she might see it from afar, and hear of it. And when they went to court, and Clorinda had a great mansion in town, and many servants who needed a house-wife's eye upon their doings to restrain them from wastefulness and riot, might it not chance to be that if she served well now, and had the courage to plead with her then, she might be permitted to serve her there, living quite apart in some quiet corner of the house. And then her wild thoughts would go so far that she would dream – reddening at her own boldness – of a child who might be born to them, a lordly infant son and heir, whose eyes might be blue and winning, and his hair in great fair locks, and whom she might nurse and tend and be a slave to – and love – and love – and love, and who might end by knowing she was his tender servant, always to be counted on, and might look at her with that wooing, laughing glance, and even love her too.

The night Clorinda laid her commands upon Mistress Wimpole concerning the coming of Sir John Oxon, that matron, after receiving them, hurried to her other charges, flurried and full of talk, and poured forth her wonder and admiration at length.

'She is a wondrous lady!' she said – 'she is indeed! It is not alone her beauty, but her spirit and her wit. Mark you how she sees all things and lets none pass, and can lay a plan as prudent as any lady old enough to be twice her mother. She knows all the ways of the world of fashion, and will guard herself against gossip in such a way that none can gainsay her high virtue. Her spirit is too great to allow that she may even seem to be as the town ladies. She will not have it! Sir John will not find his court easy to pay. She will not allow that he shall be able to say to anyone that he has seen her alone a moment. Thus, she says, he cannot boast. If all ladies were as wise and cunning, there would be no tales to tell.' She talked long and garrulously, and set forth to them how Mistress Clorinda had looked straight at her with her black eyes, until she had almost shaken as she sat, because it seemed as though she dared her to disobey her will; and how she had sat with her hair trailing upon the floor over the chair's back, and at first it had seemed that she was flushed with anger, but next as if she had smiled.

'Betimes,' said Mistress Wimpole, 'I am afraid when she smiles, but tonight some thought had crossed her mind that pleased her. I think it was that she liked to think that he who has conquered so many ladies will find that he is to be outwitted and made a mock of. She likes that others shall be beaten if she thinks them impudent. She liked it as a child, and would flog the stable boys with her little whip until they knelt to beg her pardon for their freedoms.'

That night Mistress Anne went to her bedchamber with her head full of wandering thoughts, and she had not the power to bid them disperse themselves and leave her – indeed, she scarce wished for it. She was thinking of Clorinda, and wondering sadly that she was of so high a pride that she could bear herself as though there were no human weakness in her breast, not even the womanly weakness of a heart. How could it be possible that she could treat with disdain this gallant gentleman, if he loved her, as he surely must? Herself she had been sure that she had seen an ardent flame in his blue eyes, even that first day when he had bowed to her with that air of grace as he spoke of the fragrance of the rose leaves he had thought wafted from her robe. How could a woman whom he loved resist him? How could she cause him to suffer by forcing him to stand at arm's length when he sighed to draw near and breathe his passion at her feet?

In the silence of her chamber as she disrobed, she sighed with restless pain, but did not know that her sighing was for grief that love – of which there seemed so little in some lives – could be wasted and flung away. She could not fall into slumber when she lay down upon her pillow, but tossed from side to side with a burdened heart.

'She is so young and beautiful and proud,' she thought. 'It is because I am so much older that I can see these things – that I see that this is surely the one man who should be her husband. There may be many others, but they are none of them her equals, and she would scorn and hate them when she was once bound to them for life. This one is as beautiful as she – and full of grace, and wit, and spirit. She could not look down upon him, however wrath she was at any time. Ah me! She should not spurn him, surely she should not!'

She was so restless and ill at ease that she could not lie upon her bed, but rose therefrom, as she often did in her wakeful hours, and went to her lattice, gently opening it to look out upon the night, and calm herself by sitting with her face uplifted to the stars, which from her childhood she had fancied looked down upon her kindly and as if they would give her comfort.

Tonight there were no stars. There should have been a moon three-quarters full, but, in the evening, clouds had drifted across the sky and closed over all heavily, so that no moonlight was to be seen, save when a rare sudden gust made a ragged rent, for a moment, in the blackness.

She did not sit this time, but knelt, clad in her night-rail as she was. All was sunk into the profoundest silence of the night. By this time the entire household had been long enough abed to be plunged in sleep. She alone was waking, and being of that simple mind which, like a child's, must ever bear its trouble to a protecting strength, she looked up at the darkness of the cloudy sky and prayed for the better fortune of the man who had indeed not remembered her existence after the moment he had made her his obeisance. She was too plain and sober a creature to be remembered.

'Perchance,' she murmured, 'he is at this moment also looking at the clouds from his window, because he cannot sleep for thinking that in two days he will be beneath her father's roof and will see her loveliness, and he must needs be contriving within his mind what he will say, if she do but look as if she might regard him with favour, which I pray she will.'

From the path below, that moment there rose a slight sound, so slight a one that for a moment she thought she must have been deceived in believing it had fallen upon her ear. All was still after it for full two minutes, and had she heard no more she would have surely forgotten she had heard aught, or would have believed herself but the victim of fancy. But after the long pause the same sound came again, though this time it was slighter; yet, despite its slightness, it seemed to her to be the crushing of the earth and stone beneath a cautious foot. It was a foot so cautious that it was surely stealthy and scarce dared to advance at all. And then all was still again. She was for a moment overcome with fears, not being of a courageous temper, and having heard, but of late, of a bold gipsy vagabond who, with a companion, had broken into the lower rooms of a house of the neighbourhood, and being surprised by its owner, had only been overcome and captured after a desperate fight, in which shots were exchanged, and one of the hurriedly-awakened servants killed. So she leaned forward to hearken further, wondering what she should do to best alarm the house, and, as she bent so, she heard the sound again and a smothered oath, and with her straining eyes saw that surely upon the path there stood a dark-draped figure. She rose with great care to her feet, and stood a moment shaking and clinging to the window ledge, while she bethought her of what servants she could wake first, and how she could reach her father's room. Her poor heart beat in her side, and her breath came quickly. The soundlessness of the night was broken by one of the strange sudden gusts of wind which tossed the trees, and tore at the clouds as they hurried. She heard the footsteps again, as if it feared its own sound the less when the wind might cover it. A faint pale gleam showed between two dark clouds behind which the moon had been hidden; it grew brighter, and a jagged rent was torn, so that the moon herself for a second or so shone out dazzling bright before the clouds rushed over her again and shut her in.

It was at this very instant Mistress Anne heard the footsteps once more, and saw full well a figure in dark cloak and hat which stepped quickly into the shade of a great tree. But more she saw – and clapped her hand upon her mouth to stifle the cry that would have otherwise risen in spite of her – that notwithstanding his fair locks were thrust out of sight beneath his hat, and he looked strange and almost uncomely, it was the face of Sir John Oxon, the moon, bursting through the jagged clouds, had shone upon.

Two Meet in the Deserted Rose Garden, and the Old Earl of Dunstanwolde Is Made a Happy Man

It was not until three days later, instead of two, that Sir John Oxon rode into the courtyard with his servant behind him. He had been detained on his journey, but looked as if his impatience had not caused him to suffer, for he wore his finest air of spirit and beauty, and when he was alone with Sir Jeoffry, made his compliments to the absent ladies, and enquired of their health with his best town grace.

Mistress Clorinda did not appear until the dining hour, when she swept into the room like a queen, followed by her sister, Anne, and Mistress Wimpole, this being the first occasion of Mistress Anne's dining, as it were, in state with her family.

The honour had so alarmed her, that she looked pale, and so ugly that Sir Jeoffry scowled at sight of her, and swore under his breath to Clorinda that she should have been allowed to come.

'I know my own affairs the best, by your leave, sir,' answered Clorinda, as low and with a grand flash of her eye. 'She hath been drilled well.'

This she had indeed, and so had Mistress Wimpole, and throughout Sir John Oxon's stay they were called upon to see that they played well their parts. Two weeks he stayed and then rode gaily back to town, and when Clorinda made her sweeping curtsey to the ground to him upon the threshold of the flowered room in which he bade her farewell, both Anne and Mistress Wimpole curtseyed a step behind her.

'Now that he has gone and you have shown me that you can attend me as I wish,' she said, turning to them as the sound of his horse's hoofs died away, 'it will not trouble me should he choose some day to come again. He has not carried with him much that he can boast of.'

In truth, it seemed to the outer world that she had held him well in hand. If he had come as a sighing lover, the whole county knew she had shown him but small favour. She had invited companies to the house on several occasions, and all could see how she bore herself towards him. She carried herself with a certain proud courtesy as becoming the daughter of his host, but her wit did not spare him, and sometimes when it was more than in common cutting he was seen to wince though he held himself gallantly. There were one or two who thought they now and then had seen his blue eyes fall upon her when he believed none were looking, and rest there burningly for a moment, but 'twas never for more than an instant, when he would rouse himself with a start and turn away.

She had been for a month or two less given to passionate outbreaks, having indeed decided that it was to her interest as a young lady and a future great one to curb herself. Her tire-woman, Rebecca, had begun to dare to breathe more freely when she was engaged about her person, and had, in truth, spoken of her pleasanter fortune among her fellows in the servants' hall.

But a night or two after the visitor took his departure, she gave way to such an outburst as even Rebecca had scarce ever beheld, being roused to it by a small thing in one sense, though in yet another perhaps great enough, since it touched upon the despoiling of one of her beauties.

She was at her toilet table being prepared for the night, and her long hair brushed and dressed before retiring. Mistress Wimpole had come in to the chamber to do something at her bidding, and chancing to stand gazing at her great and heavy fall of locks as she was waiting, she observed a thing which caused her, foolish woman that she was, to give a start and utter an unwise exclamation.

'Madam!' she gasped – 'madam!'

'What then!' quoth Mistress Clorinda angrily. 'You bring my heart to my throat!'

'Your hair!' stammered Wimpole, losing all her small wit – 'your beauteous hair! A lock is gone, madam!'

Clorinda started to her feet, and flung the great black mass over her white shoulder, that she might see it in the glass.

'Gone!' she cried. 'Where? How? What mean you? Ah-h!'

Her voice rose to a sound that was well-nigh a scream. She saw the rifled spot – a place where a great lock had been severed jaggedly – and it must have been five feet long.

She turned and sprang upon her woman, her beautiful face distorted with fury, and her eyes like flames of fire. She seized her by each shoulder and boxed her ears until her head spun round and bells rang within it.

''Twas you!' she shrieked. ''Twas you – she-devil-beast – slut that you are! 'Twas when you used your scissors to the new head you made for me. You set it on my hair that you might set a loop – and in your sluttish way you snipped a lock by accident and hid it from me.'

She beat her till her own black hair flew about her like the mane of a fury; and having used her hands till they were tired, she took her brush from the table and beat her with that till the room echoed with the blows on the stout shoulders.

'Mistress, 'twas not so!' cried the poor thing, sobbing and struggling. ''Twas not so, madam!'

'Madam, you will kill the woman,' wept Mistress Wimpole. 'I beseech you – ! 'Tis not seemly, I beseech –'

Mistress Clorinda flung her woman from her and threw the brush at Mistress Wimpole, crying at her with the lordly rage she had been wont to shriek with when she wore breeches.

'Damnation to thy seemliness!' she cried, 'and to thee too! Get thee gone – from me, both – get thee gone from my sight!'

And both women fled weeping, and sobbing, and gasping from the room incontinently.

She was shrewish and sullen with her woman for days after, and it was the poor creature's labour to keep from her sight, when she dressed her head, the place from whence the lock had been taken. In the servants' hall the woman vowed that it was not she who had cut it, that she had had no accident, though it was true she had used the scissors about her head, yet it was but in snipping a ribbon, and she had not touched a hair.

'If she were another lady,' she said, 'I should swear some gallant had robbed her of it; but, forsooth, she does not allow them to come near enough for such sport, and with five feet of hair wound up in coronals, how could a man unwind a lock, even if 'twas permitted him to stand at her very side.'

Two years passed, and the beauty had no greater fields to conquer than those she found in the country, since her father, Sir Jeoffry, had not the money to take her to town, he becoming more and more involved and so fallen into debt that it was even whispered that at times it went hard with him to keep even the poor household he had.

Mistress Clorinda's fortunes the gentry of the neighbourhood discussed with growing interest and curiosity. What was like to become of her great gifts and powers in the end, if she could never show them to the great world, and have the chance to carry her splendid wares to the fashionable market where there were men of quality and wealth who would be like to bid for them. She had not chosen to accept any of those who had offered themselves so far, and it was believed that for some reason she had held off my lord of Dunstanwolde in his suit. 'Twas evident that he admired her greatly, and why he had not already made her his countess was a sort of mystery which was productive of many discussions and bore much talking over. Some said that, with all her beauty and his admiration, he was wary and waited, and some were pleased to say that the reason he waited was because the young lady herself contrived that he should, it being her desire to make an open conquest of Sir John Oxon, and show him to the world as her slave, before she made up her mind to make even a much greater match. Some hinted that for all her disdainfulness and haughty pride she would marry Sir John if he asked her, but that he being as brilliant a beau as she a beauty, he was too fond of his pleasures and his gay town life to give them up even to a goddess who had no fortune. His own had not been a great one, and he had squandered it magnificently, his extravagances being renowned in the world of fashion, and having indeed founded for him his reputation.

It was, however, still his way to accept frequent hospitalities from his kinsman Eldershawe, and Sir Jeoffry was always rejoiced enough to secure him as his companion for a few days when he could lure him from the dissipation of the town. At such times it never failed that Mistress Wimpole and poor Anne kept their guard. Clorinda never allowed them to relax their vigilance, and Mistress Wimpole ceased to feel afraid, and became accustomed to her duties, but Anne never did so. She looked always her palest and ugliest when Sir John was in the house, and she would glance with sad wonder and timid adoration from him to Clorinda; but sometimes when she looked at Sir John her plain face would grow crimson, and once or twice he caught her at the folly, and when she dropped her eyes overwhelmed with shame, he faintly smiled to himself, seeing in her a new though humble conquest.

There came a day when in the hunting-field there passed from mouth to mouth a rumour, and Sir Jeoffry, hearing it, came pounding over on his big black horse to his daughter and told it to her in great spirits.

'He is a sly dog, John Oxon,' he said, a broad grin on his rubicund face. 'This very week he comes to us, and he and I are cronies, yet he has blabbed nothing of what is being buzzed about by all the world.'

'He has learned how to keep a closed mouth,' said Mistress Clorinda, without asking a question.

'But 'tis marriage he is so mum about, bless ye!' said Sir Jeoffry. 'And that is not a thing to be hid long. He is to be shortly married, they say. My lady, his mother, has found him a great fortune in a new beauty but just come to town. She hath great estates in the West Indies, as well as a fine fortune in England – and all the world is besieging her; but Jack hath come and bowed sighing before her, and writ some verses, and borne her off from them all.'

''Tis time,' said Clorinda, 'that he should marry some woman who can pay his debts and keep him out of the sponging house, for to that he will come if he does not play his cards with skill.'

Sir Jeoffry looked at her askance and rubbed his red chin.

'I wish thou hadst liked him, Clo,' he said, 'and ye had both had fortunes to match. I love the fellow, and ye would have made a handsome pair.'

Mistress Clorinda laughed, sitting straight in her saddle, her fine eyes unblenching, though the sun struck them.

'We had fortunes to match,' she said – 'I was a beggar and he was a spendthrift. Here comes Lord Dunstanwolde.'

And as the gentleman rode near, it seemed to his dazzled eyes that the sun so shone down upon her because she was a goddess and drew it from the heavens.

In the west wing of the Hall 'twas talked of between Mistress Wimpole and her charges, that a rumour of Sir John Oxon's marriage was afloat.

'Yet can I not believe it,' said Mistress Margery; 'for if ever a gentleman was deep in love, though he bitterly strove to hide it, 'twas Sir John, and with Mistress Clorinda.'

'But she,' faltered Anne, looking pale and even agitated – 'she was always disdainful to him and held him at arm's length. I – I wished she would have treated him more kindly.'

''Tis not her way to treat men kindly,' said Mistress Wimpole.

But whether the rumour was true or false – and there were those who bestowed no credit upon it, and said it was mere town talk, and that the same things had been bruited abroad before – it so chanced that Sir John paid no visit to his relative or to Sir Jeoffry for several months. 'Twas heard once that he had gone to France, and at the French Court was making as great a figure as he had made at the English one, but of this even his kinsman Lord Eldershawe could speak no more certainly than he could of the first matter.

The suit of my Lord of Dunstanwolde – if suit it was – during these months appeared to advance somewhat. All orders of surmises were made concerning it – that Mistress Clorinda had privately quarrelled with Sir John and sent him packing; that he had tired of his lovemaking, as 'twas well known he had done many times before, and having squandered his possessions and finding himself in open straits, must needs patch up his fortunes in a hurry with the first heiress whose estate suited him. But 'twas the women who said these things; the men swore that no man could tire of or desert such spirit and beauty, and that if Sir John Oxon stayed away 'twas because he had been commanded to do so, it never having been Mistress Clorinda's intention to do more than play with him awhile, she having been witty against him always for a fop, and meaning herself to accept no man as a husband who could not give her both rank and wealth.

'We know her,' said the old boon companions of her childhood, as they talked of her over their bottles. 'She knew her price and would bargain for it when she was not eight years old, and would give us songs and kisses but when she was paid for them with sweet things and knick-knacks from the toy-shops. She will marry no man who cannot make her at least a countess, and she would take him but because there was not a duke at hand. We know her, and her beauty's ways.'

But they did not know her; none knew her, save herself.

In the west wing, which grew more bare and ill-furnished as things wore out and time went by, Mistress Anne waxed thinner and paler. She was so thin in two months' time, that her soft, dull eyes looked twice their natural size, and seemed to stare piteously at people. One day, indeed, as she sat at work in her sister's room, Clorinda being there at the time, the beauty, turning and beholding her face suddenly, uttered a violent exclamation.

'Why look you at me so?' she said. 'Your eyes stand out of your head like a new-hatched, unfeathered bird's. They irk me with their strange asking look. Why do you stare at me?'

'I do not know,' Anne faltered. 'I could not tell you, sister. My eyes seem to stare so because of my thinness. I have seen them in my mirror.'

'Why do you grow thin?' quoth Clorinda harshly. 'You are not ill.'

'I – I do not know,' again Anne faltered. 'Naught ails me. I do not know. For– forgive me!'

Clorinda laughed.

'Soft little fool,' she said, 'why should you ask me to forgive you? I might as fairly ask you to forgive me, that I keep my shape and show no wasting.'

Anne rose from her chair and hurried to her sister's side, sinking upon her knees there to kiss her hand.

'Sister,' she said, 'one could never dream that you could need pardon. I love you so – that all you do, it seems to me must be right – whatsoever it might be.'

Clorinda drew her fair hands away and clasped them on the top of her head, proudly, as if she crowned herself thereby, her great and splendid eyes setting themselves upon her sister's face.

'All that I do,' she said slowly, and with the steadfast high arrogance of an empress' self – 'All that I do is right – for me. I make it so by doing it. Do you think that I am conquered by the laws that other women crouch and whine before, because they dare not break them, though they long to do so? I am my own law – and the law of some others.'

It was by this time the first month of the summer, and tonight there was again a birth-night ball, at which the beauty was to dazzle all eyes; but 'twas of greater import than the one she had graced previously, it being to celebrate the majority of the heir to an old name and estate, who had been orphaned early, and was highly connected, counting, indeed, among the members of his family the Duke of Osmonde, who was one of the richest and most envied nobles in Great Britain, his dukedom being of the oldest, his numerous estates the most splendid and beautiful, and the long history of his family full of heroic deeds. This nobleman was also a distant kinsman to the Earl of Dunstanwolde, and at this ball, for the first time for months, Sir John Oxon appeared again.

He did not arrive on the gay scene until an hour somewhat late. But there was one who had seen him early, though no human soul had known of the event.

In the rambling, ill-cared for grounds of Wildairs Hall there was an old rose-garden, which had once been the pride and pleasure of some lady of the house, though this had been long ago; and now it was but a lonely wilderness where roses only grew because the dead Lady Wildairs had loved them, and Barbara and Anne had tended them, and with their own hands planted and pruned during their childhood and young maiden days. But of late years even they had seemed to have forgotten it, having become discouraged, perchance, having no gardeners to do the rougher work, and the weeds and brambles so running riot. There were high hedges and winding paths overgrown and run wild; the stronger rose-bushes grew in tangled masses, flinging forth their rich blooms among the weeds; such as were more delicate, struggling to live among them, became more frail and scant-blossoming season by season; a careless foot would have trodden them beneath it as their branches grew long and trailed in the grass; but for many months no foot had trodden there at all, and it was a beauteous place deserted.

In the centre was an ancient broken sundial, which was in these days in the midst of a sort of thicket, where a bold tangle of the finest red roses clambered, and, defying neglect, flaunted their rich colour in the sun.

And though the place had been so long forgotten, and it was not the custom for it to be visited, about this garlanded broken sundial the grass was a little trodden, and on the morning of the young heir's coming of age someone stood there in the glowing sunlight as if waiting.

This was no less than Mistress Clorinda herself. She was clad in a morning gown of white, which seemed to make of her more than ever a tall, transcendent creature, less a woman than a conquering goddess; and she had piled the dial with scarlet red roses, which she was choosing to weave into a massive wreath or crown, for some purpose best known to herself. Her head seemed haughtier and more splendidly held on high even than was its common wont, but upon these roses her lustrous eyes were downcast and were curiously smiling, as also was her ripe, arching lip, whose scarlet the blossoms vied with but poorly. It was a smile like this, perhaps, which Mistress Wimpole feared and trembled before, for 'twas not a tender smile nor a melting one. If she was waiting, she did not wait long, nor, to be sure, would she have long waited if she had been kept by any daring laggard. This was not her way.

'Twas not a laggard who came soon, stepping hurriedly with light feet upon the grass, as though he feared the sound which might be made if he had trodden upon the gravel. It was Sir John Oxon who came towards her in his riding costume.

He came and stood before her on the other side of the dial, and made her a bow so low that a quick eye might have thought 'twas almost mocking. His feather, sweeping the ground, caught a fallen rose, which clung to it. His beauty, when he stood upright, seemed to defy the very morning's self and all the morning world; but Mistress Clorinda did not lift her eyes, but kept them upon her roses, and went on weaving.

'Why did you choose to come?' she asked.

'Why did you choose to keep the tryst in answer to my message?' he replied to her.

At this she lifted her great shining eyes and fixed them full upon him.

'I wished,' she said, 'to hear what you would say – but more to see you than to hear.'

'And I,' he began – 'I came –'

She held up her white hand with a long-stemmed rose in it – as though a queen should lift a sceptre.

'You came,' she answered, 'more to see me than to hear. You made that blunder.'

'You choose to bear yourself like a goddess, and disdain me from Olympian heights,' he said. 'I had the wit to guess it would be so.'

She shook her royal head, faintly and most strangely smiling.

'That you had not,' was her clear-worded answer. 'That is a later thought sprung up since you have seen my face. 'Twas quick – for you – but not quick enough.' And the smile in her eyes was maddening. 'You thought to see a woman crushed and weeping, her beauty bent before you, her locks dishevelled, her streaming eyes lifted to Heaven – and you – with prayers, swearing that not Heaven could help her so much as your deigning magnanimity. You have seen women do this before, you would have seen me do it – at your feet – crying out that I was lost – lost for ever. That you expected! 'Tis not here.'

Debauched as his youth was, and free from all touch of heart or conscience – for from his earliest boyhood he had been the pupil of rakes and fashionable villains – well as he thought he knew all women and their ways, betraying or betrayed – this creature taught him a new thing, a new mood in woman, a new power which came upon him like a thunderbolt.

'Gods!' he exclaimed, catching his breath, and even falling back apace, 'Damnation! you are not a woman!'

She laughed again, weaving her roses, but not allowing that his eyes should loose themselves from hers.

'But now, you called me a goddess and spoke of Olympian heights,' she said; 'I am not one – I am a woman who would show other women how to bear themselves in hours like these. Because I am a woman why should I kneel, and weep, and rave? What have I lost – in losing you? I should have lost the same had I been twice your wife. What is it women weep and beat their breasts for – because they love a man – because they lose his love. They never have them.'

She had finished the wreath, and held it up in the sun to look at it. What a strange beauty was hers, as she held it so – a heavy, sumptuous thing – in her white hands, her head thrown backward.

'You marry soon,' she asked – 'if the match is not broken?'

'Yes,' he answered, watching her – a flame growing in his eyes and in his soul in his own despite.

'It cannot be too soon,' she said. And she turned and faced him, holding the wreath high in her two hands poised like a crown above her head – the brilliant sun embracing her, her lips curling, her face uplifted as if she turned to defy the light, the crimson of her cheek. 'Twas as if from foot to brow the woman's whole person was a flame, rising and burning triumphant high above him. Thus for one second's space she stood, dazzling his very eyesight with her strange, dauntless splendour; and then she set the great rose-wreath upon her head, so crowning it.

'You came to see me,' she said, the spark in her eyes growing to the size of a star; 'I bid you look at me – and see how grief has faded me these past months, and how I am bowed down by it. Look well – that you may remember.'

'I look,' he said, almost panting.

'Then,' she said, her fine-cut nostril pinching itself with her breath, as she pointed down the path before her – 'go! – back to your kennel!'

That night she appeared at the birth-night ball with the wreath of roses on her head. No other ladies wore such things, 'twas a fashion of her own; but she wore it in such beauty and with such state that it became a crown again even as it had been the first moment that she had put it on. All gazed at her as she entered, and a murmur followed her as she moved with her father up the broad oak staircase which was known through all the country for its width and massive beauty. In the hall below guests were crowded, and there were indeed few of them who did not watch her as she mounted by Sir Jeoffry's side. In the upper hall there were guests also, some walking to and fro, some standing talking, many looking down at the arrivals as they came up.

''Tis Mistress Wildairs,' these murmured as they saw her. 'Clorinda, by God!' said one of the older men to his crony who stood near him. 'And crowned with roses! The vixen makes them look as if they were built of rubies in every leaf.'

At the top of the great staircase there stood a gentleman, who had indeed paused a moment, spellbound, as he saw her coming. He was a man of unusual height and of a majestic mien; he wore a fair periwig, which added to his tallness; his laces and embroiderings were marvels of art and richness, and his breast blazed with orders. Strangely, she did not seem to see him; but when she reached the landing, and her face was turned so that he beheld the full blaze of its beauty, 'twas so great a wonder and revelation to him that he gave a start. The next moment almost, one of the red roses of her crown broke loose from its fastenings and fell at his very feet. His countenance changed so that it seemed almost, for a second, to lose some of its colour. He stooped and picked the rose up and held it in his hand. But Mistress Clorinda was looking at my Lord of Dunstanwolde, who was moving through the crowd to greet her. She gave him a brilliant smile, and from her lustrous eyes surely there passed something which lit a fire of hope in his.

After she had made her obeisance to her entertainers, and her birthday greetings to the young heir, he contrived to draw closely to her side and speak a few words in a tone those near her could not hear.

'Tonight, madam,' he said, with melting fervour, 'you deign to bring me my answer as you promised.'

'Yes,' she murmured. 'Take me where we may be a few moments alone.'

He led her to an antechamber, where they were sheltered from the gaze of the passers-by, though all was moving gaiety about them. He fell upon his knee and bowed to kiss her fair hand. Despite the sobriety of his years, he was as eager and tender as a boy.

'Be gracious to me, madam,' he implored. 'I am not young enough to wait. Too many months have been thrown away.'

'You need wait no longer, my lord,' she said – 'not one single hour.'

And while he, poor gentleman, knelt, kissing her hand with adoring humbleness, she, under the splendour of her crown of roses, gazed down at his grey-sprinkled head with her great steady shining orbs, as if gazing at some almost uncomprehended piteous wonder.

In less than an hour the whole assemblage knew of the event and talked of it. Young men looked daggers at Dunstanwolde and at each other; and older men wore glum or envious faces. Women told each other 'twas as they had known it would be, or 'twas a wonder that at last it had come about. Upon the arm of her lord that was to be, Mistress Clorinda passed from room to room like a royal bride.

As she made her first turn of the ballroom, all eyes upon her, her beauty blazing at its highest, Sir John Oxon entered and stood at the door. He wore his gallant air, and smiled as ever; and when she drew near him he bowed low, and she stopped, and bent lower in a curtsey sweeping the ground.

'Twas but in the next room her lord led her to a gentleman who stood with a sort of court about him. It was the tall stranger, with the fair periwig, and the orders glittering on his breast – the one who had started at sight of her as she had reached the landing of the stairs. He held still in his hand a broken red rose, and when his eye fell on her crown the colour mounted to his cheek.

'My honoured kinsman, his Grace the Duke of Osmonde,' said her affianced lord. 'Your Grace – it is this lady who is to do me the great honour of becoming my Lady Dunstanwolde.'

And as the deep, tawny brown eye of the man bending before her flashed into her own, for the first time in her life Mistress Clorinda's lids fell, and as she swept her curtsey of stately obeisance her heart struck like a hammer against her side.

'I give to him the thing he craves
with all his soul – myself'

In a month she was the Countess of Dunstanwolde, and reigned
in her lord's great town house with a retinue of servants, her
powdered lackeys among the tallest, her liveries and equipages
the richest the world of fashion knew. She was presented at the
Court, blazing with the Dunstanwolde jewels, and even with
others her bridegroom had bought in his passionate desire to
heap upon her the magnificence which became her so well. From
the hour she knelt to kiss the hand of royalty she set the town
on fire. It seemed to have been ordained by Fate that her passage
through this world should be always the triumphant passage of
a conqueror. As when a baby she had ruled the servants' hall,
the kennel, and the grooms' quarters, later her father and his
boisterous friends, and from her fifteenth birthday the whole
hunting shire she lived in, so she held her sway in the great
world, as did no other lady of her rank or any higher. Those
of her age seemed but girls yet by her side, whether married or
unmarried, and howsoever trained to modish ways. She was but
scarce eighteen at her marriage, but she was no girl, nor did she
look one, glowing as was the early splendour of her bloom. Her
height was far beyond the ordinary for a woman; but her shape
so faultless and her carriage so regal, that though there were men
upon whom she was tall enough to look down with ease, the
beholder but felt that her tallness was an added grace and beauty
with which all women should have been endowed, and which,
as they were not, caused them to appear but insignificant. What
a throat her diamonds blazed on, what shoulders and bosom
her laces framed, on what a brow her coronet sat and glittered.
Her lord lived as 'twere upon his knees in enraptured adoration.
Since his first wife's death in his youth, he had dwelt almost
entirely in the country at his house there, which was fine and

stately, but had been kept gloomily half closed for a decade. His town establishment had, in truth, never been opened since his bereavement; and now – an elderly man – he returned to the gay world he had almost forgotten, with a bride whose youth and beauty set it aflame. What wonder that his head almost reeled at times and that he lost his breath before the sum of his strange late bliss, and the new lease of brilliant life which seemed to have been given to him.

In the days when, while in the country, he had heard such rumours of the lawless days of Sir Jeoffry Wildairs' daughter, when he had heard of her dauntless boldness, her shrewish temper, and her violent passions, he had been awed at the thought of what a wife such a woman would make for a gentle-man accustomed to a quiet life, and he had indeed striven hard to restrain the desperate admiration he was forced to admit she had inspired in him even at her first ball.

The effort had, in sooth, been in vain, and he had passed many a sleepless night; and when, as time went on, he beheld her again and again, and saw with his own eyes, as well as heard from others, of the great change which seemed to have taken place in her manners and character, he began devoutly to thank Heaven for the alteration, as for a merciful boon vouchsafed to him. He had been wise enough to know that even a stronger man than himself could never conquer or rule her; and when she seemed to begin to rule herself and bear herself as befitted her birth and beauty, he had dared to allow himself to dream of what perchance might be if he had great good fortune.

In these days of her union with him, he was, indeed, almost humbly amazed at the grace and kindness she showed him every hour they passed in each other's company. He knew that there were men, younger and handsomer than himself, who, being wedded to beauties far less triumphant than she, found that their wives had but little time to spare them from the world, which knelt at their feet, and that in some fashion they themselves seemed to fall into the background. But 'twas not so with this woman, powerful and worshipped though she might be. She bore herself with the high dignity of her rank, but rendered to him the gracious respect and deference due both to his position and his merit. She stood by his side and not before him, and her smiles and wit were bestowed upon him as generously as to others. If she had once been a vixen, she was surely so no longer, for he never heard a sharp or harsh word pass her lips, though it is true her manner was always somewhat imperial, and her lackeys and waiting women stood in greatest awe of her. There was that in her presence and in her eye before which all commoner or weaker creatures quailed. The men of the world who flocked to pay their court to her, and the popinjays who followed them, all knew this look, and a tone in her rich voice which could cut like a knife when she chose that it should do so. But to my Lord of Dunstanwolde she was all that a worshipped lady could be.

'Your ladyship has made of me a happier man than I ever dared to dream of being, even when I was but thirty,' he would say to her, with reverent devotion. 'I know not what I have done to deserve this late summer which hath been given me.'

'When I consented to be your wife,' she answered once, 'I swore to myself that I would make one for you,' and she crossed the hearth to where he sat – she was attired in all her splendour for a Court ball, and starred with jewels – bent over his chair and placed a kiss upon his grizzled hair.

Upon the night before her wedding with him, her sister, Mistress Anne, had stolen to her chamber at a late hour. When she had knocked upon the door, and had been commanded to enter, she had come in, and closing the door behind her, had stood leaning against it, looking before her, with her eyes wide with agitation and her poor face almost grey.

All the tapers for which places could be found had been gathered together, and the room was a blaze of light. In the midst of it, before her mirror, Clorinda stood attired in her bridal splendour of white satin and flowing rich lace, a diamond crescent on her head, sparks of light flaming from every point of her raiment. When she caught sight of Anne's reflection in the glass before her, she turned and stood staring at her in wonder.

'What – nay, what is this?' she cried. 'What do you come for? On my soul, you come for something – or you have gone mad.'

Anne started forward, trembling, her hands clasped upon her breast, and fell at her feet with sobs.

'Yes, yes,' she gasped, 'I came – for something – to speak – to pray you –! Sister – Clorinda, have patience with me – till my courage comes again!' and she clutched her robe.

Something which came nigh to being a shudder passed through Mistress Clorinda's frame; but it was gone in a second, and she touched Anne – though not ungently – with her foot, withdrawing her robe.

'Do not stain it with your tears,' she said, ''twould be a bad omen.'

Anne buried her face in her hands and knelt so before her.

''Tis not too late!' she said – ''tis not too late yet.'

'For what?' Clorinda asked. 'For what, I pray you tell me, if you can find your wits. You go beyond my patience with your folly.'

'Too late to stop,' said Anne – 'to draw back and repent.'

'What?' commanded Clorinda – 'what then should I repent me?'

'This marriage,' trembled Mistress Anne, taking her poor hands from her face to wring them. 'It should not be.'

'Fool!' quoth Clorinda. 'Get up and cease your grovelling. Did you come to tell me it was not too late to draw back and refuse to be the Countess of Dunstanwolde?' and she laughed bitterly.

'But it should not be – it must not!' Anne panted. 'I – I know, sister, I know –'

Clorinda bent deliberately and laid her strong, jewelled hand on her shoulder with a grasp like a vice. There was no hurry in her movement or in her air, but by sheer, slow strength she forced her head backward so that the terrified woman was staring in her face.

'Look at me,' she said. 'I would see you well, and be squarely looked at, that my eyes may keep you from going mad. You have pondered over this marriage until you have a frenzy. Women who live alone are sometimes so, and your brain was always weak. What is it that you know? Look – in my eyes – and tell me.'

It seemed as if her gaze stabbed through Anne's eyes to the very centre of her brain. Anne tried to bear it, and shrunk and withered; she would have fallen upon the floor at her feet a helpless, sobbing heap, but the white hand would not let her go.

'Find your courage – if you have lost it – and speak plain words,' Clorinda commanded. Anne tried to writhe away, but could not again, and burst into passionate, hopeless weeping.

'I cannot – I dare not!' she gasped. 'I am afraid. You are right; my brain is weak, and I – but that – that gentleman – who so loved you –'

'Which?' said Clorinda, with a brief scornful laugh.

'The one who was so handsome – with the fair locks and the gallant air –'

'The one you fell in love with and stared at through the window,' said Clorinda, with her brief laugh again. 'John Oxon! He has victims enough, forsooth, to have spared such an one as you are.'

'But he loved you!' cried Anne piteously, 'and it must have been that you – you too, sister – or – or else –' She choked again with sobs, and Clorinda released her grasp upon her shoulder and stood upright.

'He wants none of me – nor I of him,' she said, with strange sternness. 'We have done with one another. Get up upon your feet if you would not have me thrust you out into the corridor.'

She turned from her, and walking back to her dressing table, stood there steadying the diadem on her hair, which had loosed a fastening when Anne tried to writhe away from her. Anne half sat, half knelt upon the floor, staring at her with wet, wild eyes of misery and fear.

'Leave your kneeling,' commanded her sister again, 'and come here.'

Anne staggered to her feet and obeyed her behest. In the glass she could see the resplendent reflection; but Clorinda did not deign to turn towards her while she addressed her, changing the while the brilliants in her hair.

'Hark you, sister Anne,' she said. 'I read you better than you think. You are a poor thing, but you love me and – in my fashion – I think I love you somewhat too. You think I should not marry a gentleman whom you fancy I do not love as I might a younger, handsomer man. You are full of love, and spinster dreams of it which make you flighty. I love my Lord of Dunstanwolde as well as any other man, and better than some, for I do not hate him. He has a fine estate, and is a gentleman – and worships me. Since I have been promised to him, I own I have for a moment seen another gentleman who might – but 'twas but for a moment, and 'tis done with. 'Twas too late then. If we had met two years agone 'twould not have been so. My Lord Dunstanwolde gives to me wealth, and rank, and life at Court. I give to him the thing he craves with all his soul – myself. It is an honest bargain, and I shall bear my part of it with honesty. I have no virtues – where should I have got them from, forsooth, in a life like mine? I mean I have no women's virtues; but I have one that is sometimes – not always – a man's. 'Tis that I am not a coward and a trickster, and keep my word when 'tis given. You fear that I shall lead my lord a bitter life of it. 'Twill not be so. He shall live smoothly, and not suffer from me. What he has paid for he shall honestly have. I will not cheat him as weaker women do their husbands; for he pays – poor gentleman – he pays.'

And then, still looking at the glass, she pointed to the doorway through which her sister had come, and in obedience to her gesture of command, Mistress Anne stole silently away.

'Yes – I have marked him'

Through the brilliant, happy year succeeding to his marriage my Lord of Dunstanwolde lived like a man who dreams a blissful dream and knows it is one.

'I feel,' he said to his lady, 'as if 'twere too great rapture to last, and yet what end could come, unless you ceased to be kind to me; and, in truth, I feel that you are too noble above all other women to change, unless I were more unworthy than I could ever be since you are mine.'

Both in the town and in the country, which last place heard many things of his condition and estate through rumour, he was the man most wondered at and envied of his time – envied because of his strange happiness; wondered at because having, when long past youth, borne off this arrogant beauty from all other aspirants she showed no arrogance to him, and was as perfect a wife as could have been some woman without gifts whom he had lifted from low estate and endowed with rank and fortune. She seemed both to respect himself and her position as his lady and spouse. Her manner of reigning in his household was among his many delights the greatest. It was a great house, and an old one, built long before by a Dunstanwolde whose lavish feasts and riotous banquets had been the notable feature of his life. It was curiously rambling in its structure. The rooms of entertainment were large and splendid, the halls and staircases stately; below stairs there was space for an army of servants to be disposed of; and its network of cellars and wine vaults was so beyond all need that more than one long arched stone passage was shut up as being without use, and but letting cold, damp air into corridors leading to the servants' quarters. It was, indeed, my Lady Dunstanwolde who had ordered the closing of this part when it had been her pleasure to be shown her domain by her housekeeper, the which had greatly awed and impressed her household as signifying that, exalted lady as she was, her wit was practical as well as brilliant, and that her eyes being open to her surroundings, she meant not that her lackeys should rob her and her scullions filch, thinking that she was so high that she was ignorant of common things and blind.

'You will be well housed and fed and paid your dues,' she said to them; 'but the first man or woman who does a task ill or dishonestly will be turned from his place that hour. I deal justice – not mercy.'

'Such a mistress they have never had before,' said my lord when she related this to him. 'Nay, they have never dreamed of such a lady – one who can be at once so severe and so kind. But there is none other such, my dearest one. They will fear and worship you.'

She gave him one of her sweet, splendid smiles. It was the sweetness she at rare times gave her splendid smile which was her marvellous power.

'I would not be too grand a lady to be a good housewife,' she said. 'I may not order your dinners, my dear lord, or sweep your corridors, but they shall know I rule your household and would rule it well.'

'You are a goddess!' he cried, kneeling to her, enraptured. 'And you have given yourself to a poor mortal man, who can but worship you.'

'You give me all I have,' she said, 'and you love me nobly, and I am grateful.'

Her assemblies were the most brilliant in the town, and the most to be desired entrance to. Wits and beauties planned and intrigued that they might be bidden to her house; beaux and fine ladies fell into the spleen if she neglected them. Her lord's kinsman the Duke of Osmonde, who had been present when she first knelt to royalty, had scarce removed his eyes from her so long as he could gaze. He went to Dunstanwolde afterwards and congratulated him with stately courtesy upon his great good fortune and happiness, speaking almost with fire of her beauty and majesty, and thanking his kinsman that through him such perfections had been given to their name and house. From that time, at all special assemblies given by his kinsman he was present, the observed of all observers. He was a man of whom 'twas said that he was the most magnificent gentleman in Europe; that there was none to compare with him in the combination of gifts given both by Nature and Fortune. His beauty both of feature and carriage was of the greatest, his mind was of the highest, and his education far beyond that of the age he lived in. It was not the fashion of the day that men of his rank should devote themselves to the cultivation of their intellects instead of to a life of pleasure; but this he had done from his earliest youth, and now, in his perfect though early maturity, he had no equal in polished knowledge and charm of bearing. He was the patron of literature and art; men of genius were not kept waiting in his antechamber, but were received by him with courtesy and honour. At the Court 'twas well known there was no man who stood so near the throne in favour, and that there was no union so exalted that he might not have made his suit as rather that of a superior than an equal. The Queen both loved and honoured him, and condescended to avow as much with gracious frankness. She knew no other man, she deigned to say, who was so worthy of honour and affection, and that he had not married must be because there was no woman who could meet him on ground that was equal. If there were no scandals about him – and there were none – 'twas not because he was cold of heart or imagination. No man or woman could look into his deep eye and not know that when love came to him 'twould be a burning passion, and an evil fate if it went ill instead of happily.

'Being past his callow, youthful days, 'tis time he made some woman a duchess,' Dunstanwolde said reflectively once to his wife. ''Twould be more fitting that he should; and it is his way to honour his house in all things, and bear himself without fault as the head of it. Methinks it strange he makes no move to do it.'

'No, 'tis not strange,' said my lady, looking under her black-fringed lids at the glow of the fire, as though reflecting also. 'There is no strangeness in it.'

'Why not?' her lord asked.

'There is no mate for him,' she answered slowly. 'A man like him must mate as well as marry, or he will break his heart with silent raging at the weakness of the thing he is tied to. He is too strong and splendid for a common woman. If he married one, 'twould be as if a lion had taken to himself for mate a jackal or a sheep. Ah!' with a long drawn breath – 'he would go mad – mad with misery,' and her hands, which lay upon her knee, wrung themselves hard together, though none could see it.

'He should have a goddess, were they not so rare,' said Dunstanwolde, gently smiling. 'He should hold a bitter grudge against me, that I, his unworthy kinsman, have been given the only one.'

'Yes, he should have a goddess,' said my lady slowly again; 'and there are but women, naught but women.'

'You have marked him well,' said her lord, admiring her wisdom. 'Methinks that you – though you have spoken to him but little, and have but of late become his kinswoman – have marked and read him better than the rest of us.'

'Yes – I have marked him,' was her answer.

'He is a man to mark, and I have a keen eye.' She rose up as she spoke, and stood before the fire, lifted by some strong feeling to her fullest height, and towering there, splendid in the shadow – for 'twas by twilight they talked. 'He is a Man,' she said – 'he is a Man! Nay, he is as God meant man should be. And if men were so, there would be women great enough for them to mate with and to give the world men like them.' And but that she stood in the shadow, her lord would have seen the crimson torrent rush up her cheek and brow, and overspread her long round throat itself.

If none other had known of it, there was one man who knew that she had marked him, though she had borne herself towards him always with her stateliest grace. This man was his Grace the Duke himself. From the hour that he had stood transfixed as he watched her come up the broad oak stair, from the moment that the red rose fell from her wreath at his feet, and he had stooped to lift it in his hand, he had seen her as no other man had seen her, and he had known that had he not come but just too late, she would have been his own. Each time he had beheld her since that night he had felt this burn more deeply in his soul. He was too high and fine in all his thoughts to say to himself that in her he saw for the first time the woman who was his peer; but this was very truth – or might have been, if Fate had set her youth elsewhere, and a lady who was noble and her own mother had trained and guarded her. When he saw her at the Court surrounded, as she ever was, by a court of her own; when he saw her reigning in her lord's house, receiving and doing gracious honour to his guests and hers; when she passed him in her coach, drawing every eye by the majesty of her presence, as she drove through the town, he felt a deep pang, which was all the greater that his honour bade him conquer it. He had no ignoble thought of her, he would have scorned to sully his soul with any light passion; to him she was the woman who might have been his beloved wife and duchess, who would have upheld with him the honour and traditions of his house, whose strength and power and beauty would have been handed down to his children, who so would have been born endowed with gifts befitting the state to which Heaven had called them. It was of this he thought when he saw her, and of naught less like to do her honour. And as he had marked her so, he saw in her eyes, despite her dignity and grace, she had marked him. He did not know how closely, or that she gave him the attention he could not restrain himself from bestowing upon her. But when he bowed before her, and she greeted him with all courtesy, he saw in her great, splendid eye that had Fate willed it so, she would have understood all his thoughts, shared all his ambitions, and aided him to uphold his high ideals. Nay, he knew she understood him even now, and was stirred by what stirred him also, even though they met but rarely, and when they encountered each other, spoke but as kinsman and kinswoman who would show each other all gracious respect and honour. It was because of this pang which struck his great heart at times that he was not a frequent visitor at my Lord Dunstanwolde's mansion, but appeared there only at such assemblies as were matters of ceremony, his absence from which would have been a noted thing. His kinsman was fond of him, and though himself of so much riper age, honoured him greatly. At times he strove to lure him into visits of greater familiarity; but though his kindness was never met coldly or repulsed, a further intimacy was in some gracious way avoided.

'My lady must beguile you to be less formal with us,' said Dunstanwolde. And later her ladyship spoke as her husband had privately desired: 'My lord would be made greatly happy if your Grace would honour our house oftener,' she said one night, when at the end of a great ball he was bidding her adieu.

Osmonde's deep eye met hers gently and held it. 'My Lord Dunstanwolde is always gracious and warm of heart to his kinsman,' he replied. 'Do not let him think me discourteous or ungrateful. In truth, your ladyship, I am neither the one nor the other.'

The eyes of each gazed into the other's steadfastly and gravely. The Duke of Osmonde thought of Juno's as he looked at hers; they were of such velvet, and held such fathomless deeps.

'Your Grace is not so free as lesser men,' Clorinda said. 'You cannot come and go as you would.'

'No,' he answered gravely, 'I cannot, as I would.'

And this was all.

It having been known by all the world that, despite her beauty and her conquests, Mistress Clorinda Wildairs had not smiled with great favour upon Sir John Oxon in the country, it was not wondered at or made any matter of gossip that the Countess of

Dunstanwolde was but little familiar with him and saw him but rarely at her house in town.

Once or twice he had appeared there, it is true, at my Lord Dunstanwolde's instance, but my lady herself scarce seemed to see him after her first courtesies as hostess were over.

'You never smiled on him, my love,' Dunstanwolde said to his wife. 'You bore yourself towards him but cavalierly, as was your ladyship's way – with all but one poor servant,' tenderly; 'but he was one of the many who followed in your train, and if these gay young fellows stay away, 'twill be said that I keep them at a distance because I am afraid of their youth and gallantry. I would not have it fancied that I was so ungrateful as to presume upon your goodness and not leave to you your freedom.'

'Nor would I, my lord,' she answered. 'But he will not come often; I do not love him well enough.'

His marriage with the heiress who had wealth in the West Indies was broken off, or rather 'twas said had come to naught. All the town knew it, and wondered, and talked, because it had been believed at first that the young lady was much enamoured of him, and that he would soon lead her to the altar, the which his creditors had greatly rejoiced over as promising them some hope that her fortune would pay their bills of which they had been in despair. Later, however, gossip said that the heiress had not been so tender as was thought; that, indeed, she had been found to be in love with another man, and that even had she not, she had heard such stories of Sir John as promised but little nuptial happiness for any woman that took him to husband.

When my Lord Dunstanwolde brought his bride to town, and she soared at once to splendid triumph and renown, inflaming every heart, and setting every tongue at work, clamouring her praises, Sir John Oxon saw her from afar in all the scenes of brilliant fashion she frequented and reigned queen of. 'Twas from afar, it might be said, he saw her only, though he was often near her, because she bore herself as if she did not observe him, or as though he were a thing which did not exist. The first time that she deigned to address him was upon an occasion when she found herself standing so near him at an assembly that in the crowd she brushed him with her robe. His blue eyes were fixed burningly upon her, and as she brushed him he drew in a hard breath, which she hearing, turned slowly and let her own eyes fall upon his face.

'You did not marry,' she said.

'No, I did not marry,' he answered, in a low, bitter voice. ''Twas your ladyship who did that.'

She faintly, slowly smiled.

'I should not have been like to do otherwise,' she said; ''tis an honourable condition. I would advise you to enter it.'

Wherein a Noble Life Comes to an End

When the earl and his countess went to their house in the country, there fell to Mistress Anne a great and curious piece of good fortune. In her wildest dreams she had never dared to hope that such a thing might be.

My Lady Dunstanwolde, on her first visit home, bore her sister back with her to the manor, and there established her. She gave her a suite of rooms and a waiting woman of her own, and even provided her with a suitable wardrobe. This last she had chosen herself with a taste and fitness which only such wit as her own could have devised.

'They are not great rooms I give thee, Anne,' she said, 'but quiet and small ones, which you can make homelike in such ways as I know your taste lies. My lord has aided me to choose romances for your shelves, he knowing more of books than I do. And I shall not dress thee out like a peacock with gay colours and great farthingales. They would frighten thee, poor woman, and be a burden with their weight. I have chosen such things as are not too splendid, but will suit thy pale face and shot partridge eyes.'

Anne stood in the middle of her room and looked about at its comforts, wondering.

'Sister,' she said, 'why are you so good to me? What have I done to serve you? Why is it Anne instead of Barbara you are so gracious to?'

'Perchance because I am a vain woman and would be worshipped as you worship me.'

'But you are always worshipped,' Anne faltered.

'Ay, by men!' said Clorinda, mocking; 'but not by women. And it may be that my pride is so high that I must be worshipped by a woman too. You would always love me, sister Anne. If you saw me break the law – if you saw me stab the man I hated to the heart, you would think it must be pardoned to me.'

She laughed, and yet her voice was such that Anne lost her breath and caught at it again.

'Ay, I should love you, sister!' she cried. 'Even then I could not but love you. I should know you could not strike so an innocent creature, and that to be so hated he must have been worthy of hate. You – are not like other women, sister Clorinda; but you could not be base – for you have a great heart.'

Clorinda put her hand to her side and laughed again, but with less mocking in her laughter.

'What do you know of my heart, Anne?' she said. 'Till late I did not know it beat, myself. My lord says 'tis a great one and noble, but I know 'tis his own that is so. Have I done honestly by him, Anne, as I told you I would? Have I been fair in my bargain – as fair as an honest man, and not a puling, slippery woman?'

'You have been a great lady,' Anne answered, her great dull, soft eyes filling with slow tears as she gazed at her. 'He says that you have given to him a year of Heaven, and that you seem to him like some archangel – for the lower angels seem not high enough to set beside you.'

''Tis as I said – 'tis his heart that is noble,' said Clorinda. 'But I vowed it should be so. He paid – he paid!'

The country saw her lord's happiness as the town had done, and wondered at it no less. The manor was thrown open, and guests came down from town; great dinners and balls being given, at which all the country saw the mistress reign at her consort's side with such a grace as no lady ever had worn before. Sir Jeoffry, appearing at these assemblies, was so amazed that he forgot to muddle himself with drink, in gazing at his daughter and following her in all her movements.

'Look at her!' he said to his old boon companions and hers, who were as much awed as he. 'Lord! who would think she was the strapping, handsome shrew that swore, and sang men's songs to us, and rode to the hunt in breeches.'

He was awed at the thought of paying fatherly visits to her house, and would have kept away, but that she was kind to him in the way he was best able to understand.

'I am country-bred, and have not the manners of your town men, my lady,' he said to her, as he sat with her alone on one of the first mornings he spent with her in her private apartment. 'I am used to rap out an oath or an ill-mannered word when it comes to me. Dunstanwolde has weaned you of hearing such things – and I am too old a dog to change.'

'Wouldst have thought I was too old to change,' answered she, 'but I was not. Did I not tell thee I would be a great lady? There is naught a man or woman cannot learn who hath the wit.'

'Thou hadst it, Clo,' said Sir Jeoffry, gazing at her with a sort of slow wonder. 'Thou hadst it. If thou hadst not – !' He paused, and shook his head, and there was a rough emotion in his coarse face. 'I was not the man to have made aught but a baggage of thee, Clo. I taught thee naught decent, and thou never heard or saw aught to teach thee. Damn me!' almost with moisture in his eyes, 'if I know what kept thee from going to ruin before thou wert fifteen.'

She sat and watched him steadily.

'Nor I,' quoth she, in answer. 'Nor I – but here thou seest me, Dad – an earl's lady, sitting before thee.'

''Twas thy wit,' said he, still moved, and fairly maudlin. ''Twas thy wit and thy devil's will!'

'Ay,' she answered, ''twas they – my wit and my devil's will!'

She rode to the hunt with him as she had been wont to do, but she wore the latest fashion in hunting habit and coat; and though 'twould not have been possible for her to sit her horse better than of old, or to take hedges and ditches with greater daring and spirit, yet in some way every man who rode with her felt that 'twas a great lady who led the field. The horse she rode was a fierce, beauteous devil of a beast which Sir Jeoffry himself would scarce have mounted even in his younger days; but she carried her loaded whip, and she sat upon the brute as if she scarcely felt its temper, and held it with a wrist of steel.

My Lord Dunstanwolde did not hunt this season. He had never been greatly fond of the sport, and at this time was a little ailing, but he would not let his lady give up her pleasure because he could not join it.

'Nay,' he said, ''tis not for the queen of the hunting-field to stay at home to nurse an old man's aches. My pride would not let it be so. Your father will attend you. Go – and lead them all, my dear.'

In the field appeared Sir John Oxon, who for a brief visit was at Eldershawe. He rode close to my lady, though she had naught to say to him after her first greetings of civility. He looked not as fresh and glowing with youth as had been his wont only a year ago. His reckless wildness of life and his town debaucheries had at last touched his bloom, perhaps. He had a haggard look at moments when his countenance was not lighted by excitement. 'Twas whispered that he was deep enough in debt to be greatly straitened, and that his marriage having come to naught his creditors were besetting him without mercy. This and more than this, no one knew so well as my Lady Dunstanwolde; but of a certainty she had little pity for his evil case, if one might judge by her face, when in the course of the running he took a hedge behind her, and pressing his horse, came up by her side and spoke.

'Clorinda,' he began breathlessly, through set teeth.

She could have left him and not answered, but she chose to restrain the pace of her wild beast for a moment and look at him.

'"Your ladyship!"' she corrected his audacity. 'Or – "my Lady Dunstanwolde".'

'There was a time –' he said.

'This morning,' she said, 'I found a letter in a casket in my closet. I do not know the mad villain who wrote it. I never knew him.'

'You did not,' he cried, with an oath, and then laughed scornfully.

'The letter lies in ashes on the hearth,' she said. ''Twas burned unopened. Do not ride so close, Sir John, and do not play the madman and the beast with the wife of my Lord Dunstanwolde.'

'"The wife!"' he answered. '"My lord!" 'Tis a new game this, and well played, by God!'

She did not so much as waver in her look, and her wide eyes smiled.

'Quite new,' she answered him – 'quite new. And could I not have played it well and fairly, I would not have touched the cards. Keep your horse off, Sir John. Mine is restive, and likes not another beast near him,' and she touched the creature with her whip, and he was gone like a thunderbolt.

The next day, being in her room, Anne saw her come from her dressing table with a sealed letter in her hand. She went to the bell and rang it.

'Anne,' she said, 'I am going to rate my woman and turn her from my service. I shall not beat or swear at her as I was wont to do with my women in time past. You will be afraid, perhaps; but you must stay with me.'

She was standing by the fire with the letter held almost at arm's length in her fingertips, when the woman entered, who, seeing her face, turned pale, and casting her eyes upon the letter, paler still, and began to shake.

'You have attended mistresses of other ways than mine,' her lady said in her slow, clear voice, which seemed to cut as knives do. 'Some fool and madman has bribed you to serve him. You cannot serve me also. Come hither and put this in the fire. If 'twere to be done I would make you hold it in the live coals with your hand.'

The woman came shuddering, looking as if she thought she might be struck dead. She took the letter and kneeled, ashen pale, to burn it. When 'twas done, her mistress pointed to the door.

'Go and gather your goods and chattels together, and leave within this hour,' she said. 'I will be my own tirewoman till I can find one who comes to me honest.'

When she was gone, Anne sat gazing at the ashes on the hearth. She was pale also.

'Sister,' she said, 'do you –'

'Yes,' answered my lady. ''Tis a man who loved me, a cur and a knave. He thought for an hour he was cured of his passion. I could have told him 'twould spring up and burn more fierce than ever when he saw another man possess me. 'Tis so with knaves and curs; and 'tis so with him. He hath gone mad again.'

'Ay, mad!' cried Anne – 'mad, and base, and wicked!'

Clorinda gazed at the ashes, her lips curling.

'He was ever base,' she said – 'as he was at first, so he is now. 'Tis thy favourite, Anne,' lightly, and she delicately spurned the blackened tinder with her foot – 'thy favourite, John Oxon.'

Mistress Anne crouched in her seat and hid her face in her thin hands.

'Oh, my lady!' she cried, not feeling that she could say 'sister', 'if he be base, and ever was so, pity him, pity him! The base need pity more than all.'

For she had loved him madly, all unknowing her own passion, not presuming even to look up in his beautiful face, thinking of him only as the slave of her sister, and in dead secrecy knowing strange things – strange things! And when she had seen the letter she had known the handwriting, and the beating of her simple heart had well-nigh strangled her – for she had seen words writ by him before.

When Dunstanwolde and his lady went back to their house in town, Mistress Anne went with them. Clorinda willed that it should be so. She made her there as peaceful and retired a nest of her own as she had given to her at Dunstanwolde. By strange good fortune Barbara had been wedded to a plain gentleman, who, being a widower with children, needed a helpmeet in his modest household, and through a distant relationship to Mistress Wimpole, encountered her charge, and saw in her meekness of spirit the thing which might fall into the supplying of his needs. A beauty or a fine lady would not have suited him; he wanted but a housewife and a mother for his orphaned children, and this, a young woman who had lived straitly, and been forced to many contrivances for mere decency of apparel and ordinary comfort, might be trained to become.

So it fell that Mistress Anne could go to London without pangs of conscience at leaving her sister in the country and alone. The stateliness of the town mansion, my Lady Dunstanwolde's retinue of lackeys and serving-women, her little black page, who waited on her and took her pug dogs to walk, her wardrobe, and jewels, and equipages, were each and all marvels to her, but seemed to her mind so far befitting that she remembered, wondering, the days when she had darned the tattered tapestry in her chamber, and changed the ribands and fashions of her gowns. Being now attired fittingly, though soberly as became her, she was not in these days – at least, as far as outward seeming went – an awkward blot upon the scene when she appeared among her sister's company; but at heart she was as timid and shrinking as ever, and never mingled with the guests in the great rooms when she could avoid so doing. Once or twice she went forth with Clorinda in her coach and six, and saw the glittering world, while she drew back into her corner of the equipage and gazed with all a country-bred woman's timorous admiration.

''Twas grand and like a beautiful show!' she said, when she came home the first time. 'But do not take me often, sister; I am too plain and shy, and feel that I am naught in it.'

But though she kept as much apart from the great world of fashion as she could, she contrived to know of all her sister's triumphs; to see her when she went forth in her bravery, though 'twere but to drive in the Mall; to be in her closet with her on great nights when her tirewomen were decking her in brocades and jewels, that she might show her highest beauty at some assembly or ball of State. And at all these times, as also at all others, she knew that she but shared her own love and dazzled admiration with my Lord Dunstanwolde, whose tenderness, being so fed by his lady's unfailing graciousness of bearing and kindly looks and words, grew with every hour that passed.

They held one night a splendid assembly at which a member of the Royal House was present. That night Clorinda bade her sister appear.

'Sometimes – I do not command it always – but sometimes you must show yourself to our guests. My lord will not be pleased else. He says it is not fitting that his wife's sister should remain unseen as if we hid her away through ungraciousness. Your woman will prepare for you all things needful. I myself will see that your dress becomes you. I have commanded it already, and given much thought to its shape and colour. I would have you very comely, Anne.' And she kissed her lightly on her cheek – almost as gently as she sometimes kissed her lord's grey hair. In truth, though she was still a proud lady and stately in her ways, there had come upon her some strange subtle change Anne could not understand.

On the day on which the assembly was held, Mistress Anne's woman brought to her a beautiful robe. 'Twas flowered satin of the sheen and softness of a dove's breast, and the lace adorning it was like a spider's web for gossamer fineness. The robe was sweetly fashioned, fitting her shape wondrously; and when she was attired in it at night a little colour came into her cheeks to see herself so far beyond all comeliness she had ever known before. When she found herself in the midst of the dazzling scene in the rooms of entertainment, she was glad when at last she could feel herself lost among the crowd of guests. Her only pleasure in such scenes was to withdraw to some hidden corner and look on as at a pageant or a play. Tonight she placed herself in the shadow of a screen, from which retreat she could see Clorinda and Dunstanwolde as they received their guests. Thus she found enjoyment enough; for, in truth, her love and almost abject passion of adoration for her sister had grown as his lordship's had, with every hour. For a season there had rested upon her a black shadow beneath which she wept and trembled, bewildered and lost; though even at its darkest the object of her humble love had been a star whose brightness was not dimmed, because it could not be so whatsoever passed before it. This cloud, however, being it seemed dispelled, the star had shone but more brilliant in its high place, and she the more passionately worshipped it. To sit apart and see her idol's radiance, to mark her as she reigned and seemed the more royal when she bent the knee to royalty itself, to see the shimmer of her jewels crowning her midnight hair and crashing the warm whiteness of her noble neck, to observe the admiration in all eyes as they dwelt upon her – this was, indeed, enough of happiness.

'She is, as ever,' she murmured, 'not so much a woman as a proud lovely goddess who has deigned to descend to earth. But my lord does not look like himself. He seems shrunk in the face and old, and his eyes have rings about them. I like not that. He is so kind a gentleman and so happy that his body should not fail him. I have marked that he has looked colourless for days, and Clorinda questioned him kindly on it, but he said he suffered naught.'

'Twas but a little later than she had thought this, that she remarked a gentleman step aside and stand quite near without observing her. Feeling that she had no testimony to her fanciful-ness, she found herself thinking in a vague fashion that he, too, had come there because he chose to be unobserved. 'Twould not have been so easy for him to retire as it had been for her small-ness and insignificance to do so; and, indeed, she did not fancy that he meant to conceal himself, but merely to stand for a quiet moment a little apart from the crowd.

And as she looked up at him, wondering why this should be, she saw he was the noblest and most stately gentleman she had ever beheld.

She had never seen him before; he must either be a stranger or a rare visitor. As Clorinda was beyond a woman's height, he was beyond a man's.

He carried himself as kingly as she did nobly; he had a countenance of strong, manly beauty, and a deep tawny eye, thick-fringed and full of fire; orders glittered upon his breast, and he wore a fair periwig, which became him wondrously, and seemed to make his eye more deep and burning by its contrast.

Beside his strength and majesty of bearing the stripling beauty of John Oxon would have seemed slight and paltry, a thing for flippant women to trifle with.

Mistress Anne looked at him with an admiration somewhat like reverence, and as she did so a sudden thought rose to her mind, and even as it rose, she marked what his gaze rested on, and how it dwelt upon it, and knew that he had stepped apart to stand and gaze as she did – only with a man's hid fervour – at her sister's self.

'Twas as if suddenly a strange secret had been told her. She read it in his face, because he thought himself unobserved, and for a space had cast his mask aside. He stood and gazed as a man who, starving at soul, fed himself through his eyes, having no hope of other sustenance, or as a man weary with long carrying of a burden, for a space laid it down for rest and to gather power to go on. She heard him draw a deep sigh almost stifled in its birth, and there was that in his face which she felt it was unseemly that a stranger like herself should behold, himself unknowing of her near presence.

She gently rose from her corner, wondering if she could retire from her retreat without attracting his observation; but as she did so, chance caused him to withdraw himself a little farther within the shadow of the screen, and doing so, he beheld her.

Then his face changed; the mask of noble calmness, for a moment fallen, resumed itself, and he bowed before her with the reverence of a courtly gentleman, undisturbed by the unexpectedness of his recognition of her neighbourhood.

'Madam,' he said, 'pardon my unconsciousness that you were near me. You would pass?' And he made way for her.

She curtseyed, asking his pardon with her dull, soft eyes.

'Sir,' she answered, 'I but retired here for a moment's rest from the throng and gaiety, to which I am unaccustomed. But chiefly I sat in retirement that I might watch – my sister.'

'Your sister, madam?' he said, as if the questioning echo were almost involuntary, and he bowed again in some apology.

'My Lady Dunstanwolde,' she replied. 'I take such pleasure in her loveliness and in all that pertains to her, it is a happiness to me to but look on.'

Whatsoever the thing was in her loving mood which touched him and found echo in his own, he was so far moved that he answered to her with something less of ceremoniousness; remembering also, in truth, that she was a lady he had heard of, and recalling her relationship and name.

'It is then Mistress Anne Wildairs I am honoured by having speech with,' he said. 'My Lady Dunstanwolde has spoken of you in my presence. I am my lord's kinsman the Duke of Osmonde,' again bowing, and Anne curtseyed low once more.

Despite his greatness, she felt a kindness and grace in him which was not condescension, and which almost dispelled the timidity which, being part of her nature, so unduly beset her at all times when she addressed or was addressed by a stranger. John Oxon, bowing his bright curls, and seeming ever to mock with his smiles, had caused her to be overcome with shy awkwardness and blushes; but this man, who seemed as far above him in person and rank and mind as a god is above a graceful painted puppet, even appeared to give of his own noble strength to her poor weakness. He bore himself towards her with a courtly respect such as no human being had ever shown to her before. He besought her again to be seated in her nook, and stood before her conversing with such delicate sympathy with her mood as seemed to raise her to the pedestal on which stood less humble women. All those who passed before them he knew and could speak easily of. The high deeds of those who were statesmen, or men honoured at Court or in the field, he was familiar with; and of those who were beauties or notable gentle-women he had always something courtly to say.

Her own worship of her sister she knew full well he under-stood, though he spoke of her but little.

'Well may you gaze at her,' he said. 'So does all the world, and honours and adores.'

He proffered her at last his arm, and she, having strangely taken courage, let him lead her through the rooms and persuade her to some refreshment. Seeing her so wondrously emerge from her chrysalis, and under the protection of so distinguished a companion, all looked at her as she passed with curious amazement, and indeed Mistress Anne was all but overpowered by the reverence shown them as they made their way.

As they came again into the apartment wherein the host and hostess received their guests, Anne felt her escort pause, and looked up at him to see the meaning of his sudden hesita-tion. He was gazing intently, not at Clorinda, but at the Earl of Dunstanwolde.

'Madam,' he said, 'pardon me that I seem to detain you, but – but I look at my kinsman. Madam,' with a sudden fear in his voice, 'he is ailing – he sways as he stands. Let us go to him. Quickly! He falls!'

And, in sooth, at that very moment there arose a dismayed cry from the guests about them, and there was a surging movement; and as they pressed forward themselves through the throng, Anne saw Dunstanwolde no more above the people, for he had indeed fallen and lay outstretched and deathly on the floor.

'Twas but a few seconds before she and Osmonde were close enough to him to mark his fallen face and ghastly pallor, and a strange dew starting out upon his brow.

But 'twas his wife who knelt beside his prostrate body, waving all else aside with a great majestic gesture of her arm.

'Back! back!' she cried. 'Air! air! and water! My lord! My dear lord!'

But he did not answer, or even stir, though she bent close to him and thrust her hand within his breast. And then the frightened guests beheld a strange but beautiful and loving thing, such as might have moved any heart to tenderness and wonder. This great beauty, this worshipped creature, put her arms beneath and about the helpless, awful body – for so its pallor and stillness indeed made it – and lifted it in their powerful whiteness as if it had been the body of a child, and so bore it to a couch near and laid it down, kneeling beside it.

Anne and Osmonde were beside her. Osmonde pale himself, but gently calm and strong. He had despatched for a physician the instant he saw the fall.

'My lady,' he said, bending over her, 'permit me to approach. I have some knowledge of these seizures. Your pardon!'

He knelt also and took the moveless hand, feeling the pulse; he, too, thrust his hand within the breast and held it there, looking at the sunken face.

'My dear lord,' her ladyship was saying, as if to the prostrate man's ear alone, knowing that her tender voice must reach him if aught would – as indeed was truth. 'Edward! My dear – dear lord!'

Osmonde held his hand steadily over the heart. The guests shrunk back, stricken with terror.

There was that in this corner of the splendid room which turned faces pale.

Osmonde slowly withdrew his hand, and turning to the kneeling woman – with a pallor like that of marble, but with a noble tenderness and pity in his eyes –

'My lady,' he said, 'you are a brave woman. Your great courage must sustain you. The heart beats no more. A noble life is finished.'

The guests heard, and drew still farther back, a woman or two faintly whimpering; a hurrying lackey parted the crowd, and so, way being made for him, the physician came quickly forward.

Anne put her shaking hands up to cover her gaze. Osmonde stood still, looking down. My Lady Dunstanwolde knelt by the couch and hid her beautiful face upon the dead man's breast.

Which Treats of the Obsequies of My Lord of Dunstanwolde, of His Lady's Widowhood, and of Her Return to Town

All that remained of my Lord Dunstanwolde was borne back to his ancestral home, and there laid to rest in the ancient tomb in which his fathers slept. Many came from town to pay him respect, and the Duke of Osmonde was, as was but fitting, among them. The countess kept her own apartments, and none but her sister, Mistress Anne, beheld her.

The night before the final ceremonies she spent sitting by her lord's coffin, and to Anne it seemed that her mood was a stranger one, than ever woman had before been ruled by. She did not weep or moan, and only once kneeled down. In her sweeping black robes she seemed more a majestic creature than she had ever been, and her beauty more that of a statue than of a mortal woman. She sent away all other watchers, keeping only her sister with her, and Anne observed in her a strange protecting gentleness when she spoke of the dead man.

'I do not know whether dead men can feel and hear,' she said. 'Sometimes there has come into my mind – and made me shudder – the thought that, though they lie so still, mayhap they know what we do – and how they are spoken of as nothings whom live men and women but wait a moment to thrust away, that their own living may go on again in its accustomed way, or perchance more merrily. If my lord knows aught, he will be grateful that I watch by him tonight in this solemn room. He was ever grateful, and moved by any tenderness of mine.'

'Twas as she said, the room was solemn, and this almost to awfulness. It was a huge cold chamber at best, and draped with black, and hung with hatchments; a silent gloom filled it which made it like a tomb. Tall wax-candles burned in it dimly, but adding to its solemn shadows with their faint light; and in his rich coffin the dead man lay in his shroud, his hands like carvings of yellowed ivory clasped upon his breast.

Mistress Anne dared not have entered the place alone, and was so overcome at sight of the pinched nostrils and sunk eyes that she turned cold with fear. But Clorinda seemed to feel no dread or shrinking. She went and stood beside the great funeral-draped bed of state on which the coffin lay, and thus standing, looked down with a grave, protecting pity in her face. Then she stooped and kissed the dead man long upon the brow.

'I will sit by you tonight,' she said. 'That which lies here will be alone tomorrow. I will not leave you this last night. Had I been in your place you would not leave me.'

She sat down beside him and laid her strong warm hand upon his cold waxen ones, closing it over them as if she would give them heat. Anne knelt and prayed – that all might be forgiven, that sins might be blotted out, that this kind poor soul might find love and peace in the kingdom of Heaven, and might not learn there what might make bitter the memory of his last year of rapture and love. She was so simple that she forgot that no knowledge of the past could embitter aught when a soul looked back from Paradise.

Throughout the watches of the night her sister sat and held the dead man's hand; she saw her more than once smooth his grey hair almost as a mother might have touched a sick sleeping child's; again she kissed his forehead, speaking to him gently, as if to tell him he need not fear, for she was close at hand; just once she knelt, and Anne wondered if she prayed, and in what manner, knowing that prayer was not her habit.

'Twas just before dawn she knelt so, and when she rose and stood beside him, looking down again, she drew from the folds of her robe a little package.

'Anne,' she said, as she untied the riband that bound it, 'when first I was his wife I found him one day at his desk looking at these things as they lay upon his hand. He thought at first it would offend me to find him so; but I told him that I was gentler than he thought – though not so gentle as the poor innocent girl who died in giving him his child. 'Twas her picture he was gazing at, and a little ring and two locks of hair – one a brown ringlet from her head, and one – such a tiny wisp of down – from the head of her infant. I told him to keep them always and look at them often, remembering how innocent she had been, and that she had died for him. There were tears on my hand when he kissed it in thanking me. He kept the little package in his desk, and I have brought it to him.'

The miniature was of a sweet-faced girl with large loving childish eyes, and cheeks that blushed like the early morning. Clorinda looked at her almost with tenderness.

'There is no marrying or giving in marriage, 'tis said,' quoth she; 'but were there, 'tis you who were his wife – not I. I was but a lighter thing, though I bore his name and he honoured me. When you and your child greet him he will forget me – and all will be well.'

She held the miniature and the soft hair to his cold lips a moment, and Anne saw with wonder that her own mouth worked. She slipped the ring on his least finger, and hid the picture and the ringlets within the palms of his folded hands.

'He was a good man,' she said; 'he was the first good man that I had ever known.' And she held out her hand to Anne and drew her from the room with her, and two crystal tears fell upon the bosom of her black robe and slipped away like jewels.

When the funeral obsequies were over, the next of kin who was heir came to take possession of the estate which had fallen to him, and the widow retired to her father's house for seclusion from the world. The town house had been left to her by her deceased lord, but she did not wish to return to it until the period of her mourning was over and she laid aside her weeds. The income the earl had been able to bestow upon her made her a rich woman, and when she chose to appear again in the world it would be with the power to mingle with it fittingly.

During her stay at her father's house she did much to make it a more suitable abode for her, ordering down from London furnishings and workmen to set her own apartments and Anne's in order. But she would not occupy the rooms she had lived in heretofore. For some reason it seemed to be her whim to have begun to have an enmity for them. The first day she entered them with Anne she stopped upon the threshold.

'I will not stay here,' she said. 'I never loved the rooms – and now I hate them. It seems to me it was another woman who lived in them – in another world. 'Tis so long ago that 'tis ghostly. Make ready the old red chambers for me,' to her woman; 'I will live there. They have been long closed, and are worm-eaten and mouldy perchance; but a great fire will warm them. And I will have furnishings from London to make them fit for habitation.'

The next day it seemed for a brief space as if she would have changed even from the red chambers.

'I did not know,' she said, turning with a sudden movement from a side window, 'that one might see the old rose garden from here. I would not have taken the room had I guessed it. It is too dreary a wilderness, with its tangle of briars and its broken sundial.'

'You cannot see the dial from here,' said Anne, coming towards her with a strange paleness and haste. 'One cannot see within the garden from any window, surely.'

'Nay,' said Clorinda; ''tis not near enough, and the hedges are too high; but one knows 'tis there, and 'tis tiresome.'

'Let us draw the curtains and not look, and forget it,' said poor Anne. And she drew the draperies with a trembling hand; and ever after while they dwelt in the room they stayed so.

My lady wore her mourning for more than a year, and in her sombre trailing weeds was a wonder to behold. She lived in her father's house, and saw no company, but sat or walked and drove with her sister Anne, and visited the poor. The perfect stateliness of her decorum was more talked about than any levity would have been; those who were wont to gossip expecting that having made her fine match and been so soon rid of her lord, she would begin to show her strange wild breeding again, and indulge in fantastical whims. That she should wear her mourning with unflinching dignity and withdraw from the world as strictly as if she had been a lady of royal blood mourning her prince, was the unexpected thing, and so was talked of everywhere.

At the end of the eighteenth month she sent one day for Anne, who, coming at her bidding, found her standing in her chamber surrounded by black robes and draperies piled upon the bed, and chairs, and floor, their sombreness darkening the room like a cloud; but she stood in their midst in a trailing garment of pure white, and in her bosom was a bright red rose tied with a knot of scarlet riband, whose ends fell floating. Her woman was upon her knees before a coffer in which she was laying the weeds as she folded them.

Mistress Anne paused within the doorway, her eyes dazzled by the tall radiant shape and blot of scarlet colour as if by the shining of the sun. She knew in that moment that all was changed, and that the world of darkness they had been living in for the past months was swept from existence. When her sister had worn her mourning weeds she had seemed somehow almost pale; but now she stood in the sunlight with the rich scarlet on her cheek and lip, and the stars in her great eyes.

'Come in, sister Anne,' she said. 'I lay aside my weeds, and my woman is folding them away for me. Dost know of any poor creature newly left a widow whom some of them would be a help to? 'Tis a pity that so much sombreness should lie in chests when there are perhaps poor souls to whom it would be a godsend.'

Before the day was over, there was not a shred of black stuff left in sight; such as had not been sent out of the house to be distributed, being packed away in coffers in the garrets under the leads.

'You will wear it no more, sister?' Anne asked once. 'You will wear gay colours – as if it had never been?'

'It is as if it had never been,' Clorinda answered. 'Ere now her lord is happy with her, and he is so happy that I am forgot. I had a fancy that – perhaps at first – well, if he had looked down on earth – remembering – he would have seen I was faithful in my honouring of him. But now, I am sure –'

She stopped with a half laugh. ''Twas but a fancy,' she said. 'Perchance he has known naught since that night he fell at my feet – and even so, poor gentleman, he hath a happy fate. Yes, I will wear gay colours,' flinging up her arms as if she dropped fetters, and stretched her beauteous limbs for case – 'gay colours – and roses and rich jewels – and all things – all that will make me beautiful!'

The next day there came a chest from London, packed close with splendid raiment; when she drove out again in her chariot her servants' sad-coloured liveries had been laid by, and she was attired in rich hues, amidst which she glowed like some flower new bloomed.

Her house in town was thrown open again, and set in order for her coming. She made her journey back in state, Mistress Anne accompanying her in her travelling coach. As she passed over the highroad with her equipage and her retinue, or spent the night for rest at the best inns in the towns and villages, all seemed to know her name and state.

''Tis the young widow of the Earl of Dunstanwolde,' people said to each other – 'she that is the great beauty, and of such a wit and spirit that she is scarce like a mere young lady. 'Twas said she wed him for his rank; but afterwards 'twas known she made him a happy gentleman, though she gave him no heir. She wore weeds for him beyond the accustomed time, and is but now issuing from her retirement.'

Mistress Anne felt as if she were attending some royal lady's progress, people so gazed at them and nudged each other, wondered and admired.

'You do not mind that all eyes rest on you,' she said to her sister; 'you are accustomed to be gazed at.'

'I have been gazed at all my life,' my lady answered; 'I scarce take note of it.'

On their arrival at home they met with fitting welcome and reverence. The doors of the town house were thrown open wide, and in the hall the servants stood in line, the housekeeper at the head with her keys at her girdle, the little jet-black negro page grinning beneath his turban with joy to see his lady again, he worshipping her as a sort of fetish, after the manner of his race. 'Twas his duty to take heed to the pet dogs, and he stood holding by their little silver chains a smart-faced pug and a pretty spaniel. His lady stopped a moment to pat them and to speak to him a word of praise of their condition; and being so favoured, he spoke also, rolling his eyes in his delight at finding somewhat to impart.

'Yesterday, ladyship, when I took them out,' he said, 'a gentleman marked them, knowing whose they were. He asked me when my lady came again to town, and I answered him today. 'Twas the fair gentleman in his own hair.'

''Twas Sir John Oxon, your ladyship,' said the lackey nearest to him.

Her ladyship left caressing her spaniel and stood upright. Little Nero was frightened, fearing she was angered; she stood so straight and tall, but she said nothing and passed on.

At the top of the staircase she turned to Mistress Anne with a laugh.

'Thy favourite again, Anne,' she said. 'He means to haunt me, now we are alone. 'Tis thee he comes after.'

Wherein a Deadly War Begins

The town and the world of fashion greeted her on her return with open arms. Those who looked on when she bent the knee to kiss the hand of royalty at the next drawing room, whispered among themselves that bereavement had not dimmed her charms, which were even more radiant than they had been at her presentation on her marriage, and that the mind of no man or woman could dwell on aught as mournful as widowhood in connection with her, or, indeed, could think of anything but her brilliant beauty. 'Twas as if from this time she was launched into a new life. Being rich, of high rank, and no longer an unmarried woman, her position had a dignity and freedom which there was no creature but might have envied. As the wife of Dunstan-wolde she had been the fashion, and adored by all who dared adore her; but as his widow she was surrounded and besieged. A fortune, a toast, a wit, and a beauty, she combined all the things either man or woman could desire to attach themselves to the train of; and had her air been less regal, and her wit less keen of edge, she would have been so beset by flatterers and toadies that life would have been burdensome. But this she would not have, and was swift enough to detect the man whose debts drove him to the expedient of daring to privately think of the usefulness of her fortune, or the woman who manoeuvred to gain reputation or success by means of her position and power.

'They would be about me like vultures if I were weak fool enough to let them,' she said to Anne. 'They cringe and grovel like spaniels, and flatter till 'tis like to make one sick. 'Tis always so with toadies; they have not the wit to see that their flattery is an insolence, since it supposes adulation so rare that one may be moved by it. The men with empty pockets would marry me, forsooth, and the women be dragged into company clinging to my petticoats. But they are learning. I do not shrink from giving them sharp lessons.'

This she did without mercy, and in time cleared herself of hangers-on, so that her banquets and assemblies were the most distinguished of the time, and the men who paid their court to her were of such place and fortune that their worship could but be disinterested.

Among the earliest to wait upon her was his Grace of Osmonde, who found her one day alone, save for the presence of Mistress Anne, whom she kept often with her. When the lackey announced him, Anne, who sat upon the same seat with her, felt her slightly start, and looking up, saw in her countenance a thing she had never beheld before, nor had indeed ever dreamed of beholding. It was a strange, sweet crimson which flowed over her face, and seemed to give a wondrous deepness to her lovely orbs. She rose as a queen might have risen had a king come to her, but never had there been such pulsing softness in her look before. 'Twas in some curious fashion like the look of a girl; and, in sooth, she was but a girl in years, but so different to all others of her age, and had lived so singular a life, that no one ever thought of her but as a woman, or would have deemed it aught but folly to credit her with any tender emotion or blushing warmth girlhood might be allowed.

His Grace was as courtly of bearing as he had ever been. He stayed not long, and during his visit conversed but on such subjects as a kinsman may graciously touch upon; but Anne noted in him a new look also, though she could scarce have told what it might be. She thought that he looked happier, and her fancy was that some burden had fallen from him.

Before he went away he bent low and long over Clorinda's hand, pressing his lips to it with a tenderness which strove not to conceal itself. And the hand was not withdrawn, her ladyship standing in sweet yielding, the tender crimson trembling on her cheek. Anne herself trembled, watching her new, strange loveliness with a sense of fascination; she could scarce withdraw her eyes, it seemed so as if the woman had been reborn.

'Your Grace will come to us again,' my lady said, in a soft voice. 'We are two lonely women,' with her radiant compelling smile, 'and need your kindly countenancing.'

His eyes dwelt deep in hers as he answered, and there was a flush upon his own cheek, man and warrior though he was.

'If I might come as often as I would,' he said, 'I should be at your door, perhaps, with too great frequency.'

'Nay, your Grace,' she answered. 'Come as often as we would – and see who wearies first. 'Twill not be ourselves.'

He kissed her hand again, and this time 'twas passionately, and when he left her presence it was with a look of radiance on his noble face, and with the bearing of a king new crowned.

For a few moments' space she stood where he had parted from her, looking as though listening to the sound of his step, as if she would not lose a footfall; then she went to the window, and stood among the flowers there, looking down into the street, and Anne saw that she watched his equipage.

'Twas early summer, and the sunshine flooded her from head to foot; the window and balcony were full of flowers – yellow jonquils and daffodils, white narcissus, and all things fragrant of the spring. The scent of them floated about her like an incense, and a straying zephyr blew great puffs of their sweetness back into the room. Anne felt it all about her, and remembered it until she was an aged woman.

Clorinda's bosom rose high in an exultant, rapturous sigh.

''Tis the spring that comes,' she murmured breathlessly. 'Never hath it come to me before.'

Even as she said the words, at the very moment of her speaking, Fate – a strange Fate indeed – brought to her yet another visitor. The door was thrown open wide, and in he came, a lackey crying aloud his name. 'Twas Sir John Oxon.

Those of the world of fashion who were wont to gossip, had bestowed upon them a fruitful subject for discussion over their tea-tables, in the future of the widowed Lady Dunstanwolde. All the men being enamoured of her, 'twas not likely that she would long remain unmarried, her period of mourning being over; and, accordingly, forthwith there was every day chosen for her a new husband by those who concerned themselves in her affairs, and they were many. One week 'twas a great general she was said to smile on; again, a great beau and female conqueror, it being argued that, having made her first marriage for rank and wealth, and being a passionate and fantastic beauty, she would this time allow herself to be ruled by her caprice, and wed for love; again, a certain marquis was named, and after him a young earl renowned for both beauty and wealth; but though each and all of those selected were known to have laid themselves at her feet, none of them seemed to have met with the favour they besought for.

There were two men, however, who were more spoken of than all the rest, and whose court awakened a more lively interest; indeed, 'twas an interest which was lively enough at times to become almost a matter of contention, for those who upheld the cause of the one man would not hear of the success of the other, the claims of each being considered of such different nature. These two men were the Duke of Osmonde and Sir John Oxon. 'Twas the soberer and more dignified who were sure his Grace had but to proffer his suit to gain it, and their sole wonder lay in that he did not speak more quickly.

'But being a man of such noble mind, it may be that he would leave her to her freedom yet a few months, because, despite her stateliness, she is but young, and 'twould be like his honourableness to wish that she should see many men while she is free to choose, as she has never been before. For these days she is not a poor beauty as she was when she took Dunstanwolde.'

The less serious, or less worldly, especially the sentimental spinsters and matrons and romantic young, who had heard and enjoyed the rumours of Mistress Clorinda Wildairs' strange early days, were prone to build much upon a certain story of that time.

'Sir John Oxon was her first love,' they said. 'He went to her father's house a beautiful young man in his earliest bloom, and she had never encountered such an one before, having only known country dolts and her father's friends. 'Twas said they loved each other, but were both passionate and proud, and quarrelled bitterly. Sir John went to France to strive to forget her in gay living; he even obeyed his mother and paid court to another woman, and Mistress Clorinda, being of fierce haughtiness, revenged herself by marrying Lord Dunstanwolde.'

'But she has never deigned to forgive him,' 'twas also said. 'She is too haughty and of too high a temper to forgive easily that a man should seem to desert her for another woman's favour. Even when 'twas whispered that she favoured him, she was disdainful, and sometimes flouted him bitterly, as was her way with all men. She was never gentle, and had always a cutting wit. She will use him hardly before she relents; but if he sues patiently enough with such grace as he uses with other women, love will conquer her at last, for 'twas her first.'

She showed him no great favour, it was true; and yet it seemed she granted him more privilege than she had done during her lord's life, for he was persistent in his following her, and would come to her house whether of her will or of his own. Sometimes he came there when the Duke of Osmonde was with her – this happened more than once – and then her ladyship's face, which was ever warmly beautiful when Osmonde was near, would curiously change. It would grow pale and cold; but in her eyes would burn a strange light which one man knew was as the light in the eyes of a tigress lying chained, but crouching to leap. But it was not Osmonde who felt this, he saw only that she changed colour, and having heard the story of her girlhood, a little chill of doubt would fall upon his noble heart. It was not doubt of her, but of himself, and fear that his great passion made him blind; for he was the one man chivalrous enough to remember how young she was, and to see the cruelty of the Fate which had given her unmothered childhood into the hands of a coarse rioter and debauchee, making her his plaything and his whim. And if in her first hours of bloom she had been thrown with youthful manhood and beauty, what more in the course of nature than that she should have learned to love; and being separated from her young lover by their mutual youthful faults of pride and passionateness of temper, what more natural than, being free again, and he suing with all his soul, that her heart should return to him, even though through a struggle with pride. In her lord's lifetime he had not seen Oxon near her; and in those days when he had so struggled with his own surging love, and striven to bear himself nobly, he had kept away from her, knowing that his passion was too great and strong for any man to always hold at bay and make no sign, because at brief instants he trembled before the thought that in her eyes he had seen that which would have sprung to answer the same self in him if she had been a free woman. But now when, despite her coldness, which never melted to John Oxon, she still turned pale and seemed to fall under a restraint on his coming, a man of sufficient high dignity to be splendidly modest where his own merit was concerned, might well feel that for this there must be a reason, and it might be a grave one.

So though he would not give up his suit until he was sure that 'twas either useless or unfair, he did not press it as he would have done, but saw his lady when he could, and watched with all the tenderness of passion her lovely face and eyes. But one short town season passed before he won his prize; but to poor Anne it seemed that in its passing she lived years.

Poor woman, as she had grown thin and large-eyed in those days gone by, she grew so again. Time in passing had taught her so much that others did not know; and as she served her sister, and waited on her wishes, she saw that of which no other dreamed, and saw without daring to speak, or show by any sign, her knowledge.

The day when Lady Dunstanwolde had turned from standing among her daffodils, and had found herself confronting the open door of her saloon, and John Oxon passing through it, Mistress Anne had seen that in her face and his which had given to her a shock of terror. In John Oxon's blue eyes there had been a set fierce look, and in Clorinda's a blaze which had been like a declaration of war; and these same looks she had seen since that day, again and again. Gradually it had become her sister's habit to take Anne with her into the world as she had not done before her widowhood, and Anne knew whence this custom came. There were times when, by use of her presence, she could avoid those she wished to thrust aside, and Anne noted, with a cold sinking of the spirit, that the one she would plan to elude most frequently was Sir John Oxon; and this was not done easily. The young man's gay lightness of demeanour had changed. The few years that had passed since he had come to pay his courts to the young beauty in male attire, had brought experiences to him which had been bitter enough. He had squandered his fortune, and failed to reinstate himself by marriage; his dissipations had told upon him, and he had lost his spirit and good-humour; his mocking wit had gained a bitterness; his gallantry had no longer the gaiety of youth. And the woman he had loved for an hour with youthful passion, and had dared to dream of casting aside in boyish insolence, had risen like a phoenix, and soared high and triumphant to the very sun itself. 'He was ever base,' Clorinda had said. 'As he was at first he is now,' and in the saying there was truth. If she had been helpless and heartbroken, and had pined for him, he would have treated her as a victim, and disdained her humiliation and grief; magnificent, powerful, rich, in fullest beauty, and disdaining himself, she filled him with a mad passion of love which was strangely mixed with hatred and cruelty. To see her surrounded by her worshippers, courted by the Court itself, all eyes drawn towards her as she moved, all hearts laid at her feet, was torture to him. In such cases as his and hers, it was the woman who should sue for love's return, and watch the averted face, longing for the moment when it would deign to turn and she could catch the cold eye and plead piteously with her own. This he had seen; this, men like himself, but older, had taught him with vicious art; but here was a woman who had scorned him at the hour which should have been the moment of his greatest powerfulness, who had mocked at and lashed him in the face with the high derision of a creature above law, and who never for one instant had bent her neck to the yoke which women must bear. She had laughed it to scorn – and him – and all things – and gone on her way, crowned with her scarlet roses, to wealth, and rank, and power, and adulation; while he – the man, whose right it was to be transgressor – had fallen upon hard fortune, and was losing step by step all she had won. In his way he loved her madly – as he had loved her before, and as he would have loved any woman who embodied triumph and beauty; and burning with desire for both, and with jealous rage of all, he swore he would not be outdone, befooled, cast aside, and trampled on.

At the playhouse when she looked from her box, she saw him leaning against some pillar or stationed in some noticeable spot, his bold blue eyes fixed burningly upon her; at fashionable assemblies he made his way to her side and stood near her, gazing, or dropping words into her ear; at church he placed himself in some pew near by, that she and all the world might behold him; when she left her coach and walked in the Mall he joined her or walked behind. At such times in my lady's close-fringed eyes there shone a steady gleam; but they were ever eyes that glowed, and there were none who had ever come close enough to her to know her well, and so there were none who read its meaning. Only Anne knew as no other creature could, and looked on with secret terror and dismay. The world but said that he was a man mad with love, and desperate at the know-ledge of the powerfulness of his rivals, could not live beyond sight of her.

They did not hear the words that passed between them at times when he stood near her in some crowd, and dropped, as 'twas thought, words of burning prayer and love into her ear. 'Twas said that it was like her to listen with unchanging face, and when she deigned reply, to answer without turning towards him. But such words and replies it had more than once been Anne's ill-fortune to be near enough to catch, and hearing them she had shuddered.

One night at a grand rout, the Duke of Osmonde but just having left the reigning beauty's side, she heard the voice she hated close by her, speaking.

'You think you can disdain me to the end,' it said. 'Your lady-ship is sure so?'

She did not turn or answer, and there followed a low laugh.

'You think a man will lie beneath your feet and be trodden upon without speaking. You are too high and bold.'

She waved her painted fan, and gazed steadily before her at the crowd, now and then bending her head in gracious greeting and smiling at some passer-by.

'If I could tell the story of the rose garden, and of what the sundial saw, and what the moon shone on –' he said.

He heard her draw her breath sharply through her teeth, he saw her white bosom lift as if a wild beast leapt within it, and he laughed again.

'His Grace of Osmonde returns,' he said; and then marking, as he never failed to do, bitterly against his will, the grace and majesty of this rival, who was one of the greatest and bravest of England's gentlemen, and knowing that she marked it too, his rage so mounted that it overcame him.

'Sometimes,' he said, 'methinks that I shall kill you!'

'Would you gain your end thereby?' she answered, in a voice as low and deadly.

'I would frustrate his – and yours.'

'Do it, then,' she hissed back, 'some day when you think I fear you.'

''Twould be too easy,' he answered. 'You fear it too little. There are bitterer things.'

She rose and met his Grace, who had approached her. Always to his greatness and his noble heart she turned with that new feeling of dependence which her whole life had never brought to her before. His deep eyes, falling on her tenderly as she rose, were filled with protecting concern. Involuntarily he hastened his steps.

'Will your Grace take me to my coach?' she said. 'I am not well. May I – go?' as gently as a tender, appealing girl.

And moved by this, as by her pallor, more than his man's words could have told, he gave her his arm and drew her quickly and supportingly away.

Mistress Anne did not sleep well that night, having much to distract her mind and keep her awake, as was often in these days the case. When at length she closed her eyes her slumber was fitful and broken by dreams, and in the mid hour of the darkness she wakened with a start as if some sound had aroused her. Perhaps there had been some sound, though all was still when she opened her eyes; but in the chair by her bedside sat Clorinda in her night-rail, her hands wrung hard together on her knee, her black eyes staring under a brow knit into straight deep lines.

'Sister!' cried Anne, starting up in bed. 'Sister!'

Clorinda slowly turned her head towards her, whereupon Anne saw that in her face there was a look as if of horror which struggled with a grief, a woe, too monstrous to be borne.

'Lie down, Anne,' she said. 'Be not afraid – 'tis only I,' – bitterly – 'who need fear?'

Anne cowered among the pillows and hid her face in her thin hands. She knew so well that this was true.

'I never thought the time would come,' her sister said, 'when I should seek you for protection. A thing has come upon me – perhaps I shall go mad – tonight, alone in my room, I wanted to sit near a woman – 'twas not like me, was it?'

Mistress Anne crept near the bed's edge, and stretching forth a hand, touched hers, which were as cold as marble.

'Stay with me, sister,' she prayed. 'Sister, do not go! What – what can I say?'

'Naught,' was the steady answer. 'There is naught to be said. You were always a woman – I was never one – till now.'

She rose up from her chair and threw up her arms, pacing to and fro.

'I am a desperate creature,' she cried. 'Why was I born?'

She walked the room almost like a thing mad and caged.

'Why was I thrown into the world?' striking her breast. 'Why was I made so – and not one to watch or care through those mad years? To be given a body like this and tossed to the wolves.'

She turned to Anne, her arms outstretched, and so stood white and strange and beauteous as a statue, with drops like great pearls running down her lovely cheeks, and she caught her breath sobbingly, like a child.

'I was thrown to them,' she wailed piteously, 'and they harried me – and left the marks of their great teeth – and of the scars I cannot rid myself – and since it was my fate – pronounced from my first hour – why was not this,' clutching her breast, 'left hard as 'twas at first? Not a woman's – not a woman's, but a she-cub's. Ah! 'twas not just – not just that it should be so!'

Anne slipped from her bed and ran to her, falling upon her knees and clinging to her, weeping bitterly.

'Poor heart!' she cried. 'Poor, dearest heart!'

Her touch and words seemed to recall Clorinda to herself. She started as if wakened from a dream, and drew her form up rigid.

'I have gone mad,' she said. 'What is it I do?' She passed her hand across her brow and laughed a little wild laugh. 'Yes,' she said; 'this it is to be a woman – to turn weak and run to other women – and weep and talk. Yes, by these signs I am a woman!' She stood with her clenched hands pressed against her breast. 'In any fair fight,' she said, 'I could have struck back blow for blow – and mine would have been the heaviest; but being changed into a woman, my arms are taken from me. He who strikes, aims at my bared breast – and that he knows and triumphs in.'

She set her teeth together, and ground them, and the look, which was like that of a chained and harried tigress, lit itself in her eyes.

'But there is none shall beat me,' she said through these fierce shut teeth. 'Nay I say there is none! Get up, Anne,' bending to raise her. 'Get up, or I shall be kneeling too – and I must stand upon my feet.'

She made a motion as if she would have turned and gone from the room without further explanation, but Anne still clung to her. She was afraid of her again, but her piteous love was stronger than her fear.

'Let me go with you,' she cried. 'Let me but go and lie in your closet that I may be near, if you should call.'

Clorinda put her hands upon her shoulders, and stooping, kissed her, which in all their lives she had done but once or twice.

'God bless thee, poor Anne,' she said. 'I think thou wouldst lie on my threshold and watch the whole night through, if I should need it; but I have given way to womanish vapours too much – I must go and be alone. I was driven by my thoughts to come and sit and look at thy good face – I did not mean to wake thee. Go back to bed.'

She would be obeyed, and led Anne to her couch herself, making her lie down, and drawing the coverlet about her; after which she stood upright with a strange smile, laying her hands lightly about her own white throat.

'When I was a newborn thing and had a little throat and a weak breath,' she cried, ''twould have been an easy thing to end me. I have been told I lay beneath my mother when they found her dead. If, when she felt her breath leaving her, she had laid her hand upon my mouth and stopped mine, I should not,' with the little laugh again – 'I should not lie awake tonight.'

And then she went away.

Containing the History of the Breaking of the Horse Devil, and Relates the Returning of His Grace of Osmonde From France

There were in this strange nature, depths so awful and profound that it was not to be sounded or to be judged as others were. But one thing could have melted or caused the unconquerable spirit to bend, and this was the overwhelming passion of love – not a slight, tender feeling, but a great and powerful one, such as could be awakened but by a being of as strong and deep a nature as itself, one who was in all things its peer.

'I have been lonely – lonely all my life,' my Lady Dunstanwolde had once said to her sister, and she had indeed spoken a truth.

Even in her childhood she had felt in some strange way she stood apart from the world about her. Before she had been old enough to reason she had been conscious that she was stronger and had greater power and endurance than any human being about her. Her strength she used in these days in wilful tyranny, and indeed it was so used for many a day when she was older. The time had never been when an eye lighted on her with indifference, or when she could not rule and punish as she willed. As an infant she had browbeaten the women-servants and the stable boys and grooms; but because of her quick wit and clever tongue, and also because no humour ever made her aught but a creature well worth looking at, they had taken her bullying in good humour and loved her in their coarse way. She had tyrannised over her father and his companions, and they had adored and boasted of her; but there had not been one among them whom she could have turned to if a softer moment had come upon her and she had felt the need of a friend, nor indeed one whom she did not regard privately with contempt.

A god or goddess forced upon earth and surrounded by mere human beings would surely feel a desolateness beyond the power of common words to express, and a human being endowed with powers and physical gifts so rare as to be out of all keeping with those of its fellows of ordinary build and mental stature must needs be lonely too.

She had had no companion, because she had found none like herself, and none with whom she could have aught in common. Anne she had pitied, being struck by some sense of the unfairness of her lot as compared with her own. John Oxon had moved her, bringing to her her first knowledge of buoyant, ardent youth, and blooming strength and beauty; for Dunstanwolde she had felt gratitude and affection; but than these there had been no others who even distantly had touched her heart.

The night she had given her promise to Dunstanwolde, and had made her obeisance before his kinsman as she had met his deep and leonine eye, she had known that 'twas the only man's eye before which her own would fall and which held the power to rule her very soul.

She did not think this as a romantic girl would have thought it; it was revealed to her by a sudden tempestuous leap of her heart, and by a shock like terror. Here was the man who was of her own build, whose thews and sinews of mind and body was as powerful as her own – here was he who, had she met him one short year before, would have revolutionised her world.

In the days of her wifehood when she had read in his noble face something of that which he endeavoured to command and which to no other was apparent, the dignity of his self-restraint had but filled her with tenderness more passionate and grateful.

'Had he been a villain and a coward,' was her thought, 'he would have made my life a bitter battle; but 'tis me he loves, not himself only, and as I honour him so does he honour me.'

Now she beheld the same passion in his eyes, but no more held in leash: his look met hers, hiding from her nothing of what his high soul burned with; and she was free – free to answer when he spoke, and only feeling one bitterness in her heart – if he had but come in time – God! why had he not been sent in time?

But, late or early, he had come; and what they had to give each other should not be mocked at and lost. The night she had ended by going to Anne's chamber, she had paced her room saying this again and again, all the strength of her being rising in revolt. She had been then a caged tigress of a verity; she had wrung her hands; she had held her palm hard against her leaping heart; she had walked madly to and fro, battling in thought with what seemed awful fate; she had flung herself upon her knees and wept bitter scalding tears.

'He is so noble,' she had cried – 'he is so noble – and I so worship his nobleness – and I have been so base!'

And in her suffering her woman's nerves had for a moment betrayed her. Heretofore she had known no weakness of her sex, but the woman soul in her so being moved, she had been broken and conquered for a space, and had gone to Anne's chamber, scarcely knowing what refuge she so sought. It had been a feminine act, and she had realised all it signified when Anne sank weeping by her. Women who wept and prated together at midnight in their chambers ended by telling their secrets. So it was that it fell out that Anne saw not again the changed face to the sight of which she had that night awakened. It seemed as if my lady from that time made plans which should never for a moment leave her alone. The next day she was busied arranging a brilliant rout, the next a rich banquet, the next a great assembly; she drove in the Mall in her stateliest equipages; she walked upon its promenade, surrounded by her crowd of courtiers, smiling upon them, and answering them with shafts of graceful wit – the charm of her gaiety had never been so remarked upon, her air never so enchanting. At every notable gathering in the world of fashion she was to be seen. Being bidden to the Court, which was at Hampton, her brilliant beauty and spirit so enlivened the royal dullness that 'twas said the Queen herself was scarce resigned to part with her, and that the ladies and gentlemen in waiting all suffered from the spleen when she withdrew. She bought at this time the fiercest but most beautiful beast of a horse she had ever mounted. The creature was superbly handsome, but apparently so unconquerable and so savage that her grooms were afraid to approach it, and indeed it could not be saddled and bitted unless she herself stood near. Even the horse-dealer, rogue though he was, had sold it to her with some approach to a qualm of conscience, having confessed to her that it had killed two grooms, and been sentenced to be shot by its first owner, and was still living only because its great beauty had led him to hesitate for a few days. It was by chance that during these few days Lady Dunstanwolde heard of it, and going to see it, desired and bought it at once.

'It is the very beast I want,' she said, with a gleam in her eye. 'It will please me to teach it that there is one stronger than itself.'

She had much use for her loaded riding-whip; and indeed, not finding it heavy enough, ordered one made which was heavier. When she rode the beast in Hyde Park, her first battles with him were the town talk; and there were those who bribed her footmen to inform them beforehand, when my lady was to take out Devil, that they might know in time to be in the Park to see her. Fops and hunting-men laid wagers as to whether her ladyship would kill the horse or be killed by him, and followed her training of the creature with an excitement and delight quite wild.

'Well may the beast's name be Devil,' said more than one looker-on; 'for he is not so much horse as demon. And when he plunges and rears and shows his teeth, there is a look in his eye which flames like her own, and 'tis as if a male and female demon fought together, for surely such a woman never lived before. She will not let him conquer her, God knows; and it would seem that he was swearing in horse fashion that she should not conquer him.'

When he was first bought and brought home, Mistress Anne turned ashy at the sight of him, and in her heart of hearts grieved bitterly that it had so fallen out that his Grace of Osmonde had been called away from town by high and important matters; for she knew full well, that if he had been in the neighbourhood, he would have said some discreet and tender word of warning to which her ladyship would have listened, though she would have treated with disdain the caution of any other man or woman. When she herself ventured to speak, Clorinda looked only stern.

'I have ridden only ill-tempered beasts all my life, and that for the mere pleasure of subduing them,' she said. 'I have no liking for a horse like a bell-wether; and if this one should break my neck, I need battle with neither men nor horses again, and I shall die at the high tide of life and power; and those who think of me afterwards will only remember that they loved me – that they loved me.'

But the horse did not kill her, nor she it. Day after day she stood by while it was taken from its stall, many a time dealing with it herself, because no groom dare approach; and then she would ride it forth, and in Hyde Park force it to obey her; the wondrous strength of her will, her wrist of steel, and the fierce, pitiless punishment she inflicted, actually daunting the devilish creature's courage. She would ride from the encounter, through two lines of people who had been watching her – and some of them found themselves following after her, even to the Park gate – almost awed as they looked at her, sitting erect and splendid on the fretted, anguished beast, whose shining skin was covered with lather, whose mouth tossed blood-flecked foam, and whose great eye was so strangely like her own, but that hers glowed with the light of triumph, and his burned with the agonised protest of the vanquished. At such times there was somewhat of fear in the glances that followed her beauty, which almost seemed to blaze – her colour was so rich, the curve of her red mouth so imperial, the poise of her head, with its loosening coils of velvet black hair, so high.

'It is good for me that I do this,' she said to Anne, with a short laugh, one day. 'I was growing too soft – and I have need now for all my power. To fight with the demon in this beast, rouses all in me that I have held in check since I became my poor lord's wife. That the creature should have set his will against all others, and should resist me with such strength and devilishness, rouses in me the passion of the days when I cursed and raved and struck at those who angered me. 'Tis fury that possesses me, and I could curse and shriek at him as I flog him, if 'twould be seemly. As it would not be so, I shut my teeth hard, and shriek and curse within them, and none can hear.'

Among those who made it their custom to miss no day when she went forth on Devil that they might stand near and behold her, there was one man ever present, and 'twas Sir John Oxon. He would stand as near as might be and watch the battle, a stealthy fire in his eye, and a look as if the outcome of the fray had deadly meaning to him. He would gnaw his lip until at times the blood started; his face would by turns flush scarlet and turn deadly pale; he would move suddenly and restlessly, and break forth under breath into oaths of exclamation. One day a man close by him saw him suddenly lay his hand upon his sword, and having so done, still keep it there, though 'twas plain he quickly remembered where he was.

As for the horse's rider, my Lady Dunstanwolde, whose way it had been to avoid this man and to thrust him from her path by whatsoever adroit means she could use, on these occasions made no effort to evade him and his glances; in sooth, he knew, though none other did so, that when she fought with her horse she did it with a fierce joy in that he beheld her. 'Twas as though the battle was between themselves; and knowing this in the depths of such soul as he possessed, there were times when the man would have exulted to see the brute rise and fall upon her, crushing her out of life, or dash her to the earth and set his hoof upon her dazzling upturned face. Her scorn and deadly defiance of him, her beauty and maddening charm, which seemed but to increase with every hour that flew by, had roused his love to fury. Despite his youth, he was a villain, as he had ever been; even in his first freshness there had been older men – and hardened ones – who had wondered at the selfish mercilessness and blackness of the heart that was but that of a boy. They had said among themselves that at his years they had never known a creature who could be so gaily a dastard, one who could plan with such light remorselessness, and using all the gifts given him by Nature solely for his own ends, would take so much and give so little. In truth, as time had gone on, men who had been his companions, and had indeed small consciences to boast of, had begun to draw off a little from him, and frequent his company less. He chose to tell himself that this was because he had squandered his fortune and was less good company, being pursued by creditors and haunted by debts; but though there was somewhat in this, perchance 'twas not the entire truth.

'By Gad!' said one over his cups, 'there are things even a rake-hell fellow like me cannot do; but he does them, and seems not to know that they are to his discredit.'

There had been a time when without this woman's beauty he might have lived – indeed, he had left it of his own free vicious will; but in these days, when his fortunes had changed and she represented all that he stood most desperately in need of, her beauty drove him mad. In his haunting of her, as he followed her from place to place, his passion grew day by day, and all the more gained strength and fierceness because it was so mixed with hate. He tossed upon his bed at night and cursed her; he remembered the wild past, and the memory all but drove him to delirium. He knew of what stern stuff she was made, and that even if her love had died, she would have held to her compact like grim death, even while loathing him. And he had cast all this aside in one mad moment of boyish cupidity and folly; and now that she was so radiant and entrancing a thing, and wealth, and splendour, and rank, and luxury lay in the hollow of her hand, she fixed her beauteous devil's eyes upon him with a scorn in their black depths which seemed to burn like fires of hell.

The great brute who dashed, and plunged, and pranced beneath her seemed to have sworn to conquer her as he had sworn himself; but let him plunge and kick as he would, there was no quailing in her eye, she sat like a creature who was super-human, and her hand was iron, her wrist was steel. She held him so that he could not do his worst without such pain as would drive him mad; she lashed him, and rained on him such blows as almost made him blind. Once at the very worst, Devil dancing near him, she looked down from his back into John Oxon's face, and he cursed aloud, her eye so told him his own story and hers. In those days their souls met in such combat as it seemed must end in murder itself.

'You will not conquer him,' he said to her one morning, forcing himself near enough to speak.

'I will, unless he kills me,' she answered, 'and that methinks he will find it hard to do.'

'He will kill you,' he said. 'I would, were I in his four shoes.'

'You would if you could,' were her words; 'but you could not with his bit in your mouth and my hand on the snaffle. And if he killed me, still 'twould be he, not I, was beaten; since he could only kill what any bloody villain could with any knife. He is a brute beast, and I am that which was given dominion over such. Look on till I have done with him.'

And thus, with other beholders, though in a different mood from theirs, he did, until a day when even the most sceptical saw that the brute came to the fray with less of courage, as if there had at last come into his brain the dawning of a fear of that which rid him, and all his madness could not displace from its throne upon his back.

'By God!' cried more than one of the bystanders, seeing this, despite the animal's fury, 'the beast gives way! He gives way! She has him!' And John Oxon, shutting his teeth, cut short an oath and turned pale as death.

From that moment her victory was a thing assured. The duel of strength became less desperate, and having once begun to learn his lesson, the brute was made to learn it well. His bearing was a thing superb to behold; once taught obedience, there would scarce be a horse like him in the whole of England. And day by day this he learned from her, and being mastered, was put through his paces, and led to answer to the rein, so that he trotted, cantered, galloped, and leaped as a bird flies. Then as the town had come to see him fight for freedom, it came to see him adorn the victory of the being who had conquered him, and over their dishes of tea in the afternoon beaux and beauties of fashion gossiped of the interesting and exciting event; and there were vapourish ladies who vowed they could not have beaten a brute so, and that surely my Lady Dunstanwolde must have looked hot and blowzy while she did it, and have had the air of a great rough man; and there were some pretty tiffs and even quarrels when the men swore that never had she looked so magnificent a beauty and so inflamed the hearts of all beholding her.

On the first day after her ladyship's last battle with her horse, the one which ended in such victory to her that she rode him home hard through the streets without an outbreak, he white with lather, and marked with stripes, but his large eye holding in its velvet a look which seemed almost like a human thought – on that day after there occurred a thing which gave the town new matter to talk of.

His Grace of Osmonde had been in France, called there by business of the State, and during his absence the gossip concerning the horse Devil had taken the place of that which had before touched on himself. 'Twas not announced that he was to return to England, and indeed there were those who, speaking with authority, said that for two weeks at least his affairs abroad would not be brought to a close; and yet on this morning, as my Lady Dunstanwolde rode 'neath the trees, holding Devil well in hand, and watching him with eagle keenness of eye, many looking on in wait for the moment when the brute might break forth suddenly again, a horseman was seen approaching at a pace so rapid that 'twas on the verge of a gallop, and the first man who beheld him looked amazed and lifted his hat, and the next, seeing him, spoke to another, who bowed with him, and all along the line of loungers hats were removed, and people wore the air of seeing a man unexpectedly, and hearing a name spoken in exclamation by his side, Sir John Oxon looked round and beheld ride by my lord Duke of Osmonde. The sun was shining brilliantly, and all the park was gay with bright warmth and greenness of turf and trees. Clorinda felt the glow of the summer morning permeate her being. She kept her watch upon her beast; but he was going well, and in her soul she knew that he was beaten, and that her victory had been beheld by the one man who knew that it meant to her that which it seemed to mean also to himself. And filled with this thought and the joy of it, she rode beneath the trees, and so was riding with splendid spirit when she heard a horse behind her, and looked up as it drew near, and the rich crimson swept over her in a sweet flood, so that it seemed to her she felt it warm on her very shoulders, 'neath her habit, for 'twas Osmonde's self who had followed and reached her, and uncovered, keeping pace by her side.

Ah, what a face he had, and how his eyes burned as they rested on her. It was such a look she met, that for a moment she could not find speech, and he himself spoke as a man who, through some deep emotion, has almost lost his breath.

'My Lady Dunstanwolde,' he began; and then with a sudden passion, 'Clorinda, my beloved!' The time had come when he could not keep silence, and with great leapings of her heart she knew. Yet not one word said she, for she could not; but her beauty, glowing and quivering under his eyes' great fire, answered enough.

'Were it not that I fear for your sake the beast you ride,' he said, 'I would lay my hand upon his bridle, that I might crush your hand in mine. At post-haste I have come from France, hearing this thing – that you endangered every day that which I love so madly. My God! beloved, cruel, cruel woman – sure you must know!'

She answered with a breathless wild surrender. 'Yes, yes!' she gasped, 'I know.'

'And yet you braved this danger, knowing that you might leave me a widowed man for life.'

'But,' she said, with a smile whose melting radiance seemed akin to tears – 'but see how I have beaten him – and all is passed.'

'Yes, yes,' he said, 'as you have conquered all – as you have conquered me – and did from the first hour. But God forbid that you should make me suffer so again.'

'Your Grace,' she said, faltering, 'I – I will not!'

'Forgive me for the tempest of my passion,' he said. ''Twas not thus I had thought to come to make my suit. 'Tis scarcely fitting that it should be so; but I was almost mad when I first heard this rumour, knowing my duty would not loose me to come to you at once – and knowing you so well, that only if your heart had melted to the one who besought you, you would give up.'

'I – give up,' she answered; 'I give up.'

'I worship you,' he said; 'I worship you.' And their meeting eyes were drowned in each other's tenderness.

They galloped side by side, and the watchers looked on, exchanging words and glances, seeing in her beauteous, glowing face, in his joyous one, the final answer to the question they had so often asked each other. 'Twas his Grace of Osmonde who was the happy man, he and no other. That was a thing plain indeed to be seen, for they were too high above the common world to feel that they must play the paltry part of outward trifling to deceive it; and as the sun pierces through clouds and is stronger than they, so their love shone like the light of day itself through poor conventions. They did not know the people gazed and whispered, and if they had known it, the thing would have counted for naught with them.

'See!' said my lady, patting her Devil's neck – 'see, he knows that you have come, and frets no more.'

They rode homeward together, the great beauty and the great duke, and all the town beheld; and after they had passed him where he stood, John Oxon mounted his own horse and galloped away, white-lipped and with mad eyes.

'Let me escort you home,' the duke had said, 'that I may kneel to you there, and pour forth my heart as I have so dreamed of doing. Tomorrow I must go back to France, because I left my errand incomplete. I stole from duty the time to come to you, and I must return as quickly as I came.' So he took her home; and as they entered the wide hall together, side by side, the attendant lackeys bowed to the ground in deep, welcoming obeisance, knowing it was their future lord and master they received.

Together they went to her own sitting room, called the Panelled Parlour, a beautiful great room hung with rare pictures, warm with floods of the bright summer sunshine, and perfumed with bowls of summer flowers; and as the lackey departed, bowing, and closed the door behind him, they turned and were enfolded close in each other's arms, and stood so, with their hearts beating as surely it seemed to them human hearts had never beat before.

'Oh! my dear love, my heavenly love!' he cried. 'It has been so long – I have lived in prison and in fetters – and it has been so long!'

Even as my Lord Dunstanwolde had found cause to wonder at her gentle ways, so was this man amazed at her great sweetness, now that he might cross the threshold of her heart. She gave of herself as an empress might give of her store of imperial jewels, with sumptuous lavishness, knowing that the store could not fail. In truth, it seemed that it must be a dream that she so stood before him in all her great, rich loveliness, leaning against his heaving breast, her arms as tender as his own, her regal head thrown backward that they might gaze into the depths of each other's eyes.

'From that first hour that I looked up at you,' she said, 'I knew you were my lord – my lord! And a fierce pain stabbed my heart, knowing you had come too late by but one hour; for had it not been that Dunstanwolde had led me to you, I knew – ah! how well I knew – that our hearts would have beaten together not as two hearts but as one.'

'As they do now,' he cried.

'As they do now,' she answered – 'as they do now!'

'And from the moment that your rose fell at my feet and I raised it in my hand,' he said, 'I knew I held some rapture which was my own. And when you stood before me at Dunstanwolde's side and our eyes met, I could not understand – nay, I could scarce believe that it had been taken from me.'

There, in her arms, among the flowers and in the sweetness of the sun, he lived again the past, telling her of the days when, knowing his danger, he had held himself aloof, declining to come to her lord's house with the familiarity of a kinsman, because the pang of seeing her often was too great to bear; and relating to her also the story of the hours when he had watched her and she had not known his nearness or guessed his pain, when she had passed in her equipage, not seeing him, or giving him but a gracious smile. He had walked outside her window at midnight sometimes, too, coming because he was a despairing man, and could not sleep, and returning homeward, having found no rest, but only increase of anguish. 'Sometimes,' he said, 'I dared not look into your eyes, fearing my own would betray me; but now I can gaze into your soul itself, for the midnight is over – and joy cometh with the morning.'

As he had spoken, he had caressed softly with his hand her cheek and her crown of hair, and such was his great gentleness that 'twas as if he touched lovingly a child; for into her face there had come that look which it would seem that in the arms of the man she loves every true woman wears – a look which is somehow like a child's in its trusting, sweet surrender and appeal, whatsoever may be her stateliness and the splendour of her beauty.

Yet as he touched her cheek so and her eyes so dwelt on him, suddenly her head fell heavily upon his breast, hiding her face, even while her unwreathing arms held more closely.

'Oh! those mad days before!' she cried – 'Oh! those mad, mad days before!'

'Nay, they are long passed, sweet,' he said, in his deep, noble voice, thinking that she spoke of the wildness of her girlish years – 'and all our days of joy are yet to come.'

'Yes, yes,' she cried, clinging closer, yet with shuddering, 'they were before – the joy – the joy is all to come.'

In Which Sir John Oxon
Finds Again a Trophy He Had Lost

His Grace of Osmonde went back to France to complete his business, and all the world knew that when he returned to England 'twould be to make his preparations for his marriage with my Lady Dunstanwolde. It was a marriage not long to be postponed, and her ladyship herself was known already to be engaged with lacemen, linen-drapers, toyshop women, and goldsmiths. Mercers awaited upon her at her house, accompanied by their attendants, bearing burdens of brocades and silks, and splendid stuffs of all sorts. Her chariot was to be seen standing before their shops, and the interest in her purchases was so great that fashionable beauties would contrive to visit the counters at the same hours as herself, so that they might catch glimpses of what she chose. In her own great house all was repressed excitement; her women were enraptured at being allowed the mere handling and laying away of the glories of her wardrobe; the lackeys held themselves with greater state, knowing that they were soon to be a duke's servants; her little black Nero strutted about, his turban set upon his pate with a majestic cock, and disdained to enter into battle with such pages of his own colour as wore only silver collars, he feeling assured that his own would soon be of gold.

The world of fashion said when her ladyship's equipage drove by, that her beauty was like that of the god of day at morning, and that 'twas plain that no man or woman had ever beheld her as his Grace of Osmonde would.

'She loves at last,' a wit said. 'Until the time that such a woman loves, however great her splendour, she is as the sun behind a cloud.'

'And now this one hath come forth, and shines so that she warms us in mere passing,' said another. 'What eyes, and what a mouth, with that strange smile upon it. Whoever saw such before? and when she came to town with my Lord Dunstanwolde, who, beholding her, would have believed that she could wear such a look?'

In sooth, there was that in her face and in her voice when she spoke which almost made Anne weep, through its strange sweetness and radiance. 'Twas as if the flood of her joy had swept away all hardness and disdain. Her eyes, which had seemed to mock at all they rested on, mocked no more, but ever seemed to smile at some dear inward thought.

One night when she went forth to a Court ball, being all attired in brocade of white and silver, and glittering with the Dunstanwolde diamonds, which starred her as with great sparkling dewdrops, and yet had not the radiance of her eyes and smile, she was so purely wonderful a vision that Anne, who had been watching her through all the time when she had been under the hands of her tirewoman, and beholding her now so dazzling and white a shining creature, fell upon her knees to kiss her hand almost as one who worships.

'Oh, sister,' she said, 'you look like a spirit. It is as if with the earth you had naught to do – as if your eyes saw Heaven itself and Him who reigns there.'

The lovely orbs of Clorinda shone more still like the great star of morning.

'Sister Anne,' she said, laying her hand on her white breast, 'at times I think that I must almost be a spirit, I feel such heavenly joy. It is as if He whom you believe in, and who can forgive and wipe out sins, has forgiven me, and has granted it to me, that I may begin my poor life again. Ah! I will make it better; I will try to make it as near an angel's life as a woman can; and I will do no wrong, but only good; and I will believe, and pray every day upon my knees – and all my prayers will be that I may so live that my dear lord – my Gerald – could forgive me all that I have ever done – and seeing my soul, would know me worthy of him.

Oh! we are strange things, we human creatures, Anne,' with a tremulous smile; 'we do not believe until we want a thing, and feel that we shall die if 'tis not granted to us; and then we kneel and kneel and believe, because we must have somewhat to ask help from.'

'But all help has been given to you,' poor tender Anne said, kissing her hand again; 'and I will pray, I will pray –'

'Ay, pray, Anne, pray with all thy soul,' Clorinda answered; 'I need thy praying – and thou didst believe always, and have asked so little that has been given thee.'

'Thou wast given me, sister,' said Anne. 'Thou hast given me a home and kindness such as I never dared to hope; thou hast been like a great star to me – I have had none other, and I thank Heaven on my knees each night for the brightness my star has shed on me.'

'Poor Anne, dear Anne!' Clorinda said, laying her arms about her and kissing her. 'Pray for thy star, good, tender Anne, that its light may not be quenched.' Then with a sudden movement her hand was pressed upon her bosom again. 'Ah, Anne,' she cried, and in the music of her voice, agony itself was ringing – 'Anne, there is but one thing on this earth God rules over – but one thing that belongs – belongs to me; and 'tis Gerald Mertoun – and he is mine and shall not be taken from me, for he is a part of me, and I a part of him!'

'He will not be,' said Anne – 'he will not.'

'He cannot,' Clorinda answered – 'he shall not! 'Twould not be human.'

She drew a long breath and was calm again.

'Did it reach your ears,' she said, reclasping a band of jewels on her arm, 'that John Oxon had been offered a place in a foreign court, and that 'twas said he would soon leave England?'

'I heard some rumour of it,' Anne answered, her emotion getting the better of her usual discreet speech. 'God grant it may be true!'

'Ay!' said Clorinda, 'would God that he were gone!'

But that he was not, for when she entered the assembly that night he was standing near the door as though he lay in waiting for her, and his eyes met hers with a leaping gleam, which was a thing of such exultation that to encounter it was like having a knife thrust deep into her side and through and through it, for she knew full well that he could not wear such a look unless he had some strength of which she knew not.

This gleam was in his eyes each time she found herself drawn to them, and it seemed as though she could look nowhere without encountering his gaze. He followed her from room to room, placing himself where she could not lift her eyes without beholding him; when she walked a minuet with a royal duke, he stood and watched her with such a look in his face as drew all eyes towards him.

''Tis as if he threatens her,' one said. 'He has gone mad with disappointed love.'

But 'twas not love that was in his look, but the madness of long-thwarted passion mixed with hate and mockery; and this she saw, and girded her soul with all its strength, knowing that she had a fiercer beast to deal with, and a more vicious and dangerous one, than her horse Devil. That he kept at first at a distance from her, and but looked on with this secret exultant glow in his bad, beauteous eyes, told her that at last he felt he held some power in his hands, against which all her defiance would be as naught. Till this hour, though she had suffered, and when alone had writhed in agony of grief and bitter shame, in his presence she had never flinched. Her strength she knew was greater than his; but his baseness was his weapon, and the depths of that baseness she knew she had never reached.

At midnight, having just made obeisance before royalty retiring, she felt that at length he had drawn near and was standing at her side.

'Tonight,' he said, in the low undertone it was his way to keep for such occasions, knowing how he could pierce her ear – 'tonight you are Juno's self – a very Queen of Heaven!'

She made no answer.

'And I have stood and watched you moving among all lesser goddesses as the moon sails among the stars, and I have smiled in thinking of what these lesser deities would say if they had known what I bear in my breast tonight.'

She did not even make a movement – in truth, she felt that at his next words she might change to stone.

'I have found it,' he said – 'I have it here – the lost treasure – the tress of hair like a raven's wing and six feet long. Is there another woman in England who could give a man a lock like it?'

She felt then that she had, in sooth, changed to stone; her heart hung without moving in her breast; her eyes felt great and hollow and staring as she lifted them to him.

'I knew not,' she said slowly, and with bated breath, for the awfulness of the moment had even made her body weak as she had never known it feel before – 'I knew not truly that hell made things like you.'

Whereupon he made a movement forward, and the crowd about surged nearer with hasty exclamations, for the strange weakness of her body had overpowered her in a way mysterious to her, and she had changed to marble, growing too heavy of weight for her sinking limbs. And those in the surrounding groups saw a marvellous thing – the same being that my Lady Dunstanwolde swayed as she turned, and falling, lay stretched, as if dead, in her white and silver and flashing jewels at the startled beholders' feet.

She wore no radiant look when she went home that night. She would go home alone and unescorted, excepting by her lackeys, refusing all offers of companionship when once placed in her equipage. There were, of course, gentlemen who would not be denied leading her to her coach; John Oxon was among them, and at the last pressed close, with a manner of great ceremony, speaking a final word.

''Tis useless, your ladyship,' he murmured, as he made his obeisance gallantly, and though the words were uttered in his lowest tone and with great softness, they reached her ear as he intended that they should. 'Tomorrow morning I shall wait upon you.'

Anne had forborne going to bed, and waited for her return, longing to see her spirit's face again before she slept; for this poor tender creature, being denied all woman's loves and joys by Fate, who had made her as she was, so lived in her sister's beauty and triumphs that 'twas as if in some far-off way she shared them, and herself experienced through them the joy of being a woman transcendently beautiful and transcendently beloved. Tonight she had spent her waiting hours in her closet and upon her knees, praying with all humble adoration of the Being she approached. She was wont to pray long and fervently each day, thanking Heaven for the smallest things and the most common, and imploring continuance of the mercy which bestowed them upon her poor unworthiness. For her sister her prayers were offered up night and morning, and oft-times in hours between, and tonight she prayed not for herself at all, but for Clorinda and for his Grace of Osmonde, that their love might be crowned with happiness, and that no shadow might intervene to cloud its brightness, and the tender rapture in her sister's softened look, which was to her a thing so wonderful that she thought of it with reverence as a holy thing.

Her prayers being at length ended, she had risen from her knees and sat down, taking a sacred book to read, a book of sermons such as 'twas her simple habit to pore over with entire respect and childlike faith, and being in the midst of her favourite homily, she heard the chariot's returning wheels, and left her chair, surprised, because she had not yet begun to expect the sound.

''Tis my sister,' she said, with a soft, sentimental smile. 'Osmonde not being among the guests, she hath no pleasure in mingling with them.'

She went below to the room her ladyship usually went to first on her return at night from any gathering, and there she found her sitting as though she had dropped there in the corner of a great divan, her hands hanging clasped before her on her knee, her head hanging forward on her fallen chest, her large eyes staring into space.

'Clorinda! Clorinda!' Anne cried, running to her and kneeling at her side. 'Clorinda! God have mercy! What is't?'

Never before had her face worn such a look – 'twas colourless, and so drawn and fallen in that 'twas indeed almost as if all her great beauty was gone; but the thing most awful to poor Anne was that all the new softness seemed as if it had been stamped out, and the fierce hardness had come back and was engraven in its place, mingled with a horrible despair.

'An hour ago,' she said, 'I swooned. That is why I look thus. 'Tis yet another sign that I am a woman – a woman!'

'You are ill – you swooned?' cried Anne. 'I must send for your physician. Have you not ordered that he be sent for yourself? If Osmonde were here, how perturbed he would be!'

'Osmonde!' said my lady. 'Gerald! Is there a Gerald, Anne?'

'Sister!' cried Anne, affrighted by her strange look – 'oh, sister!'

'I have seen heaven,' Clorinda said; 'I have stood on the threshold and seen through the part-opened gate – and then have been dragged back to hell.'

Anne clung to her, gazing upwards at her eyes, in sheer despair.

'But back to hell I will not go,' she went on saying. 'Had I not seen Heaven, they might perhaps have dragged me; but now I will not go – I will not, that I swear! There is a thing which cannot be endured. Bear it no woman should. Even I, who was not born a woman, but a wolf's she-cub, I cannot. 'Twas not

158

I, 'twas Fate,' she said – ''twas not I, 'twas Fate – 'twas the great wheel we are bound to, which goes round and round that we may be broken on it. 'Twas not I who bound myself there; and I will not be broken so.'

She said the words through her clenched teeth, and with all the mad passion of her most lawless years; even at Anne she looked almost in the old ungentle fashion, as though half scorning all weaker than herself, and having small patience with them.

'There will be a way,' she said – 'there will be a way. I shall not swoon again.'

She left her divan and stood upright, the colour having come back to her face; but the look Anne worshipped not having returned with it, 'twas as though Mistress Clorinda Wildairs had been born again.

'Tomorrow morning I go forth on Devil,' she said; 'and I shall be abroad if any visitors come.'

What passed in her chamber that night no human being knew. Anne, who left her own apartment and crept into a chamber near hers to lie and watch, knew that she paced to and fro, but heard no other sound, and dared not intrude upon her.

When she came forth in the morning she wore the high look she had been wont to wear in the years gone by, when she ruled in her father's house, and rode to the hunt with a following of gay middle-aged and elderly rioters. Her eye was brilliant, and her colour matched it. She held her head with the old dauntless carriage, and there was that in her voice before which her women quaked, and her lackeys hurried to do her bidding.

Devil himself felt this same thing in the touch of her hand upon his bridle when she mounted him at the door, and seemed to glance askance at her sideways.

She took no servant with her, and did not ride to the park, but to the country. Once on the highroad, she rode fast and hard, only galloping straight before her as the way led, and having no intention. Where she was going she knew not; but why she rode on horseback she knew full well, it being because the wild, almost fierce motion was in keeping with the tempest in her soul. Thoughts rushed through her brain even as she rushed through the air on Devil's back, and each leaping after the other, seemed to tear more madly.

'What shall I do?' she was saying to herself. 'What thing is there for me to do? I am trapped like a hunted beast, and there is no way forth.'

The blood went like a torrent through her veins, so that she seemed to hear it roaring in her ears; her heart thundered in her side, or 'twas so she thought of it as it bounded, while she recalled the past and looked upon the present.

'What else could have been?' she groaned. 'Naught else – naught else. 'Twas a trick – a trick of Fate to ruin me for my punishment.'

When she had gone forth it had been with no hope in her breast that her wit might devise a way to free herself from the thing which so beset her, for she had no weak fancies that there dwelt in this base soul any germ of honour which might lead it to relenting. As she had sat in her dark room at night, crouched upon the floor, and clenching her hands, as the mad thoughts went whirling through her brain, she had stared her Fate in the face and known all its awfulness. Before her lay the rapture of a great, sweet, honourable passion, a high and noble life lived in such bliss as rarely fell to lot of woman – on this one man she knew that she could lavish all the splendour of her nature, and make his life a heaven, as hers would be. Behind her lay the mad, uncared-for years, and one black memory blighting all to come, though 'twould have been but a black memory with no power to blight if the heaven of love had not so opened to her and with its light cast all else into shadow.

'If 'twere not love,' she cried – 'if 'twere but ambition, I could defy it to the last; but 'tis love – love – love, and it will kill me to forego it.'

Even as she moaned the words she heard hoof beats near her, and a horseman leaped the hedge and was at her side. She set her teeth, and turning, stared into John Oxon's face.

'Did you think I would not follow you?' he asked.

'No,' she answered.

'I have followed you at a distance hitherto,' he said; 'now I shall follow close.'

She did not speak, but galloped on.

'Think you you can outride me?' he said grimly, quickening his steed's pace. 'I go with your ladyship to your own house. For fear of scandal you have not openly rebuffed me previous to this time; for a like reason you will not order your lackeys to shut your door when I enter it with you.'

My Lady Dunstanwolde turned to gaze at him again. The sun shone on his bright falling locks and his blue eyes as she had seen it shine in days which seemed so strangely long passed by, though they were not five years agone.

''Tis strange,' she said, with a measure of wonder, 'to live and be so black a devil.'

'Bah! my lady,' he said, 'these are fine words – and fine words do not hold between us. Let us leave them. I would escort you home, and speak to you in private.' There was that in his mocking that was madness to her, and made her sick and dizzy with the boiling of the blood which surged to her brain. The fury of passion which had been a terror to all about her when she had been a child was upon her once more, and though she had thought herself freed from its dominion, she knew it again and all it meant. She felt the thundering beat in her side, the hot flood leaping to her cheek, the flame burning her eyes themselves as if fire was within them. Had he been other than he was, her face itself would have been a warning. But he pressed her hard. As he would have slunk away a beaten cur if she had held the victory in her hands, so feeling that the power was his, he exulted over the despairing frenzy which was in her look.

'I pay back old scores,' he said. 'There are many to pay. When you crowned yourself with roses and set your foot upon my face, your ladyship thought not of this! When you gave yourself to Dunstanwolde and spat at me, you did not dream that there could come a time when I might goad as you did.'

She struck Devil with her whip, who leaped forward; but Sir John followed hard behind her. He had a swift horse too, and urged him fiercely, so that between these two there was a race as if for life or death. The beasts bounded forward, spurning the earth beneath their feet. My lady's face was set, her eyes were burning flame, her breath came short and pantingly between her teeth. Oxon's fair face was white with passion; he panted also, but strained every nerve to keep at her side, and kept there.

'Keep back! I warn thee!' she cried once, almost gasping.

'Keep back!' he answered, blind with rage. 'I will follow thee to hell!'

And in this wise they galloped over the white road until the hedges disappeared and they were in the streets, and people turned to look at them, and even stood and stared. Then she drew rein a little and went slower, knowing with shuddering agony that the trap was closing about her.

'What is it that you would say to me?' she asked him breathlessly.

'That which I would say within four walls that you may hear it all,' he answered. 'This time 'tis not idle threatening. I have a thing to show you.'

Through the streets they went, and as her horse's hoofs beat the pavement, and the passers-by, looking towards her, gazed curiously at so fine a lady on so splendid a brute, she lifted her eyes to the houses, the booths, the faces, and the sky, with a strange fancy that she looked about her as a man looks who, doomed to death, is being drawn in his cart to Tyburn tree. For 'twas to death she went, nor to naught else could she compare it, and she was so young and strong, and full of love and life, and there should have been such bliss and peace before her but for one madness of her all-unknowing days. And this beside her – this man with the fair face and looks and beauteous devil's eyes, was her hangman, and carried his rope with him, and soon would fit it close about her neck.

When they rode through the part of the town where abode the world of fashion, those who saw them knew them, and marvelled that the two should be together.

'But perhaps his love has made him sue for pardon that he has so borne himself,' some said, 'and she has chosen to be gracious to him, since she is gracious in these days to all.'

When they reached her house he dismounted with her, wearing an outward air of courtesy; but his eye mocked her, as she knew. His horse was in a lather of sweat, and he spoke to a servant.

'Take my beast home,' he said. 'He is too hot to stand, and I shall not soon be ready.'

Dealing With That Which
Was Done in the Panelled Parlour

He followed her to the Panelled Parlour, the one to which she had taken Osmonde on the day of their bliss, the one in which in the afternoon she received those who came to pay court to her over a dish of tea. In the mornings none entered it but herself or some invited guest. 'Twas not the room she would have chosen for him; but when he said to her, "Twere best your ladyship took me to some private place,' she had known there was no other so safe.

When the door was closed behind them, and they stood face to face, they were a strange pair to behold – she with mad defiance battling with mad despair in her face; he with the mocking which every woman who had ever trusted him or loved him had lived to see in his face when all was lost. Few men there lived who were as vile as he, his power of villainy lying in that he knew not the meaning of man's shame or honour.

'Now,' she said, 'tell me the worst.'

"Tis not so bad,' he answered, 'that a man should claim his own, and swear that no other man shall take it from him. That I have sworn, and that I will hold to.'

'Your own!' she said – 'your own you call it – villain!'

'My own, since I can keep it,' quoth he. 'Before you were my Lord of Dunstanwolde's you were mine – of your own free will.'

'Nay, nay,' she cried. 'God! through some madness I knew not the awfulness of – because I was so young and had known naught but evil – and you were so base and wise.'

'Was your ladyship an innocent?' he answered. 'It seemed not so to me.'

'An innocent of all good,' she cried – 'of all things good on earth – of all that I know now, having seen manhood and honour.'

'His Grace of Osmonde has not been told this,' he said; 'and I should make it all plain to him.'

'What do you ask, devil?' she broke forth. 'What is't you ask?'

'That you shall not be the Duchess of Osmonde,' he said, drawing near to her; 'that you shall be the wife of Sir John Oxon, as you once called yourself for a brief space, though no priest had mumbled over us –'

'Who was't divorced us?' she said, gasping; 'for I was an honest thing, though I knew no other virtue. Who was't divorced us?'

'I confess,' he answered, bowing, 'that 'twas I – for the time being. I was young, and perhaps fickle –'

'And you left me,' she cried, 'and I found that you had come but for a bet – and since I so bore myself that you could not boast, and since I was not a rich woman whose fortune would be of use to you, you followed another and left me – me!'

'As his Grace of Osmonde will when I tell him my story,' he answered. 'He is not one to brook that such things can be told of the mother of his heirs.'

She would have shrieked aloud but that she clutched her throat in time.

'Tell him!' she cried, 'tell him, and see if he will hear you. Your word against mine!'

'Think you I do not know that full well,' he answered, and he brought forth a little package folded in silk. 'Why have I done naught but threaten till this time? If I went to him without proof, he would run me through with his sword as I were a mad dog. But is there another woman in England from whose head her lover could ravish a lock as long and black as this?'

He unfolded the silk, and let other silk unfold itself, a great and thick ring of raven hair which uncoiled its serpent length, and though he held it high, was long enough after surging from his hand to lie upon the floor.

'Merciful God!' she cried, and shuddering, hid her face.

"'Twas a bet, I own,' he said; 'I heard too much of the mad beauty and her disdain of men not to be fired by a desire to prove to her and others, that she was but a woman after all, and so was to be won. I took an oath that I would come back some day with a trophy – and this I cut when you knew not that I did it.'

She clutched her throat again to keep from shrieking in her – impotent horror.

'Devil, craven, and loathsome – and he knows not what he is!' she gasped. 'He is a mad thing who knows not that all his thoughts are of hell.'

'Twas, in sooth, a strange and monstrous thing to see him so unwavering and bold, flinching before no ignominy, shrinking not to speak openly the thing before the mere accusation of which other men's blood would have boiled.

'When I bore it away with me,' he said, 'I lived wildly for a space, and in those days put it in a place of safety, and when I was sober again I had forgot where. Yesterday, by a strange chance, I came upon it. Think you it can be mistaken for any other woman's hair?'

At this she held up her hand.

'Wait,' she said. 'You will go to Osmonde, you will tell him this, you will –'

'I will tell him all the story of the rose garden and of the sundial, and the beauty who had wit enough to scorn a man in public that she might more safely hold tryst with him alone. She had great wit and cunning for a beauty of sixteen. 'Twould be well for her lord to have keen eyes when she is twenty.'

He should have seen the warning in her eyes, for there was warning enough in their flaming depths.

'All that you can say I know,' she said – 'all that you can say! And I love him. There is no other man on earth. Were he a beggar, I would tramp the highroad by his side and go hungered with him. He is my lord, and I his mate – his mate!'

166

'That you will not be,' he answered, made devilish by her words. 'He is a high and noble gentleman, and wants no man's cast-off plaything for his wife.'

Her breast leaped up and down in her panting as she pressed her hand upon it; her breath came in sharp puffs through her nostrils.

'And once,' she breathed – 'and once – I loved thee – cur!'

He was mad with exultant villainy and passion, and he broke into a laugh.

'Loved me!' he said. 'Thou! As thou lovedst me – and as thou lovest him – so will Moll Easy love any man – for a crown.'

Her whip lay upon the table, she caught and whirled it in the air. She was blind with the surging of her blood, and saw not how she caught or held it, or what she did – only that she struck!

And 'twas his temple that the loaded weapon met, and 'twas wielded by a wrist whose sinews were of steel, and even as it struck he gasped, casting up his hands, and thereupon fell, and lay stretched at her feet!

But the awful tempest which swept over her had her so under its dominion that she was like a branch whirled on the wings of the storm. She scarce noted that he fell, or noting it, gave it not one thought as she dashed from one end of the apartment to the other with the fierce striding of a mad woman.

'Devil!' she cried, 'and cur! and for thee I blasted all the years to come! To a beast so base I gave all that an empress' self could give – all life – all love – for ever. And he comes back – shameless – to barter like a cheating huckster, because his trade goes ill, and I – I could stock his counters once again.'

She strode towards him, raving.

'Think you I do not know, woman's bully and poltroon, that you plot to sell yourself, because your day has come, and no woman will bid for such an outcast, saving one that you may threaten. Rise, vermin – rise, lest I kill thee!'

In her blind madness she lashed him once across the face again. And he stirred not – and something in the resistless feeling of the flesh beneath the whip, and in the quiet of his lying, caused her to pause and stand panting and staring at the thing which lay before her. For it was a Thing, and as she stood staring, with wild heaving breast, this she saw. 'Twas but a thing – a thing lying inert, its fair locks outspread, its eyes rolled upward till the blue was almost lost; a purple indentation on the right temple from which there oozed a tiny thread of blood.

'There will be a way,' she had said, and yet in her most mad despair, of this way she had never thought; though strange it had been, considering her lawless past, that she had not – never of this way – never! Notwithstanding which, in one frenzied moment in which she had known naught but her delirium, her loaded whip had found it for her – the way!

And yet it being so found, and she stood staring, seeing what she had done – seeing what had befallen – 'twas as if the blow had been struck not at her own temple but at her heart – a great and heavy shock, which left her bloodless, and choked, and gasping.

'What! what!' she panted. 'Nay! nay! nay!' and her eyes grew wide and wild.

She sank upon her knees, so shuddering that her teeth began to chatter. She pushed him and shook him by the shoulder.

'Stir!' she cried in a loud whisper. 'Move thee! Why dost thou lie so? Stir!'

Yet he stirred not, but lay inert, only with his lips drawn back, showing his white teeth a little, as if her horrid agony made him begin to laugh. Shuddering, she drew slowly nearer, her eyes more awful than his own. Her hand crept shaking to his wrist and clutched it. There was naught astir – naught! It stole to his breast, and baring it, pressed close. That was still and moveless as his pulse; for life was ended, and a hundred mouldering years would not bring more of death.

'I have killed thee,' she breathed. 'I have killed thee – though I meant it not – even hell itself doth know. Thou art a dead man – and this is the worst of all!'

His hand fell heavily from hers, and she still knelt staring, such a look coming into her face as throughout her life had never been there before – for 'twas the look of a creature who, being tortured, the worst at last being reached, begins to smile at Fate.

'I have killed him!' she said, in a low, awful voice; 'and he lies here – and outside people walk, and know not. But he knows – and I – and as he lies methinks he smiles – knowing what he has done!'

She crouched even lower still, the closer to behold him, and indeed it seemed his still face sneered as if defying her now to rid herself of him! 'Twas as though he lay there mockingly content, saying, 'Now that I lie here, 'tis for you – for you to move me.'

She rose and stood up rigid, and all the muscles of her limbs were drawn as though she were a creature stretched upon a rack; for the horror of this which had befallen her seemed to fill the place about her, and leave her no air to breathe nor light to see.

'Now!' she cried, 'if I would give way – and go mad, as I could but do, for there is naught else left – if I would but give way, that which is I – and has lived but a poor score of years – would be done with for all time. All whirls before me. 'Twas I who struck the blow – and I am a woman – and I could go raving – and cry out and call them in, and point to him, and tell them how 'twas done – all! – all!'

She choked, and clutched her bosom, holding its heaving down so fiercely that her nails bruised it through her habit's cloth; for she felt that she had begun to rave already, and that the waves of such a tempest were arising as, if not quelled at their first swell, would sweep her from her feet and engulf her for ever.

'That – that!' she gasped – 'nay – that I swear I will not do! There was always One who hated me – and doomed and hunted me from the hour I lay 'neath my dead mother's corpse, a newborn thing. I know not whom it was – or why – or how – but 'twas so! I was made evil, and cast helpless amid evil fates, and having done the things that were ordained, and there was no escape from, I was shown noble manhood and high honour, and taught to worship, as I worship now. An angel might so love and be made higher. And at the gate of heaven a devil grins at me and plucks me back, and taunts and mires me, and I fall – on this!'

She stretched forth her arms in a great gesture, wherein it seemed that surely she defied earth and heaven.

'No hope – no mercy – naught but doom and hell,' she cried, 'unless the thing that is tortured be the stronger. Now – unless Fate bray me small – the stronger I will be!'

She looked down at the thing before her. How its stone face sneered, and even in its sneering seemed to disregard her. She knelt by it again, her blood surging through her body, which had been cold, speaking as if she would force her voice to pierce its deadened ear.

'Ay, mock!' she said, setting her teeth, 'thinking that I am conquered – yet am I not! 'Twas an honest blow struck by a creature goaded past all thought! Ay, mock – and yet, but for one man's sake, would I call in those outside and stand before them, crying: "Here is a villain whom I struck in madness – and he lies dead! I ask not mercy, but only justice."'

She crouched still nearer, her breath and words coming hard and quick. 'Twas indeed as if she spoke to a living man who heard – as if she answered what he had said.

'There would be men in England who would give it me,' she raved, whispering. 'That would there, I swear! But there would be dullards and dastards who would not. He would give it – he! Ay, mock as thou wilt! But between his high honour and love and me thy carrion shall not come!'

By her great divan the dead man had fallen, and so near to it he lay that one arm was hidden by the draperies; and at this moment this she saw – before having seemed to see nothing but the death in his face. A thought came to her like a flame lit on a sudden, and springing high the instant the match struck the fuel it leaped from. It was a thought so daring and so strange that even she gasped once, being appalled, and her hands, stealing to her brow, clutched at the hair that grew there, feeling it seem to rise and stand erect.

'Is it madness to so dare?' she said hoarsely, and for an instant, shuddering, hid her eyes, but then uncovered and showed them burning. 'Nay! not as I will dare it,' she said, 'for it will make me steel. You fell well,' she said to the stone-faced thing, 'and as you lie there, seem to tell me what to do, in your own despite. You would not have so helped me had you known. Now 'tis 'twixt Fate and I – a human thing – who is but a hunted woman.'

She put her strong hand forth and thrust him – he was already stiffening – backward from the shoulder, there being no shrinking on her face as she felt his flesh yield beneath her touch, for she had passed the barrier lying between that which is mere life and that which is pitiless hell, and could feel naught that was human. A poor wild beast at bay, pressed on all sides by dogs, by huntsmen, by resistless weapons, by Nature's pitiless self – glaring with bloodshot eyes, panting, with fangs bared in the savagery of its unfriended agony – might feel thus. 'Tis but a hunted beast; but 'tis alone, and faces so the terror and anguish of death.

The thing gazing with its set sneer, and moving but stiffly, she put forth another hand upon its side and thrust it farther backward until it lay stretched beneath the great broad seat, its glazed and open eyes seeming to stare upward blankly at the low roof of its strange prison; she thrust it farther backward still, and letting the draperies fall, steadily and with care so rearranged them that all was safe and hid from sight.

'Until tonight,' she said, 'you will lie well there. And then –
and then –'

She picked up the long silken lock of hair which lay like
a serpent at her feet, and threw it into the fire, watching it
burn, as all hair burns, with slow hissing, and she watched it till
'twas gone.

Then she stood with her hands pressed upon her eyeballs
and her brow, her thoughts moving in great leaps. Although it
reeled, the brain which had worked for her ever, worked clear
and strong, setting before her what was impending, arguing her
case, showing her where dangers would arise, how she must
provide against them, what she must defend and set at defiance.
The power of will with which she had been endowed at birth,
and which had but grown stronger by its exercise, was indeed
to be compared to some great engine whose lever 'tis not nature
should be placed in human hands; but on that lever her hand
rested now, and to herself she vowed she would control it, since
only thus might she be saved. The torture she had undergone
for months, the warring of the evil past with the noble present,
of that which was sweet and passionately loving woman with
that which was all but devil, had strung her to a pitch so intense
and high that on the falling of this unnatural and unforeseen
blow she was left scarce a human thing. Looking back, she saw
herself a creature doomed from birth; and here in one moment
seemed to stand a force ranged in mad battle with the fate
which had doomed her.

''Twas ordained that the blow should fall so,' she said, 'and
those who did it laugh – laugh at me.'

'Twas but a moment, and her sharp breathing became even
and regular as though at her command; her face composed
itself, and she turned to the bell and rang it as with imperious
haste.

When the lackey entered, she was standing holding papers in
her hand as if she had but just been consulting them.

'Follow Sir John Oxon,' she commanded. 'Tell him I have forgot an important thing and beg him to return at once. Lose no time. He has but just left me and can scarce be out of sight.'

The fellow saw there was no time to lose. They all feared that imperial eye of hers and fled to obey its glances. Bowing, he turned, and hastened to do her bidding, fearing to admit that he had not seen the guest leave, because to do so would be to confess that he had been absent from his post, which was indeed the truth.

She knew he would come back shortly, and thus he did, entering somewhat breathed by his haste.

'My lady,' he said, 'I went quickly to the street, and indeed to the corner of it, but Sir John was not within sight.'

'Fool, you were not swift enough!' she said angrily. 'Wait, you must go to his lodgings with a note. The matter is of importance.'

She went to a table – 'twas close to the divan, so close that if she had thrust forth her foot she could have touched what lay beneath it – and wrote hastily a few lines. They were to request that which was stiffening within three feet of her to return to her as quickly as possible that she might make inquiries of an important nature which she had forgotten at his departure.

'Take this to Sir John's lodgings,' she said. 'Let there be no loitering by the way. Deliver into his own hands, and bring back at once his answer.'

Then she was left alone again, and being so left, paced the room slowly, her gaze upon the floor.

'That was well done,' she said. 'When he returns and has not found him, I will be angered, and send him again to wait.'

She stayed her pacing, and passed her hand across her face.

''Tis like a nightmare,' she said – 'as if one dreamed, and choked, and panted, and would scream aloud, but could not. I cannot! I must not! Would that I might shriek, and dash myself upon the floor, and beat my head upon it until I lay – as he does.'

She stood a moment, breathing fast, her eyes widening, that part of her which was weak woman for the moment putting her in parlous danger, realising the which she pressed her sides with hands that were of steel.

'Wait! wait!' she said to herself. 'This is going mad. This is loosening hold, and being beaten by that One who hates me and laughs to see what I have come to.'

Naught but that unnatural engine of will could have held her within bounds and restrained the mounting female weakness that beset her; but this engine being stronger than all else, it beat her womanish and swooning terrors down.

'Through this one day I must live,' she said, 'and plan, and guard each moment that doth pass. My face must tell no tale, my voice must hint none. He will be still – God knows he will be still enough.'

Upon the divan itself there had been lying a little dog; 'twas a King Charles spaniel, a delicate pampered thing, which attached itself to her, and was not easily driven away. Once during the last hour the fierce, ill-hushed voices had disturbed it, and it had given vent to a fretted bark, but being a luxurious little beast, it had soon curled up among its cushions and gone to sleep again. But as its mistress walked about muttering low words and oft-times breathing sharp breaths, it became disturbed again. Perhaps through some instinct of which naught is known by human creatures, it felt the strange presence of a thing which roused it. It stirred, at first drowsily, and lifted its head and sniffed; then it stretched its limbs, and having done so, stood up, turning on its mistress a troubled eye, and this she saw and stopped to meet it. 'Twas a strange look she bestowed upon it, a startled and fearful one; her thought drew the blood up to her cheek, but backward again it flowed when the little beast lifted its nose and gave a low but woeful howl. Twice it did this, and then jumped down, and standing before the edge of the couch, stood there sniffing.

There was no mistake, some instinct of which it knew not the meaning had set it on, and it would not be thrust back. In all beasts this strange thing has been remarked – that they know that which ends them all, and so revolt against it that they cannot be at rest so long as it is near them, but must roar, or whinny, or howl until 'tis out of the reach of their scent. And so 'twas plain this little beast knew and was afraid and restless. He would not let it be, but roved about, sniffing and whining, and not daring to thrust his head beneath the falling draperies, but growing more and yet more excited and terrified, until at last he stopped, raised head in air, and gave vent to a longer, louder, and more dolorous howl, and albeit to one with so strange and noticeable a sound that her heart turned over in her breast as she stooped and caught him in her grasp, and shuddered as she stood upright, holding him to her side, her hand over his mouth. But he would not be hushed, and struggled to get down as if indeed he would go mad unless he might get to the thing and rave at it.

'If I send thee from the room thou wilt come back, poor Frisk,' she said. 'There will be no keeping thee away, and I have never ordered thee away before. Why couldst thou not keep still? Nay, 'twas not dog nature.'

That it was not so was plain by his struggles and the yelps but poorly stifled by her grasp.

She put her hand about his little neck, turning, in sooth, very pale.

'Thou too, poor little beast,' she said. 'Thou too, who art so small a thing and never harmed me.'

When the lackey came back he wore an air more timorous than before.

'Your ladyship,' he faltered, 'Sir John had not yet reached his lodgings. His servant knew not when he might expect him.'

'In an hour go again and wait,' she commanded. 'He must return ere long if he has not left town.'

And having said this, pointed to a little silken heap which lay outstretched limp upon the floor. "'Tis poor Frisk, who has had some strange spasm, and fell, striking his head. He hath been ailing for days, and howled loudly but an hour ago. Take him away, poor beast.'

Wherein His Grace of Osmonde's
Courier Arrives From France

The stronghold of her security lay in the fact that her household so stood in awe of her, and that this room, which was one of the richest and most beautiful, though not the largest, in the mansion, all her servitors had learned to regard as a sort of sacred place in which none dared to set foot unless invited or commanded to enter. Within its four walls she read and wrote in the morning hours, no servant entering unless summoned by her; and the apartment seeming, as it were, a citadel, none approached without previous parley. In the afternoon the doors were thrown open, and she entertained there such visitors as came with less formality than statelier assemblages demanded. When she went out of it this morning to go to her chamber that her habit might be changed and her toilette made, she glanced about her with a steady countenance.

'Until the babblers flock in to chatter of the modes and play-houses,' she said, 'all will be as quiet as the grave. Then I must stand near, and plan well, and be in such beauty and spirit that they will see naught but me.'

In the afternoon 'twas the fashion for those who had naught more serious in their hands than the killing of time to pay visits to each other's houses, and drinking dishes of tea, to dispose of their neighbours' characters, discuss the playhouses, the latest fashions in furbelows or commodes, and make love either lightly or with serious intent. One may be sure that at my Lady Dunstanwolde's many dishes of Bohea were drunk, and many ogling glances and much witticism exchanged. There was in these days even a greater following about her than ever. A triumphant beauty on the verge of becoming a great duchess is not like to be neglected by her acquaintance, and thus her ladyship held assemblies both gay and brilliantly varied, which were the delight of the fashionable triflers of the day.

This afternoon they flocked in greater numbers than usual. The episode of the breaking of Devil, the unexpected return of his Grace of Osmonde, the preparations for the union, had given an extra stimulant to that interest in her ladyship which was ever great enough to need none. Thereunto was added the piquancy of the stories of the noticeable demeanour of Sir John Oxon, of what had seemed to be so plain a rebellion against his fate, and also of my lady's open and cold displeasure at the manner of his bearing himself as a disappointed man who presumed to show anger against that to which he should gallantly have been resigned, as one who is conquered by the chance of war. Those who had beheld the two ride homeward together in the morning, were full of curiousness, and one and another, mentioning the matter, exchanged glances, speaking plainly of desire to know more of what had passed, and of hope that chance might throw the two together again in public, where more of interest might be gathered. It seemed indeed not unlikely that Sir John might appear among the tea-bibbers, and perchance 'twas for this lively reason that my lady's room was this afternoon more than usually full of gay spirits and gossip-loving ones.

They found, however, only her ladyship's self and her sister, Mistress Anne, who, of truth, did not often join her tea parties, finding them so given up to fashionable chatter and worldly witticisms that she felt herself somewhat out of place. The world knew Mistress Anne but as a dull, plain gentlewoman, whom her more brilliant and fortunate sister gave gracious protection to, and none missed her when she was absent, or observed her greatly when she appeared upon the scene. Today she was perchance more observed than usual, because her pallor was so great a contrast to her ladyship's splendour of beauty and colour. The contrast between them was ever a great one; but this afternoon Mistress Anne's always pale countenance seemed almost livid, there were rings of pain or illness round her eyes, and her features looked drawn and pinched. My Lady Dunstanwolde, clad in a great rich petticoat of crimson flowered satin, with wondrous yellow Mechlin for her ruffles, and with her glorious hair dressed like a tower, looked taller, more goddess-like and full of splendid fire than ever she had been before beheld, or so her visitors said to her and to each other; though, to tell the truth, this was no new story, she being one of those women having the curious power of inspiring the beholder with the feeling each time he encountered them that he had never before seen them in such beauty and bloom.

When she had come down the staircase from her chamber, Anne, who had been standing at the foot, had indeed started somewhat at the sight of her rich dress and brilliant hues.

'Why do you jump as if I were a ghost, Anne?' she asked. 'Do I look like one? My looking-glass did not tell me so.'

'No,' said Anne; 'you – are so – so crimson and splendid – and I –'

Her ladyship came swiftly down the stairs to her.

'You are not crimson and splendid,' she said. ''Tis you who are a ghost. What is it?'

Anne let her soft, dull eyes rest upon her for a moment helplessly, and when she replied her voice sounded weak.

'I think – I am ill, sister,' she said. 'I seem to tremble and feel faint.'

'Go then to bed and see the physician. You must be cared for,' said her ladyship. 'In sooth, you look ill indeed.'

'Nay,' said Anne; 'I beg you, sister, this afternoon let me be with you; it will sustain me. You are so strong – let me –'

She put out her hand as if to touch her, but it dropped at her side as though its strength was gone.

'But there will be many babbling people,' said her sister, with a curious look. 'You do not like company, and these days my rooms are full. 'Twill irk and tire you.'

'I care not for the people – I would be with you,' Anne said, in strange imploring. 'I have a sick fancy that I am afraid to sit alone in my chamber. 'Tis but weakness. Let me this afternoon be with you.'

'Go then and change your robe,' said Clorinda, 'and put some red upon your cheeks. You may come if you will. You are a strange creature, Anne.'

And thus saying, she passed into her apartment. As there are blows and pain which end in insensibility or delirium, so there are catastrophes and perils which are so great as to produce something near akin to these. As she had stood before her mirror in her chamber watching her reflection, while her woman attired her in her crimson flowered satin and builded up her stately headdress, this other woman had felt that the hour when she could have shrieked and raved and betrayed herself had passed by, and left a deadness like a calm behind, as though horror had stunned all pain and yet left her senses clear. She forgot not the thing which lay staring upward blankly at the underpart of the couch which hid it – the look of its fixed eyes, its outspread locks, and the purple indentation on the temple she saw as clearly as she had seen them in that first mad moment when she had stood staring downward at the thing itself; but the coursing of her blood was stilled, the gallop of her pulses, and that wild hysteric leaping of her heart into her throat, choking her and forcing her to gasp and pant in that way which in women must ever end in shrieks and cries and sobbing beatings of the air. But for the feminine softness to which her nature had given way for the first time, since the power of love had mastered her, there was no thing of earth could have happened to her which would have brought this rolling ball to her throat, this tremor to her body – since the hour of her birth she had never been attacked by such a female folly, as she would indeed have regarded it once; but now 'twas different – for a while she had been a woman – a woman who had flung herself upon the bosom of him who was her soul's lord, and resting there, her old rigid strength had been relaxed.

But 'twas not this woman who had known tender yielding who returned to take her place in the Panelled Parlour, knowing of the companion who waited near her unseen – for it was as her companion she thought of him, as she had thought of him when he followed her in the Mall, forced himself into her box at the play, or stood by her shoulder at assemblies; he had placed himself by her side again, and would stay there until she could rid herself of him.

'After tonight he will be gone, if I act well my part,' she said, 'and then may I live a freed woman.'

'Twas always upon the divan she took her place when she received her visitors, who were accustomed to finding her enthroned there. This afternoon when she came into the room she paused for a space, and stood beside it, the parlour being yet empty. She felt her face grow a little cold, as if it paled, and her underlip drew itself tight across her teeth.

'In a graveyard,' she said, 'I have sat upon the stone ledge of a tomb, and beneath there was – worse than this, could I but have seen it. This is no more.'

When the Sir Humphreys and Lord Charleses, Lady Bettys and Mistress Lovelys were announced in flocks, fluttering and chattering, she rose from her old place to meet them, and was brilliant graciousness itself. She hearkened to their gossipings, and though 'twas not her way to join in them, she was this day witty in such way as robbed them of the dullness in which sometimes gossip ends. It was a varied company which gathered about her; but to each she gave his or her moment, and in that moment said that which they would afterwards remember. With those of the Court she talked royalty, the humours of Her Majesty, the severities of her Grace of Marlborough; with statesmen she spoke with such intellect and discretion that they went away pondering on the good fortune which had befallen one man when it seemed that it was of such proportions as might have satisfied a dozen, for it seemed not fair to them that his Grace of Osmonde, having already rank, wealth, and fame, should have added to them a gift of such magnificence as this beauteous woman would bring; with beaux and wits she made dazzling jests; and to the beauties who desired their flatteries she gave praise so adroit that they were stimulated to plume their feathers afresh and cease to fear the rivalry of her loveliness.

And yet while she so bore herself, never once did she cease to feel the presence of that which, lying near, seemed to her racked soul as one who lay and listened with staring eyes which mocked; for there was a thought which would not leave her, which was, that it could hear, that it could see through the glazing on its blue orbs, and that knowing itself bound by the moveless irons of death and dumbness it impotently raged and cursed that it could not burst them and shriek out its vengeance, rolling forth among her worshippers at their feet and hers.

'But he cannot,' she said, within her clenched teeth, again and again – 'that he cannot.'

Once as she said this to herself she caught Anne's eyes fixed helplessly upon her, it seeming to be as the poor woman had said, that her weakness caused her to desire to abide near her sister's strength and draw support from it; for she had remained at my lady's side closely since she had descended to the room, and now seemed to implore some protection for which she was too timid to openly make request.

'You are too weak to stay, Anne,' her ladyship said. ''Twould be better that you should retire.'

'I am weak,' the poor thing answered, in low tones – 'but not too weak to stay. I am always weak. Would that I were of your strength and courage. Let me sit down – sister – here.' She touched the divan's cushions with a shaking hand, gazing upward wearily – perchance remembering that this place seemed ever a sort of throne none other than the hostess queen herself presumed to encroach upon.

'You are too meek, poor sister,' quoth Clorinda. ''Tis not a chair of coronation or the woolsack of a judge. Sit! sit! – and let me call for wine!'

She spoke to a lackey and bade him bring the drink, for even as she sank into her place Anne's cheeks grew whiter.

When 'twas brought, her ladyship poured it forth and gave it to her sister with her own hand, obliging her to drink enough to bring her colour back. Having seen to this, she addressed the servant who had obeyed her order.

'Hath Jenfry returned from Sir John Oxon?' she demanded, in that clear, ringing voice of hers, whose music ever arrested those surrounding her, whether they were concerned in her speech or no; but now all felt sufficient interest to prick up ears and hearken to what was said.

'No, my lady,' the lackey answered. 'He said that you had bidden him to wait.'

'But not all day, poor fool,' she said, setting down Anne's empty glass upon the salver. 'Did he think I bade him stand about the door all night? Bring me his message when he comes.'

''Tis ever thus with these dull serving folk,' she said to those nearest her. 'One cannot pay for wit with wages and livery. They can but obey the literal word. Sir John, leaving me in haste this morning, I forgot a question I would have asked, and sent a lackey to recall him.'

Anne sat upright.

'Sister – I pray you – another glass of wine.'

My lady gave it to her at once, and she drained it eagerly.

'Was he overtaken?' said a curious matron, who wished not to see the subject closed.

'No,' quoth her ladyship, with a light laugh – 'though he must have been in haste, for the man was sent after him in but a moment's time. 'Twas then I told the fellow to go later to his lodgings and deliver my message into Sir John's own hand, whence it seems that he thinks that he must await him till he comes.'

Upon a table near there lay the loaded whip; for she had felt it bolder to let it lie there as if forgotten, because her pulse had sprung so at first sight of it when she came down, and she had so quailed before the desire to thrust it away, to hide it from her sight. 'And that I quail before,' she had said, 'I must have the will to face – or I am lost.' So she had let it stay.

A languishing beauty, with melting blue eyes and a pretty fashion of ever keeping before the world of her admirers her waxen delicacy, lifted the heavy thing in her frail white hand.

'How can your ladyship wield it?' she said. 'It is so heavy for a woman – but your ladyship is – is not –'

'Not quite a woman,' said the beautiful creature, standing at her full great height, and smiling down at this blue and white piece of frailty with the flashing splendour of her eyes.

'Not quite a woman,' cried two wits at once. 'A goddess rather – an Olympian goddess.'

The languisher could not endure comparisons which so seemed to disparage her ethereal charms. She lifted the weapon with a great effort, which showed the slimness of her delicate fair wrist and the sweet tracery of blue veins upon it.

'Nay,' she said lispingly, 'it needs the muscle of a great man to lift it. I could not hold it – much less beat with it a horse.' And to show how coarse a strength was needed and how far her femininity lacked such vigour, she dropped it upon the floor – and it rolled beneath the edge of the divan.

'Now,' the thought shot through my lady's brain, as a bolt shoots from the sky – 'now – he laughs!'

She had no time to stir – there were upon their knees three beaux at once, and each would sure have thrust his arm below the seat and rummaged, had not God saved her! Yes, 'twas of

God she thought in that terrible mad second – God! – and only a mind that is not human could have told why.

For Anne – poor Mistress Anne – white-faced and shaking, was before them all, and with a strange adroitness stooped, and thrust her hand below, and drawing the thing forth, held it up to view.

''Tis here,' she said, 'and in sooth, sister, I wonder not at its falling – its weight is so great.'

Clorinda took it from her hand.

'I shall break no more beasts like Devil,' she said, 'and for quieter ones it weighs too much; I shall lay it by.'

She crossed the room and laid it upon a shelf.

'It was ever heavy – but for Devil. 'Tis done with,' she said; and there came back to her face – which for a second had lost hue – a flood of crimson so glowing, and a smile so strange, that those who looked and heard, said to themselves that 'twas the thought of Osmonde who had so changed her, which made her blush. But a few moments later they beheld the same glow mount again. A lackey entered, bearing a salver on which lay two letters. One was a large one, sealed with a ducal coronet, and this she saw first, and took in her hand even before the man had time to speak.

'His Grace's courier has arrived from France,' he said; 'the package was ordered to be delivered at once.'

'It must be that his Grace returns earlier than we had hoped,' she said, and then the other missive caught her eye.

''Tis your ladyship's own,' the lackey explained somewhat anxiously. ''Twas brought back, Sir John not having yet come home, and Jenfry having waited three hours.'

''Twas long enough,' quoth her ladyship. ''Twill do to-morrow.'

She did not lay Osmonde's letter aside, but kept it in her hand, and seeing that she waited for their retirement to read it, her guests began to make their farewells. One by one or in groups of twos and threes they left her, the men bowing low, and going away fretted by the memory of the picture she made – a tall and regal figure in her flowered crimson, her stateliness seeming relaxed and softened by the mere holding of the sealed missive in her hand. But the women were vaguely envious, not of Osmonde, but of her before whom there lay outspread as far as life's horizon reached, a future of such perfect love and joy; for Gerald Mertoun had been marked by feminine eyes since his earliest youth, and had seemed to embody all that woman's dreams or woman's ambitions or her love could desire.

When the last was gone, Clorinda turned, tore her letter open, and held it hard to her lips. Before she read a word she kissed it passionately a score of times, paying no heed that Anne sat gazing at her; and having kissed it so, she fell to reading it, her cheeks warm with the glow of a sweet and splendid passion, her bosom rising and falling in a tempest of tender, fluttering breaths – and 'twas these words her eyes devoured:

'If I should head this page I write to you "Goddess and Queen, and Empress of my deepest soul", what more should I be saying than "My Love" and "My Clorinda", since these express all the soul of man could crave for or his body desire. The body and soul of me so long for thee, sweetheart, and sweetest beautiful woman that the hand of Nature ever fashioned for the joy of mortals, that I have had need to pray Heaven's help to aid me to endure the passing of the days that lie between me and the hour which will make me the most strangely, rapturously, happy man, not in England, not in the world, but in all God's universe. I must pray Heaven again, and indeed do and will, for humbleness which shall teach me to remember that I am not deity, but mere man – mere man – though I shall hold a goddess to my breast and gaze into eyes which are like deep pools of Paradise, and yet answer mine with the marvel of such love as none but such a soul could make a woman's, and so fit to mate with man's. In the heavy days when I was wont to gaze at you from afar with burning heart, my unceasing anguish was that even high honour itself could not subdue and conquer the thoughts which leaped within me even as my pulse leaped, and even as my pulse could not be stilled unless by death. And one that for ever haunted – aye, and taunted – me was the image of how your tall, beauteous body would yield itself to a strong man's arm, and your noble head with its heavy tower of hair resting upon his shoulder – the centres of his very being would be thrilled and shaken by the uplifting of such melting eyes as surely man ne'er gazed within on earth before, and the ripe and scarlet bow of a mouth so beauteous and so sweet with womanhood. This beset me day and night, and with such torture that I feared betimes my brain might reel and I become a lost and ruined madman. And now – it is no more forbidden me to dwell upon it – nay, I lie waking at night, wooing the picture to me, and at times I rise from my dreams to kneel by my bedside and thank God that He hath given me at last what surely is my own! – for so it seems to me, my love, that each of us is but a part of the other, and that such forces of Nature rush to meet together in us, that Nature herself would cry out were we rent apart. If there were aught to rise like a ghost between us, if there were aught that could sunder us – noble soul, let us but swear that it shall weld us but the closer together, and that locked in each other's arms its blows shall not even make our united strength to sway. Sweetest lady, your lovely lip will curve in smiles, and you will say, "He is mad with his joy – my Gerald" (for never till my heart stops at its last beat and leaves me still, a dead man, cold upon my bed, can I forget the music of your speech when you spoke those words, "My Gerald! My Gerald.") And indeed I crave your pardon, for a man so filled with rapture cannot be quite sane, and sometimes I wonder if I walk through the palace gardens like one who is drunk, so does my brain reel. But soon, my heavenly, noble love, my exile will be over, and this is in truth what my letter is to tell you, that in four days your lackeys will throw open your doors to me and I shall enter, and being led to you, shall kneel at your feet and kiss the hem of your robe, and then rise standing to fold her who will so soon be my very wife to my throbbing breast.'

Back to her face had come all the softness which had been lost, the hard lines were gone, the tender curves had returned, her lashes looked as if they were moist. Anne, sitting rigidly and gazing at her, was afraid to speak, knowing that she was not for the time on earth, but that the sound of a voice would bring her back to it, and that 'twas well she should be away as long as she might.

She read the letter, not once, but thrice, dwelling upon every word, 'twas plain; and when she had reached the last one, turning back the pages and beginning again. When she looked up at last, 'twas with an almost wild little smile, for she had indeed for that one moment forgotten.

'Locked in each other's arms,' she said – 'locked in each other's arms. My Gerald! My Gerald! "What surely is my own – my own"!'

Anne rose and came to her, laying her hand on her arm. She spoke in a voice low, hushed, and strained.

'Come away, sister,' she said, 'for a little while – come away.'

My Lady Dunstanwolde
Sits Late Alone and Writes

That she must leave the Panelled Parlour at her usual hour, or attract attention by doing that to which her household was unaccustomed, she well knew, her manner of life being ever stately and ceremonious in its regularity. When she dined at home she and Anne partook of their repast together in the large dining room, the table loaded with silver dishes and massive glittering glass, their powdered, gold-laced lackeys in attendance, as though a score of guests had shared the meal with them. Since her lord's death there had been nights when her ladyship had sat late writing letters and reading documents pertaining to her estates, the management of which, though in a measure controlled by stewards and attorneys, was not left to them, as the business of most great ladies is generally left to others. All papers were examined by her, all leases and agreements clearly understood before she signed them, and if there were aught unsatisfactory, both stewards and lawyers were called to her presence to explain.

'Never did I – or any other man – meet with such a head upon a woman's shoulders,' her attorney said. And the head steward of Dunstanwolde and Helversly learned to quake at the sight of her bold handwriting upon the outside of a letter.

'Such a lady!' he said – 'such a lady! Lie to her if you can; palter if you know how; try upon her the smallest honest shrewd trick, and see how it fares with you. Were it not that she is generous as she is piercing of eye, no man could serve her and make an honest living.'

She went to her chamber and was attired again sumptuously for dinner. Before she descended she dismissed her woman for a space on some errand, and when she was alone, drawing near to her mirror, gazed steadfastly within it at her face. When she had read Osmonde's letter her cheeks had glowed; but when she had come back to earth, and as she had sat under her woman's hands at her toilette, bit by bit the crimson had died out as she had thought of what was behind her and of what lay before. The thing was so stiffly rigid by this time, and its eyes still stared so. Never had she needed to put red upon her cheeks before, Nature having stained them with such richness of hue; but as no lady of the day was unprovided with her crimson, there was a little pot among her toilette ornaments which contained all that any emergency might require. She opened this small receptacle and took from it the red she for the first time was in want of.

'I must not wear a pale face, God knows,' she said, and rubbed the colour on her cheeks with boldness.

It would have seemed that she wore her finest crimson when she went forth full dressed from her apartment; little Nero grinned to see her, the lackeys saying among themselves that his Grace's courier had surely brought good news, and that they might expect his master soon. At the dinner-table 'twas Anne who was pale and ate but little, she having put no red upon her cheeks, and having no appetite for what was spread before her. She looked strangely as though she were withered and shrunken, and her face seemed even wrinkled. My lady had small leaning towards food, but she sent no food away untouched, forcing herself to eat, and letting not the talk flag – though it was indeed true that 'twas she herself who talked, Mistress Anne speaking rarely; but as it was always her way to be silent, and a listener rather than one who conversed, this was not greatly noticeable.

Her Ladyship of Dunstanwolde talked of her guests of the afternoon, and was charming and witty in her speech of them; she repeated the mots of the wits, and told some brilliant stories of certain modish ladies and gentlemen of fashion; she had things to say of statesmen and politics, and was sparkling indeed in speaking of the lovely languisher whose little wrist was too delicate and slender to support the loaded whip. While she talked, Mistress Anne's soft, dull eyes were fixed upon her with a sort of wonder which had some of the quality of bewilderment; but this was no new thing either, for to the one woman the other was ever something to marvel at.

'It is because you are so quiet a mouse, Anne,' my lady said, with her dazzling smile, 'that you seem never in the way; and yet I should miss you if I knew you were not within the house. When the duke takes me to Camylotte you must be with me even then. It is so great a house that in it I can find you a bower in which you can be happy even if you see us but little. 'Tis a heavenly place I am told, and of great splendour and beauty. The park and flower-gardens are the envy of all England.'

'You – will be very happy, sister,' said Anne, 'and – and like a queen.'

'Yes,' was her sister's answer – 'yes.' And 'twas spoken with a deep indrawn breath.

After the repast was ended she went back to the Panelled Parlour.

'You may sit with me till bedtime if you desire, Anne,' she said; 'but 'twill be but dull for you, as I go to sit at work. I have some documents of import to examine and much writing to do. I shall sit up late.' And upon this she turned to the lackey holding open the door for her passing through. 'If before half-past ten there comes a message from Sir John Oxon,' she gave order, 'it must be brought to me at once; but later I must not be disturbed – it will keep until morning.'

Yet as she spoke there was before her as distinct a picture as ever of what lay waiting and gazing in the room to which she went.

Until twelve o'clock she sat at her table, a despatch box by her side, papers outspread before her. Within three feet of her was the divan, but she gave no glance to it, sitting writing, reading, and comparing documents. At twelve o'clock she rose and rang the bell.

'I shall be later than I thought,' she said. 'I need none of you who are below stairs. Go you all to bed. Tell my woman that she also may lie down. I will ring when I come to my chamber and have need of her. There is yet no message from Sir John?'

'None, my lady,' the man answered.

He went away with a relieved countenance, as she made no comment. He knew that his fellows as well as himself would be pleased enough to be released from duty for the night. They were a pampered lot, and had no fancy for late hours when there were no great entertainments being held which pleased them and gave them chances to receive vails.

Mistress Anne sat in a large chair, huddled into a small heap, and looking colourless and shrunken. As she heard bolts being shot and bars put up for the closing of the house, she knew that her own dismissal was at hand. Doors were shut below stairs, and when all was done the silence of night reigned as it does in all households when those who work have gone to rest. 'Twas a common thing enough, and yet this night there was one woman who felt the stillness so deep that it made her breathing seem a sound too loud.

'Go to bed, Anne,' she said. 'You have stayed up too long.'

Anne arose from her chair and drew near to her.

'Sister,' said she, as she had said before, 'let me stay.'

She was a poor weak creature, and so she looked with her pale insignificant face and dull eyes, a wisp of loose hair lying damp on her forehead. She seemed indeed too weak a thing to stand even for a moment in the way of what must be done this night, and 'twas almost irritating to be stopped by her.

'Nay,' said my Lady Dunstanwolde, her beautiful brow knitting as she looked at her. 'Go to your chamber, Anne, and to sleep. I must do my work, and finish tonight what I have begun.'

'But – but –' Anne stammered, dominated again, and made afraid, as she ever was, by this strong nature, 'in this work you must finish – is there not something I could do to – aid you – even in some small and poor way. Is there – naught?'

'Naught,' answered Clorinda, her form drawn to its great full height, her lustrous eyes darkening. 'What should there be that you could understand?'

'Not some small thing – not some poor thing?' Anne said, her fingers nervously twisting each other, so borne down was she by her awful timorousness, for awful it was indeed when she saw clouds gather on her sister's brow. 'I have so loved you, sister – I have so loved you that my mind is quickened somehow at times, and I can understand more than would be thought – when I hope to serve you. Once you said – once you said –'

She knew not then nor ever afterwards how it came to pass that in that moment she found herself swept into her sister's white arms and strained against her breast, wherein she felt the wild heart bounding; nor could she, not being given to subtle reasoning, have comprehended the almost fierce kiss on her cheek nor the hot drops that wet it.

'I said that I believed that if you saw me commit murder,' Clorinda cried, 'you would love me still, and be my friend and comforter.'

'I would, I would!' cried Anne.

'And I believe your word, poor, faithful soul – I do believe it,' my lady said, and kissed her hard again, but the next instant set her free and laughed. 'But you will not be put to the test,' she said, 'for I have done none. And in two days' time my Gerald will be here, and I shall be safe – saved and happy for evermore – for evermore. There, leave me! I would be alone and end my work.'

And she went back to her table and sat beside it, taking her pen to write, and Anne knew that she dare say no more, and turning, went slowly from the room, seeing for her last sight as she passed through the doorway, the erect and splendid figure at its task, the light from the candelabras shining upon the rubies round the snow-white neck and wreathed about the tower of raven hair like lines of crimson.

A Piteous Story Is Told,
and the Old Cellars Walled In

It is, indeed, strangely easy in the great world for a man to lose his importance, and from having been the target for all eyes and the subject of all conversation, to step from his place, or find it so taken by some rival that it would seem, judging from the general obliviousness to him, that he had never existed. But few years before no fashionable gathering would have been felt complete had it not been graced by the presence of the young and fascinating Lovelace, Sir John Oxon. Women favoured him, and men made themselves his boon companions; his wit was repeated; the fashion of his hair and the cut of his waistcoat copied. He was at first rich and gay enough to be courted and made a favourite; but when his fortune was squandered, and his marriage with the heiress came to naught, those qualities which were vicious and base in him were more easy to be seen. Besides, there came new male beauties and new dandies with greater resources and more of prudence, and these, beginning to set fashion, win ladies' hearts, and make conquests, so drew the attention of the public mind that he was less noticeable, being only one of many, instead of ruling singly as it had seemed that by some strange chance he did at first. There were indeed so many stories told of his light ways, that their novelty being worn off and new ones still repeated, such persons as concerned themselves with matters of reputation either through conscience or policy, began to speak of him with less of warmth or leniency.

''Tis not well for a matron with daughters to marry and with sons to keep an eye to,' it was said, 'to have in her household too often a young gentleman who has squandered his fortune in dice and drink and wild living, and who 'twas known was cast off by a reputable young lady of fortune.'

So there were fine ladies who began to avoid him, and those in power at Court and in the world who regarded him with lessening favour day by day! In truth, he had such debts, and his creditors pressed him so ceaselessly, that even had the world's favour continued, his life must have changed its aspect greatly. His lodgings were no longer the most luxurious in the fashionable part of the town, his brocades and laces were no longer of the richest, nor his habit of the very latest and most modish cut; he had no more an equipage attracting every eye as he drove forth, nor a gentleman's gentleman whose swagger and pomp outdid that of all others in his world. Soon after the breaking of his marriage with the heiress, his mother had died, and his relatives being few, and those of an order strictly averse to the habits of ill-provided and extravagant kinsmen, he had but few family ties. Other ties he had, 'twas true, but they were not such as were accounted legal or worthy of attention either by himself or those related to him.

So it befell that when my Lady Dunstanwolde's lackey could not find him at his lodgings, and as the days went past neither his landlady nor his creditors beheld him again, his absence from the scene was not considered unaccountable by them, nor did it attract the notice it would have done in times gone by.

'He hath made his way out of England to escape us,' said the angry tailors and mercers – who had besieged his door in vain for months, and who were now infuriated at the thought of their own easiness and the impudent gay airs which had befooled them. 'A good four hundred pounds of mine hath he carried with him,' said one. 'And two hundred of mine!' 'And more of mine, since I am a poor man to whom a pound means twenty guineas!' 'We are all robbed, and he has cheated the debtors' prison, wherein, if we had not been fools, he would have been clapped six months ago.'

'Think ye he will not come back, gentlemen?' quavered his landlady. 'God knows when I have seen a guinea of his money

– but he was such a handsome, fine young nobleman, and had such a way with a poor body, and ever a smile and a chuck o' the chin for my Jenny.'

'Look well after poor Jenny if he hath left her behind,' said the tailor.

He did not come back, indeed; and hearing the rumour that he had fled his creditors, the world of fashion received the news with small disturbance, all modish persons being at that time much engaged in discussion of the approaching nuptials of her ladyship of Dunstanwolde and the Duke of Osmonde. Close upon the discussions of the preparations came the nuptials themselves, and then all the town was agog, and had small leisure to think of other things. For those who were bidden to the ceremonials and attendant entertainments, there were rich habits and splendid robes to be prepared; and to those who had not been bidden, there were bitter disappointments and thwarted wishes to think of.

'Sir John Oxon has fled England to escape seeing and hearing it all,' was said.

'He has fled to escape something more painful than the spleen,' others answered. 'He had reached his rope's end, and finding that my Lady Dunstanwolde was not of a mind to lengthen it with her fortune, having taken a better man, and that his creditors would have no more patience, he showed them a light pair of heels.'

Before my Lady Dunstanwolde left her house she gave orders that it be set in order for closing for some time, having it on her mind that she should not soon return. It was, however, to be left in such condition that at any moment, should she wish to come to it, all could be made ready in two days' time. To this end various repairs and changes she had planned were to be carried out as soon as she went away from it. Among other things was the closing with brickwork of the entrance to the passage leading to the unused cellars.

''Twill make the servants' part more wholesome and less damp and draughty,' she said; 'and if I should sell the place, will be to its advantage. 'Twas a builder with little wit who planned such passages and black holes. In spite of all the lime spread there, they were ever mouldy and of evil odour.'

It was her command that there should be no time lost, and men were set at work, carrying bricks and mortar. It so chanced that one of them, going in through a back entrance with a hod over his shoulder, and being young and lively, found his eye caught by the countenance of a pretty, frightened-looking girl, who seemed to be loitering about watching, as if curious or anxious. Seeing her near each time he passed, and observing that she wished to speak, but was too timid, he addressed her –

'Would you know aught, mistress?' he said.

She drew nearer gratefully, and then he saw her eyes were red as if with weeping.

'Think you her ladyship would let a poor girl speak a word with her?' she said. 'Think you I dare ask so much of a servant – or would they flout me and turn me from the door? Have you seen her? Does she look like a hard, shrewish lady?'

'That she does not, though all stand in awe of her,' he answered, pleased to talk with so pretty a creature. 'I but caught a glimpse of her when she gave orders concerning the closing with brick of a passageway below. She is a tall lady, and grand and stately, but she hath a soft pair of eyes as ever man would wish to look into, be he duke or ditcher.'

The tears began to run down the girl's cheeks.

'Ay!' she said; 'all men love her, they say. Many a poor girl's sweetheart has been false through her – and I thought she was cruel and ill-natured. Know you the servants that wait on her? Would you dare to ask one for me, if he thinks she would deign to see a poor girl who would crave the favour to be allowed to speak to her of – of a gentleman she knows?'

'They are but lackeys, and I would dare to ask what was in my mind,' he answered; 'but she is near her wedding day, and little as I know of brides' ways, I am of the mind that she will not like to be troubled.'

'That I stand in fear of,' she said; 'but, oh! I pray you, ask someone of them – a kindly one.'

The young man looked aside. 'Luck is with you,' he said. 'Here comes one now to air himself in the sun, having naught else to do. Here is a young woman who would speak with her ladyship,' he said to the strapping powdered fellow.

'She had best begone,' the lackey answered, striding towards the applicant. 'Think you my lady has time to receive traipsing wenches?'

''Twas only for a moment I asked,' the girl said. 'I come from – I would speak to her of – of Sir John Oxon – whom she knows.'

The man's face changed. It was Jenfry.

'Sir John Oxon,' he said. 'Then I will ask her. Had you said any other name I would not have gone near her today.'

Her ladyship was in her new closet with Mistress Anne, and there the lackey came to her to deliver his errand.

'A country-bred young woman, your ladyship,' he said, 'comes from Sir John Oxon –'

'From Sir John Oxon!' cried Anne, starting in her chair.

My Lady Dunstanwolde made no start, but turned a steady countenance towards the door, looking into the lackey's face.

'Then he hath returned?' she said.

'Returned!' said Anne.

'After the morning he rode home with me,' my lady answered, ''twas said he went away. He left his lodgings without warning. It seems he hath come back. What does the woman want?' she ended.

'To speak with your ladyship,' replied the man, 'of Sir John himself, she says.'

'Bring her to me,' her ladyship commanded.

The girl was brought in, overawed and trembling. She was a country-bred young creature, as the lackey had said, being of the simple rose-and-white freshness of seventeen years perhaps, and having childish blue eyes and fair curling locks.

She was so frightened by the grandeur of her surroundings, and the splendid beauty of the lady who was so soon to be a duchess, and was already a great earl's widow, that she could only stand within the doorway, curtseying and trembling, with tears welling in her eyes.

'Be not afraid,' said my Lady Dunstanwolde. 'Come hither, child, and tell me what you want.' Indeed, she did not look a hard or shrewish lady; she spoke as gently as woman could, and a mildness so unexpected produced in the young creature such a revulsion of feeling that she made a few steps forward and fell upon her knees, weeping, and with uplifted hands.

'My lady,' she said, 'I know not how I dared to come, but that I am so desperate – and your ladyship being so happy, it seemed – it seemed that you might pity me, who am so helpless and know not what to do.'

Her ladyship leaned forward in her chair, her elbow on her knee, her chin held in her hand, to gaze at her.

'You come from Sir John Oxon?' she said.

Anne, watching, clutched each arm of her chair.

'Not from him, asking your ladyship's pardon,' said the child, 'but – but – from the country to him,' her head falling on her breast, 'and I know not where he is.'

'You came to him,' asked my lady. 'Are you,' and her speech was pitiful and slow – 'are you one of those whom he has – ruined?'

The little suppliant looked up with widening orbs.

'How could that be, and he so virtuous and pious a gentleman?' she faltered.

Then did my lady rise with a sudden movement.

'Was he so?' says she.

'Had he not been,' the child answered, 'my mother would have been afraid to trust him. I am but a poor country widow's daughter, but was well brought up, and honestly – and when he came to our village my mother was afraid, because he was a gentleman; but when she saw his piety, and how he went to church and sang the psalms and prayed for grace, she let me listen to him.'

'Did he go to church and sing and pray at first?' my lady asks.

''Twas in church he saw me, your ladyship,' she was answered. 'He said 'twas his custom to go always when he came to a new place, and that often there he found the most heavenly faces, for 'twas piety and innocence that made a face like to an angel's; and 'twas innocence and virtue stirred his heart to love, and not mere beauty which so fades.'

'Go on, innocent thing,' my lady said; and she turned aside to Anne, flashing from her eyes unseen a great blaze, and speaking in a low and hurried voice. 'God's house,' she said – 'God's prayers – God's songs of praise – he used them all to break a tender heart, and bring an innocent life to ruin – and yet was he not struck dead?'

Anne hid her face and shuddered.

'He was a gentleman,' the poor young thing cried, sobbing – 'and I no fit match for him, but that he loved me. 'Tis said love makes all equal; and he said I was the sweetest, innocent young thing, and without me he could not live. And he told my mother that he was not rich or the fashion now, and had no modish friends or relations to flout any poor beauty he might choose to wed.'

'And he would marry you?' my lady's voice broke in. 'He said that he would marry you?'

'A thousand times, your ladyship, and so told my mother, but said I must come to town and be married at his lodgings, or 'twould not be counted a marriage by law, he being a town gentleman, and I from the country.'

'And you came,' said Mistress Anne, down whose pale cheeks the tears were running – 'you came at his command to follow him?'

'What day came you up to town?' demands my lady, breathless and leaning forward. 'Went you to his lodgings, and stayed you there with him, even for an hour?'

The poor child gazed at her, paling.

'He was not there!' she cried. 'I came alone because he said all must be secret at first; and my heart beat so with joy, my lady, that when the woman of the house whereat he lodges let me in I scarce could speak. But she was a merry woman and good-natured, and only laughed and cheered me when she took me to his rooms, and I sat trembling.'

'What said she to you?' my lady asks, her breast heaving with her breath.

'That he was not yet in, but that he would sure come to such a young and pretty thing as I, and I must wait for him, for he would not forgive her if she let me go. And the while I waited there came a man in bands and cassock, but he had not a holy look, and late in the afternoon I heard him making jokes with the woman outside, and they both laughed in such an evil way that I was affrighted, and waiting till they had gone to another part of the house, stole away.'

'But he came not back that night – thank God!' my lady said – 'he came not back.'

The girl rose from her knees, trembling, her hands clasped on her breast.

'Why should your ladyship thank God?' she says, pure drops falling from her eyes. 'I am so humble, and had naught else but that great happiness, and it was taken away – and you thank God.'

Then drops fell from my lady's eyes also, and she came forward and caught the child's hand, and held it close and warm and strong, and yet with her full lip quivering.

"'Twas not that your joy was taken away that I thanked God,' said she. 'I am not cruel – God Himself knows that, and when He smites me 'twill not be for cruelty. I knew not what I said, and yet – tell me what did you then? Tell me?'

'I went to a poor house to lodge, having some little money he had given me,' the simple young thing answered. ''Twas an honest house, though mean and comfortless. And the next day I went back to his lodgings to question, but he had not come, and I would not go in, though the woman tried to make me enter, saying, Sir John would surely return soon, as he had the day before rid with my Lady Dunstanwolde and been to her house; and 'twas plain he had meant to come to his lodgings, for her ladyship had sent her lackey thrice with a message.'

The hand with which Mistress Anne sat covering her eyes began to shake. My lady's own hand would have shaken had she not been so strong a creature.

'And he has not yet returned, then?' she asked. 'You have not seen him?'

The girl shook her fair locks, weeping with piteous little sobs.

'He has not,' she cried, 'and I know not what to do – and the great town seems full of evil men and wicked women. I know not which way to turn, for all plot wrong against me, and would drag me down to shamefulness – and back to my poor mother I cannot go.'

'Wherefore not, poor child?' my lady asked her.

'I have not been made an honest, wedded woman, and none would believe my story, and – and he might come back.'

'And if he came back?' said her ladyship.

At this question the girl slipped from her grasp and down upon her knees again, catching at her rich petticoat and holding it, her eyes searching the great lady's in imploring piteousness, her own streaming.

'I love him,' she wept – 'I love him so – I cannot leave the place where he might be. He was so beautiful and grand a gentleman, and, sure, he loved me better than all else – and I cannot thrust away from me that last night when he held me to his breast near our cottage door, and the nightingale sang in the roses, and he spake such words to me. I lie and sob all night on my hard pillow – I so long to see him and to hear his voice – and hearing he had been with you that last morning, I dared to come, praying that you might have heard him let drop some word that would tell me where he may be, for I cannot go away thinking he may come back longing for me – and I lose him and never see his face again. Oh! my lady, my lady, this place is so full of wickedness and fierce people – and dark kennels where crimes are done. I am affrighted for him, thinking he may have been struck some blow, and murdered, and hid away; and none will look for him but one who loves him – who loves him. Could it be so? – could it be? You know the town's ways so well. I pray you, tell me – in God's name I pray you!'

'God's mercy!' Anne breathed, and from behind her hands came stifled sobbing. My Lady Dunstanwolde bent down, her colour dying.

'Nay, nay,' she said, 'there has been no murder done – none! Hush, poor thing, hush thee. There is somewhat I must tell thee.'

She tried to raise her, but the child would not be raised, and clung to her rich robe, shaking as she knelt gazing upward.

'It is a bitter thing,' my lady said, and 'twas as if her own eyes were imploring. 'God help you bear it – God help us all. He told me nothing of his journey. I knew not he was about to take it; but wheresoever he has travelled, 'twas best that he should go.'

'Nay! nay!' the girl cried out – 'to leave me helpless. Nay! it could not be so. He loved me – loved me – as the great duke loves you!'

'He meant you evil,' said my lady, shuddering, 'and evil he would have done you. He was a villain – a villain who meant to

204

trick you. Had God struck him dead that day, 'twould have been mercy to you. I knew him well.'

The young thing gave a bitter cry and fell swooning at her feet; and down upon her knees my lady went beside her, loosening her gown, and chafing her poor hands as though they two had been of sister blood.

'Call for hartshorn, Anne, and for water,' she said; 'she will come out of her swooning, poor child, and if she is cared for kindly in time her pain will pass away. God be thanked she knows no pain that cannot pass! I will protect her – aye, that will I, as I will protect all he hath done wrong to and deserted.'

She was so strangely kind through the poor victim's swoons and weeping that the very menials who were called to aid her went back to their hall wondering in their talk of the noble grandness of so great a lady, who on the very brink of her own joy could stoop to protect and comfort a creature so far beneath her, that to most ladies her sorrow and desertion would have been things which were too trivial to count; for 'twas guessed, and talked over with great freedom and much shrewdness, that this was a country victim of Sir John Oxon's, and he having deserted his creditors, was ready enough to desert his rustic beauty, finding her heavy on his hands.

Below stairs the men closing the entrance to the passage with brick, having caught snatches of the servants' gossip, talked of what they heard among themselves as they did their work.

'Ay, a noble lady indeed,' they said. 'For 'tis not a woman's way to be kindly with the cast-off fancy of a man, even when she does not want him herself. He was her own worshipper for many a day, Sir John; and before she took the old earl 'twas said that for a space people believed she loved him. She was but fifteen and a high mettled beauty; and he as handsome as she, and had a blue eye that would melt any woman – but at sixteen he was a town rake, and such tricks as this one he hath played

since he was a lad. 'Tis well indeed for this poor thing her ladyship hath seen her. She hath promised to protect her, and sends
her down to Dunstanwolde with her mother this very week.
Would all fine ladies were of her kind. To hear such things of her
puts a man in the humour to do her work well.'

A Noble Marriage

When the duke came back from France, and to pay his first eager visit to his bride that was to be, her ladyship's lackeys led him not to the Panelled Parlour, but to a room which he had not entered before, it being one she had had the fancy to have remodelled and made into a beautiful closet for herself, her great wealth rendering it possible for her to accomplish changes without the loss of time the owners of limited purses are subjected to in the carrying out of plans. This room she had made as unlike the Panelled Parlour as two rooms would be unlike one another. Its panellings were white, its furnishings were bright and delicate, its draperies flowered with rosebuds tied in clusters with love-knots of pink and blue; it had a large bow window, through which the sunlight streamed, and it was blooming with great rose-bowls overrunning with sweetness.

From a seat in the morning sunshine among the flowers and plants in the bow window, there rose a tall figure in a snow-white robe – a figure like that of a beautiful stately girl who was half an angel. It was my lady, who came to him with blushing cheeks and radiant shining eyes, and was swept into his arms in such a passion of love and blessed tenderness as Heaven might have smiled to see.

'My love! my love!' he breathed. 'My life! my life and soul!'

'My Gerald!' she cried. 'My Gerald – let me say it on your breast a thousand times!'

'My wife!' he said – 'so soon my wife and all my own until life's end.'

'Nay, nay,' she cried, her cheek pressed to his own, 'through all eternity, for Love's life knows no end.'

As it had seemed to her poor lord who had died, so it seemed to this man who lived and so worshipped her – that the wonder of her sweetness was a thing to marvel at with passionate reverence. Being a man of greater mind and poetic imagination than Dunstanwolde, and being himself adored by her, as that poor gentleman had not had the good fortune to be, he had ten thousandfold the power and reason to see the tender radiance of her. As she was taller than other women, so her love seemed higher and greater, and as free from any touch of earthly poverty of feeling as her beauty was from any flaw. In it there could be no doubt, no pride; it could be bounded by no limit, measured by no rule, its depths sounded by no plummet.

His very soul was touched by her great longing to give to him the feeling, and to feel herself, that from the hour that she had become his, her past life was a thing blotted out.

'I am a new created thing,' she said; 'until you called me "Love" I had no life! All before was darkness. 'Twas you, my Gerald, who said, "Let there be light, and there was light."'

'Hush, hush, sweet love,' he said. 'Your words would make me too near God's self.'

'Sure Love is God,' she cried, her hands upon his shoulders, her face uplifted. 'What else? Love we know; Love we worship and kneel to; Love conquers us and gives us Heaven. Until I knew it, I believed naught. Now I kneel each night and pray, and pray, but to be pardoned and made worthy.'

Never before, it was true, had she knelt and prayed, but from this time no nun in her convent knelt oftener or prayed more ardently, and her prayer was ever that the past might be forgiven her, the future blessed, and she taught how to so live that there should be no faintest shadow in the years to come.

'I know not What is above me,' she said. 'I cannot lie and say I love It and believe, but if there is aught, sure It must be a power which is great, else had the world not been so strange a thing, and I – and those who live in it – and if He made us, He must know He is to blame when He has made us weak or evil. And He must understand why we have been so made, and when we throw ourselves into the dust before Him, and pray for help and pardon, surely – surely He will lend an ear! We know naught, we have been told naught; we have but an old book which has been handed down through strange hands and strange tongues, and may be but poor history. We have so little, and we are threatened so; but for love's sake I will pray the poor prayers we are given, and for love's sake there is no dust too low for me to lie in while I plead.'

This was the strange truth – though 'twas not so strange if the world feared not to admit such things – that through her Gerald, who was but noble and high-souled man, she was led to bow before God's throne as the humblest and holiest saint bows, though she had not learned belief and only had learned love.

'But life lasts so short a while,' she said to Osmonde. 'It seems so short when it is spent in such joy as this; and when the day comes – for, oh! Gerald, my soul sees it already – when the day comes that I kneel by your bedside and see your eyes close, or you kneel by mine, it must be that the one who waits behind shall know the parting is not all.'

'It could not be all, beloved,' Osmonde said. 'Love is sure, eternal.'

Often in these blissful hours her way was almost like a child's, she was so tender and so clinging. At times her beauteous, great eyes were full of an imploring which made them seem soft with tears, and thus they were now as she looked up at him.

'I will do all I can,' she said. 'I will obey every law, I will pray often and give alms, and strive to be dutiful and – holy, that in the end He will not thrust me from you; that I may stay near – even in the lowest place, even in the lowest – that I may see your face and know that you see mine. We are so in His power, He can do aught with us; but I will so obey Him and so pray that He will let me in.'

To Anne she went with curious humility, questioning her as to her religious duties and beliefs, asking her what books she read, and what services she attended.

'All your life you have been a religious woman,' she said. 'I used to think it folly, but now –'

'But now –' said Anne.

'I know not what to think,' she answered. 'I would learn.'

But when she listened to Anne's simple homilies, and read her weighty sermons, they but made her restless and unsatisfied.

'Nay, 'tis not that,' she said one day, with a deep sigh. ''Tis more than that; 'tis deeper, and greater, and your sermons do not hold it. They but set my brain to questioning and rebellion.'

But a short time elapsed before the marriage was solemnised, and such a wedding the world of fashion had not taken part in for years, 'twas said. Royalty honoured it; the greatest of the land were proud to count themselves among the guests; the retainers, messengers, and company of the two great houses were so numerous that in the west end of the town the streets wore indeed quite a festal air, with the passing to and fro of servants and gentlefolk with favours upon their arms.

'Twas to the Tower of Camylott, the most beautiful and remote of the bridegroom's several notable seats, that they removed their household, when the irksomeness of the extended ceremonies and entertainments were over – for these they were of too distinguished rank to curtail as lesser personages might have done. But when all things were over, the stately town houses closed, and their equipages rolled out beyond the sight of town into the country roads, the great duke and his great duchess sat hand in hand, gazing into each other's eyes with as simple and ardent a joy as they had been but young 'prentice and country maid, flying to hide from the world their love.

'There is no other woman who is so like a queen,' Osmonde said, with tenderest smiling. 'And yet your eyes wear a look so young in these days that they are like a child's. In all their beauty, I have never seen them so before.'

'It is because I am a new created thing, as I have told you, love,' she answered, and leaned towards him. 'Do you not know

I never was a child. I bring myself to you new born. Make of me then what a woman should be – to be beloved of husband and of God. Teach me, my Gerald. I am your child and servant.'

'Twas ever thus, that her words when they were such as these were ended upon his breast as she was swept there by his impassioned arm. She was so goddess-like and beautiful a being, her life one strangely dominant and brilliant series of triumphs, and yet she came to him with such softness and humility of passion, that scarcely could he think himself a waking man.

'Surely,' he said, 'it is a thing too wondrous and too full of joy's splendour to be true.'

In the golden afternoon, when the sun was deepening and mellowing towards its setting, they and their retinue entered Camylott. The bells pealed from the grey belfry of the old church; the villagers came forth in clean smocks and Sunday cloaks of scarlet, and stood in the street and by the roadside curtseying and baring their heads with rustic cheers; little country girls with red cheeks threw posies before the horses' feet, and into the equipage itself when they were of the bolder sort. Their chariot passed beneath archways of flowers and boughs, and from the battlements of the Tower of Camylott there floated a flag in the soft wind.

'God save your Graces,' the simple people cried. 'God give your Graces joy and long life! Lord, what a beautiful pair they be. And though her Grace was said to be a proud lady, how sweetly she smiles at a poor body. God love ye, madam! Madam, God love ye!'

Her Grace of Osmonde leaned forward in her equipage and smiled at the people with the face of an angel.

'I will teach them to love me, Gerald,' she said. 'I have not had love enough.'

'Has not all the world loved you?' he said.

'Nay,' she answered, 'only you, and Dunstanwolde and Anne.'

Late at night they walked together on the broad terrace before the Tower. The blue-black vault of heaven above them was studded with myriads of God's brilliants; below them was spread out the beauty of the land, the rolling plains, the soft low hills, the forests and moors folded and hidden in the swathing robe of the night; from the park and gardens floated upward the freshness of acres of thick sward and deep fern thicket, the fragrance of roses and a thousand flowers, the tender sighing of the wind through the huge oaks and beeches bordering the avenues, and reigning like kings over the seeming boundless grassy spaces.

As lovers have walked since the days of Eden they walked together, no longer duke and duchess, but man and woman – near to Paradise as human beings may draw until God breaks the chain binding them to earth; and, indeed, it would seem that such hours are given to the straining human soul that it may know that somewhere perfect joy must be, since sometimes the gates are for a moment opened that Heaven's light may shine through, so that human eyes may catch glimpses of the white and golden glories within.

His arm held her, she leaned against him, their slow steps so harmonising the one with the other that they accorded with the harmony of music; the nightingales trilling and bubbling in the rose trees were not affrighted by the low murmur of their voices; perchance, this night they were so near to Nature that the barriers were o'erpassed, and they and the singers were akin.

'Oh! to be a woman,' Clorinda murmured. 'To be a woman at last. All other things I have been, and have been called "Huntress", "Goddess", "Beauty", "Empress", "Conqueror", – but never "Woman". And had our paths not crossed, I think I never could have known what 'twas to be one, for to be a woman one must close with the man who is one's mate. It must not be that one looks down, or only pities or protects and guides; and only to a few a mate seems given. And I – Gerald, how dare I walk thus at your side and feel your heart so beat near mine, and know you love me, and so worship you – so worship you –'

She turned and threw herself upon his breast, which was so near.

'Oh, woman! woman!' he breathed, straining her close. 'Oh, woman who is mine, though I am but man.'

'We are but one,' she said; 'one breath, one soul, one thought, and one desire. Were it not so, I were not woman and your wife, nor you man and my soul's lover as you are. If it were not so, we were still apart, though we were wedded a thousand times. Apart, what are we but like lopped-off limbs; welded together, we are – this.' And for a moment they spoke not, and a nightingale on the rose vine, clambering o'er the terrace's balustrade, threw up its little head and sang as if to the myriads of golden stars. They stood and listened, hand in hand, her sweet breast rose and fell, her lovely face was lifted to the bespangled sky.

'Of all this,' she said, 'I am a part, as I am a part of you. Tonight, as the great earth throbs, and as the stars tremble, and as the wind sighs, so I, being woman, throb and am tremulous and sigh also. The earth lives for the sun, and through strange mysteries blooms forth each season with fruits and flowers; love is my sun, and through its sacredness I may bloom too, and be as noble as the earth and that it bears.'

An Heir Is Born

In a fair tower whose windows looked out upon spreading woods, and rich lovely plains stretching to the freshness of the sea, Mistress Anne had her abode which her duchess sister had given to her for her own living in as she would. There she dwelt and prayed and looked on the new life which so beauteously unfolded itself before her day by day, as the leaves of a great tree unfold from buds and become noble branches, housing birds and their nests, shading the earth and those sheltering beneath them, braving centuries of storms.

To this simile her simple mind oft reverted, for indeed it seemed to her that naught more perfect and more noble in its high likeness to pure Nature and the fulfilling of God's will than the passing days of these two lives could be.

'As the first two lived – Adam and Eve in their garden of Eden – they seem to me,' she used to say to her own heart; 'but the Tree of Knowledge was not forbidden them, and it has taught them naught ignoble.'

As she had been wont to watch her sister from behind the ivy of her chamber windows, so she often watched her now, though there was no fear in her hiding, only tenderness, it being a pleasure to her full of wonder and reverence to see this beautiful and stately pair go lovingly and in high and gentle converse side by side, up and down the terrace, through the paths, among the beds of flowers, under the thick branched trees and over the sward's softness.

'It is as if I saw Love's self, and dwelt with it – the love God's nature made,' she said, with gentle sighs.

For if these two had been great and beauteous before, it seemed in these days as if life and love glowed within them, and shone through their mere bodies as a radiant light shines through alabaster lamps. The strength of each was so the being of the other that no thought could take form in the brain of one without the other's stirring with it.

'Neither of us dare be ignoble,' Osmonde said, 'for 'twould make poor and base the one who was not so in truth.'

''Twas not the way of my Lady Dunstanwolde to make a man feel that he stood in church,' a frivolous court wit once said, 'but in sooth her Grace of Osmonde has a look in her lustrous eyes which accords not with scandalous stories and playhouse jests.'

And true it was that when they went to town they carried with them the illumining of the pure fire which burned within their souls, and bore it all unknowing in the midst of the trivial or designing world, which knew not what it was that glowed about them, making things bright which had seemed dull, and revealing darkness where there had been brilliant glare.

They returned not to the house which had been my Lord of Dunstanwolde's, but went to the duke's own great mansion, and there lived splendidly and in hospitable state. Royalty honoured them, and all the wits came there, some of those gentlemen who writ verses and dedications being by no means averse to meeting noble lords and ladies, and finding in their loves and graces material which might be useful. 'Twas not only Mr Addison and Mr Steele, Dr Swift and Mr Pope, who were made welcome in the stately rooms, but others who were more humble, not yet having won their spurs, and how these worshipped her Grace for the generous kindness which was not the fashion, until she set it, among great ladies, their odes and verses could scarce express.

'They are so poor,' she said to her husband. 'They are so poor, and yet in their starved souls there is a thing which can less bear flouting than the dull content which rules in others. I know not whether 'tis a curse or a boon to be born so. 'Tis a bitter thing when the bird that flutters in them has only little wings. All the more should those who are strong protect and comfort them.'

She comforted so many creatures. In strange parts of the town, where no other lady would have dared to go to give alms, it was rumoured that she went and did noble things privately.

In dark kennels, where thieves hid and vagrants huddled, she carried her beauty and her stateliness, the which when they shone on the poor rogues and victims housed there seemed like the beams of the warm and golden sun.

Once in a filthy hovel in a black alley she came upon a poor girl dying of a loathsome ill, and as she stood by her bed of rags she heard in her delirium the uttering of one man's name again and again, and when she questioned those about she found that the sufferer had been a little country wench enticed to town by this man for a plaything, and in a few weeks cast off to give birth to a child in the almshouse, and then go down to the depths of vice in the kennel.

'What is the name she says?' her Grace asked the hag nearest to her, and least maudlin with liquor. 'I would be sure I heard it aright.'

''Tis the name of a gentleman, your ladyship may be sure,' the beldam answered; ''tis always the name of a gentleman. And this is one I know well, for I have heard more than one poor soul mumbling it and raving at him in her last hours. One there was, and I knew her, a pretty rosy thing in her country days, not sixteen, and distraught with love for him, and lay in the street by his door praying him to take her back when he threw her off, until the watch drove her away. And she was so mad with love and grief she killed her girl child when 'twas born i' the kennel, sobbing and crying that it should not live to be like her and bear others. And she was condemned to death, and swung for it on Tyburn Tree. And, Lord! how she cried his name as she jolted on her coffin to the gallows, and when the hangman put the rope round her shuddering little fair neck. "Oh, John," screams she, "John Oxon, God forgive thee! Nay, 'tis God should be forgiven for letting thee to live and me to die like this." Aye, 'twas a bitter sight! She was so little and so young, and so affrighted. The hangman could scarce hold her. I was i' the midst o' the crowd and cried to her to strive to stand still, 'twould be the sooner over. But that she could not. "Oh, John," she screams, "John Oxon, God forgive thee! Nay, 'tis God should be forgiven for letting thee to live and me to die like this!"'

Till the last hour of the poor creature who lay before her when she heard this thing, her Grace of Osmonde saw that she was tended, took her from her filthy hovel, putting her in a decent house and going to her day by day, until she received her last breath, holding her hand while the poor wench lay staring up at her beauteous face and her great deep eyes, whose lustrousness held such power to sustain, protect, and comfort.

'Be not afraid, poor soul,' she said, 'be not afraid. I will stay near thee. Soon all will end in sleep, and if thou wakest, sure there will be Christ who died, and wipes all tears away. Hear me say it to thee for a prayer,' and she bent low and said it soft and clear into the deadening ear, 'He wipes all tears away – He wipes all tears away.'

The great strength she had used in the old days to conquer and subdue, to win her will and to defend her way, seemed now a power but to protect the suffering and uphold the weak, and this she did, not alone in hovels but in the brilliant court and world of fashion, for there she found suffering and weakness also, all the more bitter and sorrowful since it dared not cry aloud. The grandeur of her beauty, the elevation of her rank, the splendour of her wealth would have made her a protector of great strength, but that which upheld all those who turned to her was that which dwelt within the high soul of her, the courage and power of love for all things human which bore upon itself, as if upon an eagle's outspread wings, the woes dragging themselves broken and halting upon earth. The starving beggar in the kennel felt it, and, not knowing wherefore, drew a longer, deeper breath, as if of purer, more exalted air; the poor poet in his garret was fed by it, and having stood near or spoken to her, went back to his lair with lightening eyes and soul warmed to believe that the words his Muse might speak the world might stay to hear.

From the hour she stayed the last moments of John Oxon's victim she set herself a work to do. None knew it but herself at first, and later Anne, for 'twas done privately. From the hag who had told her of the poor girl's hanging upon Tyburn Tree, she learned things by close questioning, which to the old woman's dull wit seemed but the curiousness of a great lady, and from others who stood too deep in awe of her to think of her as a mere human being, she gathered clues which led her far in the tracing of the evils following one wicked, heartless life. Where she could hear of man, woman, or child on whom John Oxon's sins had fallen, or who had suffered wrong by him, there she went to help, to give light, to give comfort and encouragement. Strangely, as it seemed to them, and as if done by the hand of Heaven, the poor tradesmen he had robbed were paid their dues, youth he had led into evil ways was checked mysteriously and set in better paths; women he had dragged downward were given aid and chance of peace or happiness; children he had cast upon the world, unfathered, and with no prospect but the education of the gutter, and a life of crime, were cared for by a powerful unseen hand. The pretty country girl saved by his death, protected by her Grace, and living innocently at Dunstanwolde, memory being merciful to youth, forgot him, gained back her young roses, and learned to smile and hope as though he had been but a name.

'Since 'twas I who killed him,' said her Grace to her inward soul, ''tis I must live his life which I took from him, and making it better I may be forgiven – if there is One who dares to say to the poor thing He made, "I will not forgive."'

Surely it was said there had never been lives so beautiful and noble as those the Duke of Osmonde and his lady lived as time went by. The Tower of Camylott, where they had spent the first months of their wedded life, they loved better than any other of their seats, and there they spent as much time as their duties of Court and State allowed them. It was indeed a splendid and beautiful estate, the stately tower being built upon an eminence, and there rolling out before it the most lovely land in England, moorland and hills, thick woods and broad meadows, the edge of the heather dipping to show the soft silver of the sea.

Here was this beauteous woman chatelaine and queen, wife of her husband as never before, he thought, had wife blessed and glorified the existence of mortal man. All her great beauty she gave to him in tender, joyous tribute; all her great gifts of mind and wit and grace it seemed she valued but as they were joys to him; in his stately households in town and country she reigned a lovely empress, adored and obeyed with reverence by every man or woman who served her and her lord. Among the people on his various estates she came and went a tender goddess of benevolence. When she appeared amid them in the first months of her wedded life, the humble souls regarded her with awe not unmixed with fear, having heard such wild stories of her youth at her father's house, and of her proud state and bitter wit in the great London world when she had been my Lady Dunstanwolde; but when she came among them all else was forgotten in their wonder at her graciousness and noble way.

'To see her come into a poor body's cottage, so tall and grand a lady, and with such a carriage as she hath,' they said, hobnobbing together in their talk of her, 'looking as if a crown of gold should sit on her high black head, and then to hear her gentle speech and see the look in her eyes as if she was but a simple new-married girl, full of her joy, and her heart big with the wish that all other women should be as happy as herself, it is, forsooth, a beauteous sight to see.'

'Ay, and no hovel too poor for her, and no man or woman too sinful,' was said again.

'Heard ye how she found that poor wench of Haylits lying sobbing among the fern in the Tower woods, and stayed and knelt beside her to hear her trouble? The poor soul has gone to ruin at fourteen, and her father, finding her out, beat her and thrust her from his door, and her Grace coming through the wood at sunset – it being her way to walk about for mere pleasure as though she had no coach to ride in – the girl says she came through the golden glow as if she had been one of God's angels – and she kneeled and took the poor wench in her arms – as strong as a man, Betty says, but as soft as a young mother – and she said to her things surely no mortal lady ever said before – that she knew naught of a surety of what God's true will might be, or if His laws were those that have been made by man concerning marriage by priests saying common words, but that she surely knew of a man whose name was Christ, and He had taught love and helpfulness and pity, and for His sake, He having earned our trust in Him, whether He was God or man, because He hung and died in awful torture on the Cross – for His sake all of us must love and help and pity – "I you, poor Betty," were her very words, "and you me." And then she went to the girl's father and mother, and so talked to them that she brought them to weeping, and begging Betty to come home; and also she went to her sweetheart, Tom Beck, and made so tender a story to him of the poor pretty wench whose love for him had brought her to such trouble, that she stirred him up to falling in love again, which is not man's way at such times, and in a week's time he and Betty went to church together, her Grace setting them up in a cottage on the estate.'

'I used all my wit and all my tenderest words to make a picture that would fire and touch him, Gerald,' her Grace said, sitting at her husband's side, in a great window, from which they often watched the sunset in the valley spread below; 'and that with which I am so strong sometimes – I know not what to call it, but 'tis a power people bend to, that I know – that I used upon him to waken his dull soul and brain. Whose fault is it that they are dull? Poor lout, he was born so, as I was born strong and passionate, and as you were born noble and pure and high.

I led his mind back to the past, when he had been made happy by the sight of Betty's little smiling, blushing face, and when he had kissed her and made love in the hayfields. And this I said – though 'twas not a thing I have learned from any chaplain – that when 'twas said he should make an honest woman of her, it was my thought that she had been honest from the first, being too honest to know that the world was not so, and that even the man a woman loved with all her soul, might be a rogue, and have no honesty in him. And at last – 'twas when I talked to him about the child – and that I put my whole soul's strength in – he burst out a-crying like a schoolboy, and said indeed she was a fond little thing and had loved him, and he had loved her, and 'twas a shame he had so done by her, and he had not meant it at the first, but she was so simple, and he had been a villain, but if he married her now, he would be called a fool, and laughed at for his pains. Then was I angry, Gerald, and felt my eyes flash, and I stood up tall and spoke fiercely: "Let them dare," I said – "let any man or woman dare, and then will they see what his Grace will say."'

Osmonde drew her to his breast, laughing into her lovely eyes.

'Nay, 'tis not his Grace who need be called on,' he said; ''tis her Grace they love and fear, and will obey; though 'tis the sweetest, womanish thing that you should call on me when you are power itself, and can so rule all creatures you come near.'

'Nay,' she said, with softly pleading face, 'let me not rule. Rule for me, or but help me; I so long to say your name that they may know I speak but as your wife.'

'Who is myself,' he answered – 'my very self.'

'Ay,' she said, with a little nod of her head, 'that I know – that I am yourself; and 'tis because of this that one of us cannot be proud with the other, for there is no other, there is only one. And I am wrong to say, "Let me not rule," for 'tis as if I said, "You must not rule." I meant surely, "God give me strength to be as noble in ruling as our love should make me." But just as one tree is a beech and one an oak, just as the grass stirs when the summer wind blows over it, so a woman is a woman, and 'tis her nature to find her joy in saying such words to the man who loves her, when she loves as I do. Her heart is so full that she must joy to say her husband's name as that of one she cannot think without – who is her life as is her blood and her pulses beating. 'Tis a joy to say your name, Gerald, as it will be a joy' – and she looked far out across the sun-goldened valley and plains, with a strange, heavenly sweet smile – 'as it will be a joy to say our child's – and put his little mouth to my full breast.'

'Sweet love,' he cried, drawing her by the hand that he might meet the radiance of her look – 'heart's dearest!'

She did not withhold her lovely eyes from him, but withdrew them from the sunset's mist of gold, and the clouds piled as it were at the gates of heaven, and they seemed to bring back some of the far-off glory with them. Indeed, neither her smile nor she seemed at that moment to be things of earth. She held out her fair, noble arms, and he sprang to her, and so they stood, side beating against side.

'Yes, love,' she said – 'yes, love – and I have prayed, my Gerald, that I may give you sons who shall be men like you. But when I give you women children, I shall pray with all my soul for them – that they may be just and strong and noble, and life begin for them as it began not for me.'

In the morning of a spring day when the cuckoos cried in the woods, and May blossomed thick, white and pink, in all the hedges, the bells in the grey church-steeple at Camylott rang out a joyous, jangling peal, telling all the village that the heir had been born at the Tower. Children stopped in their play to listen, men at their work in field and barn; good gossips ran out of their cottage door, wiping their arms dry, from their tubs and scrubbing-buckets, their honest red faces broadening into maternal grins.

'Ay, 'tis well over, that means surely,' one said to the other; 'and a happy day has begun for the poor lady – though God knows she bore herself queenly to the very last, as if she could have carried her burden for another year, and blenched not a bit as other women do. Bless mother and child, say I.'

'And 'tis an heir,' said another. 'She promised us that we should know almost as quick as she did, and commanded old Rowe to ring a peal, and then strike one bell loud between if 'twere a boy, and two if 'twere a girl child. 'Tis a boy, heard you, and 'twas like her wit to invent such a way to tell us.'

In four other villages the chimes rang just as loud and merrily, and the women talked, and blessed her Grace and her young child, and casks of ale were broached, and oxen roasted, and work stopped, and dancers footed it upon the green.

'Surely the newborn thing comes here to happiness,' 'twas said everywhere, 'for never yet was woman loved as is his mother.'

In her stately bed her Grace the duchess lay, with the face of the Mother Mary, and her man-child drinking from her breast. The duke walked softly up and down, so full of joy that he could not sit still. When he had entered first, it was his wife's self who had sat upright in her bed, and herself laid his son within his arms.

'None other shall lay him there,' she said, 'I have given him to you. He is a great child, but he has not taken from me my strength.'

He was indeed a great child, even at his first hour, of limbs and countenance so noble that nurses and physicians regarded him amazed. He was the offspring of a great love, of noble bodies and great souls. Did such powers alone create human beings, the earth would be peopled with a race of giants.

Amid the veiled spring sunshine and the flower-scented silence, broken only by the twittering of birds nesting in the ivy, her Grace lay soft asleep, her son resting on her arm, when

Anne stole to look at her and her child. Through the night she had knelt praying in her chamber, and now she knelt again. She kissed the newborn thing's curled rose-leaf hand and the lace frill of his mother's night-rail. She dared not further disturb them.

'Sure God forgives,' she breathed – 'for Christ's sake. He would not give this little tender thing a punishment to bear.'

Mother Anne

There was no punishment. The tender little creature grew as a blossom grows from bud to fairest bloom. His mother flowered as he, and spent her days in noble cherishing of him and tender care. Such motherhood and wifehood as were hers were as fair statues raised to Nature's self.

'Once I thought that I was under ban,' she said to her lord in one of their sweetest hours; 'but I have been given love and a life, and so I know it cannot be. Do I fill all your being, Gerald?'

'All, all!' he cried, 'my sweet, sweet woman.'

'Leave I no longing unfulfilled, no duty undone, to you, dear love, to the world, to human suffering I might aid? I pray Christ with all passionate humbleness that I may not.'

'He grants your prayer,' he answered, his eyes moist with worshipping tenderness.

'And this white soul given to me from the outer bounds we know not – it has no stain; and the little human body it wakened to life in – think you that Christ will help me to fold them in love high and pure enough, and teach the human body to do honour to its soul? 'Tis not monkish scorn of itself that I would teach the body; it is so beautiful and noble a thing, and so full of the power of joy. Surely That which made it – in His own image – would not that it should despise itself and its own wonders, but do them reverence, and rejoice in them nobly, knowing all their seasons and their changes, counting not youth folly, and manhood sinful, or age aught but gentle ripeness passing onward? I pray for a great soul, and great wit, and greater power to help this fair human thing to grow, and love, and live.'

These had been born and had rested hid within her when she lay a babe struggling 'neath her dead mother's corpse. Through the darkness of untaught years they had grown but slowly, being so unfitly and unfairly nourished; but Life's sun but falling on her, they seemed to strive to fair fruition with her days.

'Twas not mere love she gave her offspring – for she bore others as years passed, until she was the mother of four sons and two girls, children of strength and beauty as noted as her own; she gave them of her constant thought, and an honour of their humanity such as taught them reverence of themselves as of all other human things. Their love for her was such a passion as their father bore her. She was the noblest creature that they knew; her beauty, her great unswerving love, her truth, were things bearing to their child eyes the unchangingness of God's stars in heaven.

'Why is she not the Queen?' a younger one asked his father once, having been to London and seen the Court. 'The Queen is not so beautiful and grand as she, and she could so well reign over the people. She is always just and honourable, and fears nothing.'

From her side Mistress Anne was rarely parted. In her fair retreat at Camylott she had lived a life all undisturbed by outward things. When the children were born strange joy came to her.

'Be his mother also,' the duchess had said when she had drawn the clothes aside to show her first-born sleeping in her arm. 'You were made to be the mother of things, Anne.'

'Nay, or they had been given to me,' Anne had answered.

'Mine I will share with you,' her Grace had said, lifting her Madonna face. 'Kiss me, sister – kiss him, too, and bless him. Your life has been so innocent it must be good that you should love and guard him.'

'Twas sweet to see the wit she showed in giving to poor Anne the feeling that she shared her motherhood. She shared her tenderest cares and duties with her. Together they bathed and clad the child in the morning, this being their high festival, in which the nurses shared but in the performance of small duties. Each day they played with him and laughed as women will at such dear times, kissing his grand round limbs, crying out at their growth, worshipping his little rosy feet, and smothering him with caresses. And then they put him to sleep, Anne sitting close while his mother fed him from her breast until his small red mouth parted and slowly released her.

When he could toddle about and was beginning to say words, there was a morning when she bore him to Anne's tower that they might joy in him together, as was their way. It was a beautiful thing to see her walk carrying him in the strong and lovely curve of her arm as if his sturdy babyhood were of no more weight than a rose, and he cuddling against her, clinging and crowing, his wide brown eyes shining with delight.

'He has come to pay thee court, Anne,' she said. 'He is a great gallant, and knows how we are his loving slaves. He comes to say his new word that I have taught him.'

She set him down where he stood holding to Anne's knee and showing his new pearl teeth, in a rosy grin; his mother knelt beside him, beginning her coaxing.

'Who is she?' she said, pointing with her finger at Anne's face, her own full of lovely fear lest the child should not speak rightly his lesson. 'What is her name? Mammy's man say –' and she mumbled softly with her crimson mouth at his ear.

The child looked up at Anne, with baby wit and laughter in his face, and stammered sweetly –

'Muz – Muzzer – Anne,' he said, and then being pleased with his cleverness, danced on his little feet and said it over and over.

Clorinda caught him up and set him on Anne's lap.

'Know you what he calls you?' she said. ''Tis but a mumble, his little tongue is not nimble enough for clearness, but he says it his pretty best. 'Tis Mother Anne, he says – 'tis Mother Anne.'

And then they were in each other's arms, the child between them, he kissing both and clasping both, with little laughs of joy as if they were but one creature.

Each child born they clasped and kissed so, and were so clasped and kissed by; each one calling the tender unwed woman

'Mother Anne', and having a special lovingness for her, she being the creature each one seemed to hover about with innocent protection and companionship.

The wonder of Anne's life grew deeper to her hour by hour, and where she had before loved, she learned to worship, for 'twas indeed worship that her soul was filled with. She could not look back and believe that she had not dreamed a dream of all the fears gone by and that they held. This – this was true – the beauty of these days, the love of them, the generous deeds, the sweet courtesies, and gentle words spoken. This beauteous woman dwelling in her husband's heart, giving him all joy of life and love, ruling queenly and gracious in his house, bearing him noble children, and tending them with the very genius of tenderness and wisdom.

But in Mistress Anne herself life had never been strong; she was of the fibre of her mother, who had died in youth, crushed by its cruel weight, and to her, living had been so great and terrible a thing. There had not been given to her the will to battle with the Fate that fell to her, the brain to reason and disentangle problems, or the power to set them aside. So while her Grace of Osmonde seemed but to gain greater state and beauty in her ripening, her sister's frail body grew more frail, and seemed to shrink and age. Yet her face put on a strange worn sweetness, and her soft, dull eyes had a look almost like a saint's who looks at heaven. She prayed much, and did many charitable works both in town and country. She read her books of devotion, and went much to church, sitting with a reverend face through many a dull and lengthy sermon she would have felt it sacrilegious to think of with aught but pious admiration. In the middle of the night it was her custom to rise and offer up prayers through the dark hours. She was an humble soul who greatly feared and trembled before her God.

'I waken in the night sometimes,' the fair, tall child Daphne said once to her mother, 'and Mother Anne is there – she kneels and prays beside my bed. She kneels and prays so by each one of us many a night.'

''Tis because she is so pious a woman and so loves us,' said young John, in his stately, generous way. The house of Osmonde had never had so fine and handsome a creature for its heir. He o'ertopped every boy of his age in height, and the bearing of his lovely youthful body was masculine grace itself.

The town and the Court knew these children, and talked of their beauty and growth as they had talked of their mother's.

'To be the mate of such a woman, the father of such heirs, is a fate a man might pray God for,' 'twas said. 'Love has not grown stale with them. Their children are the very blossoms of it. Her eyes are deeper pools of love each year.'

'In One who will do justice, and demands that it shall be done to each thing He has made, by each who bears His image'

'Twas in these days Sir Jeoffry came to his end, it being in such way as had been often prophesied; and when this final hour came, there was but one who could give him comfort, and this was the daughter whose youth he had led with such careless evilness to harm.

If he had wondered at her when she had been my Lady Dunstanwolde, as her Grace of Osmonde he regarded her with heavy awe. Never had she been able to lead him to visit her at her house in town or at any other which was her home. ''Tis all too grand for me, your Grace,' he would say; 'I am a country yokel, and have hunted and drank, and lived too hard to look well among town gentlemen. I must be drunk at dinner, and when I am in liquor I am no ornament to a duchess' drawing room. But what a woman you have grown,' he would say, staring at her and shaking his head. 'Each time I clap eyes on you 'tis to marvel at you, remembering what a baggage you were, and how you kept from slipping by the way. There was Jack Oxon, now,' he added one day – 'after you married Dunstanwolde, I heard a pretty tale of Jack – that he had made a wager among his friends in town – he was a braggart devil, Jack – that he would have you, though you were so scornful; and knowing him to be a liar, his fellows said that unless he could bring back a raven lock six feet long to show them, he had lost his bet, for they would believe no other proof. And finely they scoffed at him when he came back saying that he had had one, but had hid it away for safety when he was drunk, and could not find it again. They so flouted and jeered at him that swords were drawn, and blood as well. But though he was a beauty and a crafty rake-hell fellow, you were too sharp for him. Had you not had so shrewd a wit and strong a will, you would not have been the greatest duchess in England, Clo, as well as the finest woman.'

'Nay,' she answered – 'in those days – nay, let us not speak of them! I would blot them out – out.'

As time went by, and the years spent in drink and debauchery began to tell even on the big, strong body which should have served any other man bravely long past his threescore and ten, Sir Jeoffry drank harder and lived more wildly, sometimes being driven desperate by dullness, his coarse pleasures having lost their potency.

'Liquor is not as strong as it once was,' he used to grumble, 'and there are fewer things to stir a man to frolic. Lord, what roaring days and nights a man could have thirty years ago.'

So in his efforts to emulate such nights and days, he plunged deeper and deeper into new orgies; and one night, after a heavy day's hunting, sitting at the head of his table with his old companions, he suddenly leaned forward, staring with starting eyes at an empty chair in a dark corner. His face grew purple, and he gasped and gurgled.

'What is't, Jeoff?' old Eldershawe cried, touching his shoulder with a shaking hand. 'What's the man staring at, as if he had gone mad?'

'Jack,' cried Sir Jeoffry, his eyes still farther starting from their sockets. 'Jack! what say you? I cannot hear.'

The next instant he sprang up, shrieking, and thrusting with his hands as if warding something off.

'Keep back!' he yelled. 'There is green mould on thee. Where hast thou been to grow mouldy? Keep back! Where hast thou been?'

His friends at table started up, staring at him and losing colour; he shrieked so loud and strangely, he clutched his hair with his hands, and fell into his chair, raving, clutching, and staring, or dashing his head down upon the table to hide his face, and then raising it as if he could not resist being drawn in his affright to gaze again. There was no soothing him. He shouted, and struggled with those who would have held him. 'Twas Jack Oxon who was there, he swore – Jack, who kept stealing slowly nearer to him, his face and his fine clothes damp and green, he beat at the air with mad hands, and at last fell upon the floor, and rolled, foaming at the mouth.

They contrived, after great strugglings, to bear him to his chamber, but it took the united strength of all who would stay near him to keep him from making an end of himself. By the dawn of day his boon companions stood by him with their garments torn to tatters, their faces drenched with sweat, and their own eyes almost starting from their sockets; the doctor who had been sent for, coming in no hurry, but scowled and shook his head when he beheld him.

'He is a dead man,' he said, 'and the wonder is that this has not come before. He is sodden with drink and rotten with ill-living, besides being past all the strength of youth. He dies of the life he has lived.'

'Twas little to be expected that his boon companions could desert their homes and pleasures and tend his horrors longer than a night. Such a sight as he presented did not inspire them to cheerful spirits.

'Lord,' said Sir Chris Crowell, 'to see him clutch his flesh and shriek and mouth, is enough to make a man live sober for his remaining days,' and he shook his big shoulders with a shudder.

'Ugh!' he said, 'God grant I may make a better end. He writhes as in hellfire.'

'There is but one on earth who will do aught for him,' said Eldershawe. ''Tis handsome Clo, who is a duchess; but she will come and tend him, I could swear. Even when she was a lawless devil of a child she had a way of standing by her friends and fearing naught.'

So after taking counsel together they sent for her, and in as many hours as it took to drive from London, her coach stood before the door. By this time all the household was panic-stricken and in hopeless disorder, the women-servants scattered and shuddering in far corners of the house; such men as could get out of the way having found work to do afield or in the kennels, for none had nerve to stay where they could hear the madman's shrieks and howls.

Her Grace, entering the house, went with her woman straight to her chamber, and shortly emerged therefrom, stripped of her rich apparel, and clad in a gown of strong blue linen, her hair wound close, her white hands bare of any ornament, save the band of gold which was her wedding ring. A servingwoman might have been clad so; but the plainness of her garb but made her height, and strength, so reveal themselves, that the mere sight of her woke somewhat that was like to awe in the eyes of the servants who beheld her as she passed.

She needed not to be led, but straightway followed the awful sounds, until she reached the chamber behind whose door they were shut. Upon the huge disordered bed, Sir Jeoffry writhed, and tried to tear himself, his great sinewy and hairy body almost stark. Two of the stable men were striving to hold him.

The duchess went to his bedside and stood there, laying her strong white hand upon his shuddering shoulder.

'Father,' she said, in a voice so clear, and with such a ring of steady command, as, the men said later, might have reached a dead man's ear. 'Father, 'tis Clo!'

Sir Jeoffry writhed his head round and glared at her, with starting eyes and foaming mouth.

'Who says 'tis Clo?' he shouted. ''Tis a lie! She was ever a bigger devil than any other, though she was but a handsome wench. Jack himself could not manage her. She beat him, and would beat him now. 'Tis a lie!'

All through that day and night the power of her Grace's white arm was the thing which saved him from dashing out his brains. The two men could not have held him, and at his greatest frenzy they observed that now and then his bloodshot eye would glance aside at the beauteous face above him. The sound of the word 'Clo' had struck upon his brain and wakened an echo.

She sent away the men to rest, calling for others in their places; but leave the bedside herself she would not. 'Twas a strange thing to see her strength and bravery, which could not be beaten down. When the doctor came again he found her there, and changed his surly and reluctant manner in the presence of a duchess, and one who in her close linen gown wore such a mien.

'You should not have left him,' she said to him unbendingly, 'even though I myself can see there is little help that can be given. Thought you his Grace and I would brook that he should die alone if we could not have reached him?'

Those words 'his Grace and I' put a new face upon the matter, and all was done that lay within the man's skill; but most was he disturbed concerning the lady, who would not be sent to rest, and whose noble consort would be justly angered if she were allowed to injure her superb health.

'His Grace knew what I came to do and how I should do it,' the duchess said, unbending still. 'But for affairs of State which held him, he would have been here at my side.'

She held her place throughout the second night, and that was worse than the first – the paroxysms growing more and more awful; for Jack was within a yard, and stretched out a green and mouldy hand, the finger-bones showing through the flesh, the while he smiled awfully.

At last one pealing scream rang out after another, until after making his shuddering body into an arc resting on heels and head, the madman fell exhausted, his flesh all quaking before the eye. Then the duchess waved the men who helped, away. She sat upon the bed's edge close – close to her father's body, putting her two firm hands on either of his shoulders, holding him so, and bent down, looking into his wild face, as if she fixed upon his very soul all the power of her wondrous will.

'Father,' she said, 'look at my face. Thou canst if thou wilt. Look at my face. Then wilt thou see 'tis Clo – and she will stand by thee.'

She kept her gaze upon his very pupils; and though 'twas at first as if his eyes strove to break away from her look, their effort was controlled by her steadfastness, and they wandered back at last, and her great orbs held them. He heaved a long breath, half a big, broken sob, and lay still, staring up at her.

'Ay,' he said, ''tis Clo! 'tis Clo!'

The sweat began to roll from his forehead, and the tears down his cheeks. He broke forth, wailing like a child.

'Clo – Clo,' he said, 'I am in hell.'

She put her hand on his breast, keeping will and eyes set on him.

'Nay,' she answered; 'thou art on earth, and in thine own bed, and I am here, and will not leave thee.'

She made another sign to the men who stood and stared aghast in wonder at her, but feeling in the very air about her the spell to which the madness had given way.

''Twas not mere human woman who sat there,' they said afterwards in the stables among their fellows. ''Twas somewhat more. Had such a will been in an evil thing a man's hair would have risen on his skull at the seeing of it.'

'Go now,' she said to them, 'and send women to set the place in order.'

She had seen delirium and death enough in the doings of her deeds of mercy, to know that his strength had gone and death was coming. His bed and room were made orderly, and at last he lay in clean linen, with all made straight. Soon his eyes seemed to sink into his head and stare from hollows, and his skin grew grey, but ever he stared only at his daughter's face.

'Clo,' he said at last, 'stay by me! Clo, go not away!'

'I shall not go,' she answered.

She drew a seat close to his bed and took his hand. It lay knotted and gnarled and swollen-veined upon her smooth palm, and with her other hand she stroked it. His breath came weak and quick, and fear grew in his eyes.

'What is it, Clo?' he said. 'What is't?'

''Tis weakness,' replied she, soothing him. 'Soon you will sleep.'

'Ay,' he said, with a breath like a sob. ''Tis over.'

His big body seemed to collapse, he shrank so in the bed-clothes.

'What day o' the year is it?' he asked.

'The tenth of August,' was her answer.

'Sixty-nine years from this day was I born,' he said, 'and now 'tis done.'

'Nay,' said she – 'nay – God grant –'

'Ay,' he said, 'done. Would there were nine and sixty more. What a man I was at twenty. I want not to die, Clo. I want to live – to live – live, and be young,' gulping, 'with strong muscle and moist flesh. Sixty-nine years – and they are gone!'

He clung to her hand, and stared at her with awful eyes. Through all his life he had been but a great, strong, human carcass; and he was now but the same carcass worn out, and at death's door. Of not one human thing but of himself had he ever thought, not one creature but himself had he ever loved – and now he lay at the end, harking back only to the wicked years gone by.

'None can bring them back,' he shuddered. 'Not even thou, Clo, who art so strong. None – none! Canst pray, Clo?' with the gasp of a craven.

'Not as chaplains do,' she answered. 'I believe not in a God who clamours but for praise.'

'What dost believe in, then?'

'In One who will do justice, and demands that it shall be done to each thing He has made, by each who bears His image – ay,

236

and mercy too – but justice always, for justice is mercy's highest self.'

Who knows the mysteries of the human soul – who knows the workings of the human brain? The God who is just alone. In this man's mind, which was so near a simple beast's in all its movings, some remote, unborn consciousness was surely reached and vaguely set astir by the clear words thus spoken.

'Clo, Clo!' he cried, 'Clo, Clo!' in terror, clutching her the closer, 'what dost thou mean? In all my nine and sixty years –' and rolled his head in agony.

In all his nine and sixty years he had shown justice to no man, mercy to no woman, since he had thought of none but Jeoffry Wildairs; and this truth somehow dimly reached his long-dulled brain and wakened there.

'Down on thy knees, Clo!' he gasped – 'down on thy knees!'

It was so horrible, the look struggling in his dying face, that she went down upon her knees that moment, and so knelt, folding his shaking hands within her own against her breast.

'Thou who didst make him as he was born into Thy world,' she said, 'deal with that to which Thou didst give life – and death. Show him in this hour, which Thou mad'st also, that Thou art not Man who would have vengeance, but that justice which is God.'

'Then – then,' he gasped – 'then will He damn me!'

'He will weigh thee,' she said; 'and that which His own hand created will He separate from that which was thine own wilful wrong – and this, sure, He will teach thee how to expiate.'

'Clo,' he cried again – 'thy mother – she was but a girl, and died alone – I did no justice to her! – Daphne! Daphne!' And he shook beneath the bedclothes, shuddering to his feet, his face growing more grey and pinched.

'She loved thee once,' Clorinda said. 'She was a gentle soul, and would not forget. She will show thee mercy.'

'Birth she went through,' he muttered, 'and death – alone. Birth and death! Daphne, my girl –' And his voice trailed off to nothingness, and he lay staring at space, and panting.

The duchess sat by him and held his hand. She moved not, though at last he seemed to fall asleep. Two hours later he began to stir. He turned his head slowly upon his pillows until his gaze rested upon her, as she sat fronting him. 'Twas as though he had awakened to look at her.

'Clo!' he cried, and though his voice was but a whisper, there was both wonder and wild question in it – 'Clo!'

But she moved not, her great eyes meeting his with steady gaze; and even as they so looked at each other his body stretched itself, his lids fell – and he was a dead man.

The Doves Sat Upon the Window Ledge and Lowly Cooed and Cooed

When they had had ten years of happiness, Anne died. 'Twas of no violent illness, it seemed but that through these years of joy she had been gradually losing life. She had grown thinner and whiter, and her soft eyes bigger and more prayerful. 'Twas in the summer, and they were at Camylott, when one sweet day she came from the flower-garden with her hands full of roses, and sitting down by her sister in her morning room, swooned away, scattering her blossoms on her lap and at her feet.

When she came back to consciousness she looked up at the duchess with a strange, far look, as if her soul had wandered back from some great distance.

'Let me be borne to bed, sister,' she said. 'I would lie still. I shall not get up again.'

The look in her face was so unearthly and a thing so full of mystery, that her Grace's heart stood still, for in some strange way she knew the end had come.

They bore her to her tower and laid her in her bed, when she looked once round the room and then at her sister.

''Tis a fair, peaceful room,' she said. 'And the prayers I have prayed in it have been answered. Today I saw my mother, and she told me so.'

'Anne! Anne!' cried her Grace, leaning over her and gazing fearfully into her face; for though her words sounded like delirium, her look had no wildness in it. And yet – 'Anne, Anne! you wander, love,' the duchess cried.

Anne smiled a strange, sweet smile. 'Perchance I do,' she said. 'I know not truly, but I am very happy. She said that all was over, and that I had not done wrong. She had a fair, young face, with eyes that seemed to have looked always at the stars of heaven. She said I had done no wrong.'

The duchess' face laid itself down upon the pillow, a river of clear tears running down her cheeks.

'Wrong!' she said – 'you! dear one – woman of Christ's heart, if ever lived one. You were so weak and I so strong, and yet as I look back it seems that all of good that made me worthy to be wife and mother I learned from your simplicity.'

Through the tower window and the ivy closing round it, the blueness of the summer sky was heavenly fair; soft, and light white clouds floated across the clearness of its sapphire. On this Anne's eyes were fixed with an uplifted tenderness until she broke her silence.

'Soon I shall be away,' she said. 'Soon all will be left behind. And I would tell you that my prayers were answered – and so, sure, yours will be.'

No man could tell what made the duchess then fall on her knees, but she herself knew. 'Twas that she saw in the exalted dying face that turned to hers concealing nothing more.

'Anne! Anne!' she cried. 'Sister Anne! Mother Anne of my children! You have known – you have known all the years and kept it hid!'

She dropped her queenly head and shielded the whiteness of her face in the coverlid's folds.

'Ay, sister,' Anne said, coming a little back to earth, 'and from the first. I found a letter near the sundial – I guessed – I loved you – and could do naught else but guard you. Many a day have I watched within the rose-garden – many a day – and night – God pardon me – and night. When I knew a letter was hid, 'twas my wont to linger near, knowing that my presence would keep others away. And when you approached – or he – I slipped aside and waited beyond the rose hedge – that if I heard a step, I might make some sound of warning. Sister, I was your sentinel, and being so, knelt while on my guard, and prayed.'

'My sentinel!' Clorinda cried. 'And knowing all, you so guarded me night and day, and prayed God's pity on my poor madness and girl's frenzy!' And she gazed at her in amaze, and with humblest, burning tears.

'For my own poor self as well as for you, sister, did I pray God's pity as I knelt,' said Anne. 'For long I knew it not – being so ignorant – but alas! I loved him too! – I loved him too! I have loved no man other all my days. He was unworthy any woman's love – and I was too lowly for him to cast a glance on; but I was a woman, and God made us so.'

Clorinda clutched her pallid hand.

'Dear God,' she cried, 'you loved him!'

Anne moved upon her pillow, drawing weakly, slowly near until her white lips were close upon her sister's ear.

'The night,' she panted – 'the night you bore him – in your arms –'

Then did the other woman give a shuddering start and lift her head, staring with a frozen face.

'What! what!' she cried.

'Down the dark stairway,' the panting voice went on, 'to the far cellar – I kept watch again.'

'You kept watch – you?' the duchess gasped.

'Upon the stair which led to the servants' place – that I might stop them if – if aught disturbed them, and they oped their doors – that I might send them back, telling them – it was I.'

Then stooped the duchess nearer to her, her hands clutching the coverlid, her eyes widening.

'Anne, Anne,' she cried, 'you knew the awful thing that I would hide! That too? You knew that he was there!'

Anne lay upon her pillow, her own eyes gazing out through the ivy-hung window of her tower at the blue sky and the fair, fleecy clouds. A flock of snow-white doves were flying back and forth across it, and one sat upon the window's deep ledge and cooed. All was warm and perfumed with summer's sweetness. There seemed naught between her and the uplifting blueness, and naught of the earth was near but the dove's deep-throated cooing and the laughter of her Grace's children floating upward from the garden of flowers below.

'I lie upon the brink,' she said – 'upon the brink, sister, and methinks my soul is too near to God's pure justice to fear as human things fear, and judge as earth does. She said I did no wrong. Yes, I knew.'

'And knowing,' her sister cried, 'you came to me that afternoon!'

'To stand by that which lay hidden, that I might keep the rest away. Being a poor creature and timorous and weak –'

'Weak! weak!' the duchess cried, amid a greater flood of streaming tears – 'ay, I have dared to call you so, who have the heart of a great lioness. Oh, sweet Anne – weak!'

''Twas love,' Anne whispered. 'Your love was strong, and so was mine. That other love was not for me. I knew that my long woman's life would pass without it – for woman's life is long, alas! if love comes not. But you were love's self, and I worshipped you and it; and to myself I said – praying forgiveness on my knees – that one woman should know love if I did not. And being so poor and imperfect a thing, what mattered if I gave my soul for you – and love, which is so great, and rules the world. Look at the doves, sister, look at them, flying past the heavenly blueness – and she said I did no wrong.'

Her hand was wet with tears fallen upon it, as her duchess sister knelt, and held and kissed it, sobbing.

'You knew, poor love, you knew!' she cried.

'Ay, all of it I knew,' Anne said – 'his torture of you and the madness of your horror. And when he forced himself within the Panelled Parlour that day of fate, I knew he came to strike some deadly blow; and in such anguish I waited in my chamber for the end, that when it came not, I crept down, praying that somehow I might come between – and I went in the room!'

'And there – what saw you?' quoth the duchess, shuddering. 'Somewhat you must have seen, or you could not have known.'

'Ay,' said Anne, 'and heard!' and her chest heaved.

'Heard!' cried Clorinda. 'Great God of mercy!'

'The room was empty, and I stood alone. It was so still I was afraid; it seemed so like the silence of the grave; and then there came a sound – a long and shuddering breath – but one – and then –'

The memory brought itself too keenly back, and she fell a-shivering.

'I heard a slipping sound, and a dead hand fell on the floor – lying outstretched, its palm turned upwards, showing beneath the valance of the couch.'

She threw her frail arms round her sister's neck, and as Clorinda clasped her own, breathing gaspingly, they swayed together.

'What did you then?' the duchess cried, in a wild whisper.

'I prayed God keep me sane – and knelt – and looked below. I thrust it back – the dead hand, saying aloud, "Swoon you must not, swoon you must not, swoon you shall not – God help! God help!" – and I saw! – the purple mark – his eyes upturned – his fair curls spread; and I lost strength and fell upon my side, and for a minute lay there – knowing that shudder of breath had been the very last expelling of his being, and his hand had fallen by its own weight.'

'O God! O God! O God!' Clorinda cried, and over and over said the word, and over again.

'How was't – how was't?' Anne shuddered, clinging to her. 'How was't 'twas done? I have so suffered, being weak – I have so prayed! God will have mercy – but it has done me to death, this knowledge, and before I die, I pray you tell me, that I may speak truly at God's throne.'

'O God! O God! O God!' Clorinda groaned – 'O God!' and having cried so, looking up, was blanched as a thing struck with death, her eyes like a great stag's that stands at bay.

'Stay, stay!' she cried, with a sudden shock of horror, for a new thought had come to her which, strangely, she had not had before. 'You thought I murdered him?'

Convulsive sobs heaved Anne's poor chest, tears sweeping her hollow cheeks, her thin, soft hands clinging piteously to her sister's.

'Through all these years I have known nothing,' she wept – 'sister, I have known nothing but that I found him hidden there, a dead man, whom you so hated and so feared.'

Her hands resting upon the bed's edge, Clorinda held her body upright, such passion of wonder, love, and pitying adoring awe in her large eyes as was a thing like to worship.

'You thought I murdered him, and loved me still,' she said. 'You thought I murdered him, and still you shielded me, and gave me chance to live, and to repent, and know love's highest sweetness. You thought I murdered him, and yet your soul had mercy. Now do I believe in God, for only a God could make a heart so noble.'

'And you – did not –' cried out Anne, and raised upon her elbow, her breast panting, but her eyes growing wide with light as from stars from heaven. 'Oh, sister love – thanks be to Christ who died!'

The duchess rose, and stood up tall and great, her arms outthrown.

'I think 'twas God Himself who did it,' she said, 'though 'twas I who struck the blow. He drove me mad and blind, he tortured me, and thrust to my heart's core. He taunted me with that vile thing Nature will not let women bear, and did it in my Gerald's name, calling on him. And then I struck with my whip, knowing nothing, not seeing, only striking, like a goaded dying thing. He fell – he fell and lay there – and all was done!'

'But not with murderous thought – only through frenzy and a cruel chance – a cruel, cruel chance. And of your own will blood is not upon your hand,' Anne panted, and sank back upon her pillow.

'With deepest oaths I swear,' Clorinda said, and she spoke through her clenched teeth, 'if I had not loved, if Gerald had not been my soul's life and I his, I would have stood upright and laughed in his face at the devil's threats. Should I have feared? You know me. Was there a thing on earth or in heaven or hell I feared until love rent me? 'Twould but have fired my blood, and made me mad with fury that dares all. "Spread it abroad!" I would have cried to him. "Tell it to all the world, craven and outcast, whose vileness all men know, and see how I shall bear myself, and how I shall drive through the town with head erect. As I bore myself when I set the rose crown on my head, so shall I bear myself then. And you shall see what comes!" This would I have said, and held to it, and gloried. But I knew love, and there was an anguish that I could not endure – that my Gerald should look at me with changed eyes, feeling that somewhat of his rightful meed was gone. And I was all distraught and conquered. Of ending his base life I never thought, never at my wildest, though I had thought to end my own; but when Fate struck the blow for me, then I swore that carrion should not taint my whole life through. It should not – should not – for 'twas Fate's self had doomed me to my ruin. And there it lay until the night; for this I planned, that being of such great strength for a woman, I could bear his body in my arms to the farthest of that labyrinth of cellars I had commanded to be cut off from the rest and closed; and so I did when all were sleeping – but you, poor Anne – but you! And there I laid him, and there he lies today – an evil thing turned to a handful of dust.'

'It was not murder,' whispered Anne – 'no, it was not.' She lifted to her sister's gaze a quivering lip. 'And yet once I had loved him – years I had loved him,' she said, whispering still. 'And in a woman there is ever somewhat that the mother creature feels' – the hand which held her sister's shook as with an ague, and her poor lip quivered – 'Sister, I – saw him again!'

The duchess drew closer as she gasped, 'Again!'

'I could not rest,' the poor voice said. 'He had been so base, he was so beautiful, and so unworthy love – and he was dead, none knowing, untouched by any hand that even pitied him that he was so base a thing, for that indeed is piteous when death comes and none can be repentant. And he lay so hard, so hard upon the stones.'

Her teeth were chattering, and with a breath drawn like a wild sob of terror, the duchess threw her arm about her and drew her nearer.

'Sweet Anne,' she shuddered – 'sweet Anne – come back – you wander!'

'Nay, 'tis not wandering,' Anne said. ''Tis true, sister. There is no night these years gone by I have not remembered it again – and seen. In the night after that you bore him there – I prayed until the mid-hours, when all were sleeping fast – and then I stole down – in my bare feet, that none could hear me – and at last I found my way in the black dark – feeling the walls until I reached that farthest door in the stone – and then I lighted my taper and opened it.'

'Anne!' cried the duchess – 'Anne, look through the tower window at the blueness of the sky – at the blueness, Anne!' But drops of cold water had started out and stood upon her brow.

'He lay there in his grave – it was a little black place with its stone walls – his fair locks were tumbled,' Anne went on, whispering. 'The spot was black upon his brow – and methought he had stopped mocking, and surely looked upon some great and awful thing which asked of him a question. I knelt, and laid his curls straight, and his hands, and tried to shut his eyes, but close they would not, but stared at that which questioned. And having loved him so, I kissed his poor cheek as his mother might have done, that he might not stand outside, having carried not

one tender human thought with him. And, oh, I prayed, sister –
I prayed for his poor soul with all my own. "If there is one noble
or gentle thing he has ever done through all his life," I prayed,
"Jesus remember it – Christ do not forget." We who are human
do so few things that are noble – oh, surely one must count.'

The duchess' head lay near her sister's breast, and she had
fallen a-sobbing – a-sobbing and weeping like a young broken
child.

'Oh, brave and noble, pitiful, strong, fair soul!' she cried. 'As
Christ loved you have loved, and He would hear your praying.
Since you so pleaded, He would find one thing to hang His
mercy on.'

She lifted her fair, tear-streaming face, clasping her hands as
one praying.

'And I – and I,' she cried – 'have I not built a temple on his
grave? Have I not tried to live a fair life, and be as Christ bade
me? Have I not loved, and pitied, and succoured those in pain?
Have I not filled a great man's days with bliss, and love, and
wifely worship? Have I not given him noble children, bred
in high lovingness, and taught to love all things God made,
even the very beasts that perish, since they, too, suffer as all
do? Have I left aught undone? Oh, sister, I have so prayed that
I left naught. Even though I could not believe that there was
One who, ruling all, could yet be pitiless as He is to some,
I have prayed That – which sure it seems must be, though we
comprehend it not – to teach me faith in something greater than
my poor self, and not of earth. Say this to Christ's self when you
are face to face – say this to Him, I pray you! Anne, Anne, look
not so strangely through the window at the blueness of the sky,
sweet soul, but look at me.'

For Anne lay upon her pillow so smiling that 'twas a strange
thing to behold. It seemed as she were smiling at the whiteness
of the doves against the blue. A moment her sister stood up
watching her, and then she stirred, meaning to go to call one of

the servants waiting outside; but though she moved not her gaze from the tower window, Mistress Anne faintly spoke.

'Nay – stay,' she breathed. 'I go – softly – stay.'

Clorinda fell upon her knees again and bent her lips close to her ear. This was death, and yet she feared it not – this was the passing of a soul, and while it went it seemed so fair and loving a thing that she could ask it her last question – her greatest – knowing it was so near to God that its answer must be rest.

'Anne, Anne,' she whispered, 'must he know – my Gerald? Must I – must I tell him all? If so I must, I will – upon my knees.'

The doves came flying downward from the blue, and lighted on the window stone and cooed – Anne's answer was as low as her soft breath and her still eyes were filled with joy at that she saw but which another could not.

'Nay,' she breathed. 'Tell him not. What need? Wait, and let God tell him – who understands.'

Then did her soft breath stop, and she lay still, her eyes yet open and smiling at the blossoms, and the doves who sat upon the window ledge and lowly cooed and cooed.

'Twas her duchess sister who clad her for her last sleeping, and made her chamber fair – the hand of no other touched her; and while 'twas done the tower chamber was full of the golden sunshine, and the doves ceased not to flutter about the window, and coo as if they spoke lovingly to each other of what lay within the room.

Then the children came to look, their arms full of blossoms and flowering sprays. They had been told only fair things of death, and knowing but these fair things, thought of it but as the opening of a golden door. They entered softly, as entering the chamber of a queen, and moving tenderly, with low and gentle speech, spread all their flowers about the bed – laying them round her head, on her breast, and in her hands, and strewing them thick everywhere.

'She lies in a bower and smiles at us,' one said. 'She hath grown beautiful like you, mother, and her face seems like a white star in the morning.'

'She loves us as she ever did,' the fair child Daphne said; 'she will never cease to love us, and will be our angel. Now have we an angel of our own.'

When the duke returned, who had been absent since the day before, the duchess led him to the tower chamber, and they stood together hand in hand and gazed at her peace.

'Gerald,' the duchess said, in her tender voice, 'she smiles, does not she?'

'Yes,' was Osmonde's answer – 'yes, love, as if at God, who has smiled at herself – faithful, tender woman heart!'

The hand which he held in his clasp clung closer. The other crept to his shoulder and lay there tremblingly.

'How faithful and how tender, my Gerald,' Clorinda said, 'I only know. She is my saint – sweet Anne, whom I dared treat so lightly in my poor wayward days. Gerald, she knows all my sins, and today she has carried them in her pure hands to God and asked His mercy on them. She had none of her own.'

'And so having done, dear heart, she lies amid her flowers, and smiles,' he said, and he drew her white hand to press it against his breast.

While her body slept beneath soft turf and flowers, and that which was her self was given in God's heaven, all joys for which her earthly being had yearned, even when unknowing how to name its longing, each year that passed made more complete and splendid the lives of those she so had loved. Never, 'twas said, had woman done such deeds of gentleness and shown so sweet and generous a wisdom as the great duchess. None who were weak were in danger if she used her strength to aid them; no man or woman was a lost thing whom she tried to save: such tasks she set herself as no lady had ever given herself before; but 'twas not her way to fail – her will being so powerful, her brain so clear, her heart so purely noble. Pauper and prince, noble and hind honoured her and her lord alike, and all felt wonder at their happiness. It seemed that they had learned life's meaning and the honouring of love, and this they taught to their children, to the enriching of a long and noble line. In the ripeness of years they passed from earth in as beauteous peace as the sun sets, and upon a tablet above the resting-place of their ancestors there are inscribed lines like these:

'Here sleeps by her husband the purest and noblest lady God e'er loved, yet the high and gentle deeds of her chaste sweet life sleep not, but live and grow, and so will do so long as earth is earth.'

Biographical Note

Frances Hodgson Burnett (1849–1924) was born in Cheetham, Manchester, the third of five children. Her family struggled financially following the death of her father, eventually moving to Tennessee.

It was in the US that Hodgson Burnett began writing stories to support her family. By the time of her marriage to Swan Burnett in 1872, her work was being published regularly in literary magazines. She began writing her first full-length novel in the same year and gave birth to the first of two sons.

Her first book for children, *Little Lord Fauntleroy*, was a runaway success when it was serialising in St Nicholas magazine in 1885 and 1886. Readers eager for the next instalment bought related merchandise and dressed their children in velvet suits like the eponymous hero. Hodgson Burnett later wrote two other enduring classics of children's literature, *A Little Princess* (1905) and *The Secret Garden* (1911). Although these are the books for which she is best remembered today, she was a popular writer of historical fiction in her lifetime, beginning with *A Lady of Quality* (1896) which was the second highest selling book in the US in 1896.

The death of her elder son in 1890 led to a period of mourning and depression for Hodgson Burnett, but she persevered with her writing and plunged herself into charity work. In 1898 she divorced her husband and later remarried although this marriage too ended in divorce.

Despite many extended stays in England, Hodgson Burnett lived most of her life in the US and became a citizen in 1905. She continued to write into her old age, producing many of her most famous works towards the end of her life. She died in New York in 1924.

Under our three imprints, Hesperus Press publishes over 300 books by many of the greatest figures in worldwide literary history, as well as contemporary and debut authors well worth discovering.

Hesperus Classics handpicks the best of worldwide and translated literature, introducing forgotten and neglected books to new generations.

Hesperus Nova showcases quality contemporary fiction and non-fiction designed to entertain and inspire.

Hesperus Minor rediscovers well-loved children's books from the past – these are books which will bring back fond memories for adults, which they will want to share with their children and loved ones.

To find out more visit www.hesperuspress.com
@HesperusPress

SELECTED TITLES FROM HESPERUS PRESS